AF148417

The Opiate
Books

This Rescue Thing

By Penny Allen

For Marjorie

This novel is inspired by a true story from the author's life.

"The leaf was darkish, and had prickles on it,/
But in another country, as he said,/
Bore a bright golden flow'r, but not in this soil."

-John Milton, *Comus*

Foreword

It's hard to imagine, anymore, having a friend that would truly go to great lengths for you. That would quite literally travel to the ends of the Earth to get you out of a bind. Or, worse still, a prison-like mental institution (or mental institution-like prison, depending on one's perspective). Most people, "in this day and age," don't have that sense of loyalty or devotion to someone. Not romantically and certainly not platonically. The world, in short, has forced people to become more adherent to the adage, "Every man for himself" (amend that how you will to allow for more gender inclusivity). Sometimes referred to as, "Look out for number one."

It's a philosophy that tends to take a greater hold on people during times of scarcity. And in the present, there is a scarcity of empathy. In the mid-90s, apparently, there was not. Or at least that's the impression our narrator in *This Rescue Thing* gives based on her dangerous leap of faith into the unknown to save a friend she knew from Portland, and one that she hadn't seen in years. This leap of faith was made all the more dangerous by the paucity of communication-oriented technology during this era.

This was not just any friend, though. But a legend, a force of nature. The kind of person you spend time with and always end up coming away with some crazy story. In this tale, that person is Sandra Sandra a.k.a. Sansan.

Many of us have all had "that one friend" like Sansan. Someone who is wilder than us, more audacious. And someone who we aspire to be more like precisely because of those qualities we lack in our meeker, more mild-mannered selves. Friends who make us more interesting by proxy. Even after moving to Paris, our narrator seemed to miss some of that spark from her old friend. Why else would she feel so compelled to fly all the way to Thailand upon learning that Sansan was being held captive in a mental facility (though, again, by Thai standards, that was a prison)? Despite having a full-time job and limited means, our narrator decides to drop everything to rescue the friend she admired so much back in Portland, where Sansan would regale audiences at open mic nights with her exploits in far-flung places such as Afghanistan. Yes, Afghanistan.

Appropriately enough, not once in the book is our narrator ever named directly. It is a creative decision that seems to be an extension of the selflessness of this act, this rescue thing she performed for a friend she truly loved. Because, regardless of how different they might appear, the narrator clearly sees herself in San. A woman as perennially out-of-place and unique as she is. In fact, both women left the U.S. for good reason, for it's not exactly the easiest country to be a "freak" (read: in any way non-normie at all) in.

This underlying motive for turning expatriate brims to the surface when Sansan confesses to our narrator, "You know why I can't go back to the States? I am too weird. I don't fit. I never did. Simply stated, I don't like the way people over there think." A limiting way of thinking that also extends to ageism. Indeed, Sansan is a woman coming to grips with the reality that ageism isn't limited to U.S. soil. That where she once might have been able to easily manipulate/flirt her way into getting what she wanted, living on the kindness of strangers because of her looks—the "beauty bias," as it were—it's becoming more of a challenge to do so thanks to the rigors of aging. Especially when one lives as unrootedly and devil-may-care as Sansan.

At a certain point, Sansan describes being taunted by some Thai kids who ask her, "Why don't you sell your pussy, or is it too old?" Although the narrator finds it harsh, she can't help but later ask herself of Sansan's fate, "How long would she be able to keep up her survival mode as a seductress, growing older in a changing world?"

It's a query that brings up many unpleasant realities that seem to only ever apply to women. And one that hits the hardest for women accustomed to being beautiful, only to watch that beauty, once considered their greatest asset, fade. And yet, that's why there's something to be said for the purity of platonic female friendship. Because it entails that somebody will always be there for you, to love you as you are at your core—which has no bearing whatsoever on what you look like.

Seeing this kind of unconditional love emanating from our narrator, San tells her, "I love you, whatever that means." Cornball as it is, *Love Story* posited that it means never having to say you're sorry and, in a sense, that is what it means for San and our narrator, with the former constantly getting into jams and scrapes that the narrator doesn't expect an apology for.

Perhaps it is their kindredness that makes the narrator so understanding, so empathetic toward Sansan. After all, both women are adrift in strange lands and have no lingering emotional connection to where they're from. Inevitably, that can lead to an unspeakable form of loneliness. As the narrator later puts it, "How do people from different cultures ever successfully communicate at all? I was beginning to think they don't."

Nonetheless, people like San and our narrator continue to search for a tribe in locations well-beyond their native land. People that can relate to and accept them for who they are. For San, that endless quest comes at a great price: her mental health. Thus, the fair questions: was her tribe always in Portland? Was she better off having never gone to Thailand at all, if it meant returning to the U.S. as a husk of her former self?

4

That, dear readers, is something you must decide on your own as you embark upon the following journey with our narrator to rescue Sansan…not just from Thailand, but from herself.

Genna Rivieccio
Editor, The Opiate Books
Spring 2024

Sansan was wonderful to look at in the late seventies: abundant long, red hair; high, prominent cheekbones; olive skin; a space between her front teeth; slender and graceful as a dancer. A beauty.

She was a storyteller, which is what she was doing when I first saw her, practicing her honorable vocation. She wasn't just telling stories though, she was performing them onstage at a rowdy poetry bar, where being outrageous was a necessity. Her imagination and startling use of language enticed me, and her constantly moving hands and flamboyance compelled the crowds to shut up, watch and listen. She compelled *me* to enter her world.

After seeing her perform several times, I noticed that Sansan's stories were often about the times she had narrowly escaped death. What's more, I felt that what she was saying was essentially true. I believed that she really *had* lived the risky life she shared onstage, and it was obvious she took a giddy pleasure in recounting her flirtations with the narrowly avoided final exit. She always got right into her subject, "performing," for example, the time she'd nearly choked to death in a marsh. She'd been escaping from a bunch of *pachucas* somewhere in San Francisco, only to run straight into mucky, shit-filled waters where she sank and nearly drowned. The girls chasing her had laughed as she gagged and struggled. She was heroic, repulsive, funny, original. Her stories shocked people out of their complacency—like her story about what her aborted fetus looked and smelled and tasted like. "My little teaspoon of tissue," she called it. When I heard that story, I felt as though her fetus sloshed around in my own stomach for days afterwards.

Another time at the poetry bar, her story was about when she nearly bled to death in Afghanistan after sitting down forcefully on the gearshift in a crowded van far from a hospital. She hadn't been wearing panties, so the gear's entry into her vagina had been opportune. As she relayed the lurid tale to a spellbound crowd, she lifted her velvet skirt higher and higher and shouted, "I had an orgasm!" As the reactions rang out, she flounced and preened, basking in the limelight. I was impressed.

Gradually, I noted that Sansan's accounts always took place in real cultural, social and historical contexts. She was painstakingly sociological or anthropological in her approach. She would throw in everything she knew about a place, then move on to what had happened to her there, the people, their lives, their jokes, always circling back to her personal involvement, and then, the near-death experience, and often that was the end. She wasn't into denouement. Her listeners were left with scenes of great peril fixed in their memory.

It was my boyfriend, Sammy, who finally officially introduced me to Sansan. Sammy was a lively, spiky-haired New Yorker who had come out West to live in Portland. He'd first heard of San the day he arrived from New York by bus, when he was in his early twenties. Everyone in the tumbledown Victorian house where he was staying—ten or twelve people—had been preoccupied with whether they should pay, as a group, for some woman named Sansan's plane ticket back to Portland from Hawaii. The idea was for all of them to chip in to bring her back from her shack in the Maui rainforest so they could have her for themselves once again. And then they would all share her living expenses. They were going to support her collectively, Sammy told me, still floored by the discussion long after.

"It was like culture shock," he told me in his jivey way, moving his shoulders for punctuation. Sammy's body was angular, with long limbs and fingers that came alive when he was putting a fine point on his portrayal of someone. "She ran wild in my imagination before I ever laid eyes on her. There I was"—his left hand carving out the "there" and holding on to it, all the while lounging on my bed in black silk pajamas given to him by Sansan—"just in from another planet, and all I heard was Sandra Sandra, Sandra Sandra. That's really her name, Sandra Sandra, by the way. That's why she's called Sansan." When she was born, he went on, her parents each picked a name. Both chose Sandra, so they decided to use the name twice. "With a name like that, they launched her as a myth right from the beginning," he summed up, obviously very taken with her.

Sammy told me his housemates had vigorously debated the meaning of San's behavior, and their own actions on her behalf. There'd been an actual fight about moral legitimacy, a feminist argument, some approving the collective "keeping" of a woman, some finding it degrading to the woman in question. Telling me all this, Sammy added, quite jollily, that his household had finally voted to take San on financially, the way followers might support a prophet. That's how they justified what they were going to do. "We decided to pay for her ticket back from Hawaii, and then to pay her keep, and I paid my share." Saying this, he slapped his thighs and laughed himself around in a circle, enjoying the show all over again.

When he got to this point in his story, I nearly walked out. Or actually, I did walk away, into the kitchen. I couldn't take hearing all this from the man I was falling for. It was so early in our relationship, I didn't know how to react. I was confused. I wasn't half as interesting as Sansan was, I couldn't compete was how I saw it at that moment. Why would Sammy want to spend time with me instead of her? They were all living in intimacy at Sammy's house. Why not stick with that? I felt blindsided, like I had lost

Sammy before I ever came on the scene. I got a glass of water, drank it, lifted myself up and came back to Sammy on my bed.

"What happened when she came back from Hawaii?" I asked, sitting down next to him, fixing on his gentle brown eyes.

"What I remember is that there she was, this gorgeous, golden-skinned woman with a flower in her wild red hair, this goddess. And I saw her sitting on the couch in our living room, everyone vibrating around her in sexual thrall!" That vision, that expression—"in sexual thrall"—didn't help me out much at that moment, but Sansan was already running wild in my imagination before I ever saw her, just like she had for Sammy and, over the years, as it would turn out, for a hell of a lot of other people.

"She was married three times before she was twenty!" Sammy announced when he finally got me together with San. We were sitting three across, San in the middle, all of us squeezed tight in the front seat of Sammy's old two-seat Honda, a beige blur zigzagging across Portland on tree-lined back streets. I noticed San was sitting astride the Honda's gearshift, caressing it with her thighs. This was after I'd already heard about her accidentally sitting on a gearshift in Pakistan. "Sounds pretty lively," I offered.

"Lively?" San shot back, tossing her mane as she rode the shift, her hands and arms moving gracefully up through her hair, then slicing the air rhythmically, overcoming my reluctance to know more of the potency and zest she might bring to an exchange.

"Like grease on a hot skillet," she laughed, observing her effect on me as she fixed on me, eye-to-eye, with her electrifying gaze, reaching out to fluff my hair. "You're cute," she said and laughed softly in the back of her throat like a baby gurgling as Sammy sped wildly on the very scary, narrow two-lane Ross Island Bridge across the Willamette. If I was looking for a jump off the rails, that seemed like an invitation. I jumped—not off the bridge, but out of what I had known up to that point. I wanted to know what she knew, from her point of view.

Sansan held court regularly for five or six people in her room located in a transient, cheap neighborhood. In the morning, she would have done her second-hand thing, finding treasures at little dusty junk shops she knew, or else at the big Goodwill store where she bought stuff for ten cents a pound. She unearthed treasures from those bins, like Japanese kimonos picked up decades before on travels by Portland's rich West Hills matrons and now finally tossed out. Or even older Japanese treasures sold for a song to occupying soldiers or other visitors to Japan just after World War II—not just kimonos or prints, but also some *netsuke*—tiny and precious ivory or wood carvings of animals. Sansan was idealistically committed to this kind of bottom-feeding that was sometimes rewarding. And she did it with bejeweled fingers and great taste, arranging her life accordingly. She cultivated a mixed entourage of artists and writers, of contributing gentlemen and ladies, clever minds who often bought her wares.

The first time I was invited into her intimate surroundings, we were six. The canaries were outside their cage, flitting around on the loose, and San was churning the air, making the birds catch in everyone's hair as they flew wilder and closer. So there was a lot of physical movement as everyone tried to avoid the birds, which added energy to Sansan's story about her lawless chase through an airport to escape with her son who she had just kidnapped from his foster parents. And there the story ended. With the chase. I was leaning forward in anticipation, following San's tale, but she turned her back to light a hand-rolled cigarette she'd peppered with hashish. After she smoked and we waited, she began again in a reflective tone: "Risk and survival are in my genes, so I have no choice about the situations I find myself in. I do what I am, take it or leave it."

Later, after everyone except me had departed, Sansan stared at me with her pale, emerald-green eyes and declared that she was descended from San Francisco saloonkeepers mixed with artsy bohemian immigrants, including one Chinese great-grandparent, whose tinted photo she showed me. It all sounded about right, but we were both stoned. San did look a bit Chinese around those green eyes though, which were slightly slanted and hooded. "Here, this is for you," she effused. She reached down to her boot and pulled out a silk scarf, then another, like a magician pulling doves from a hat. Last, she offered a cherry, fifties-era snakeskin beaded cowgirl belt and held it out for me on her open palms.

The belt was an actual treasure and Sansan was a sideshow gypsy tendering a snake caught in a trance. Her flashing green eyes were blinding. She was snagging me.

Paris, France
Many Years Later

The mail flew in under the door on a wintry gust of wind, crossing the room toward me as I lay asleep in my small, noisy apartment in an animated sector of Paris. I woke up, cursed the clumping feet resounding through the ceiling then got up and threw a rug against the gaping space at the bottom of the door. It was Paris in midwinter, a winter dark as a nightmare.

Hailstones knocked against the windows. Across the cobblestone courtyard, an older gentleman named Roger opened his tall windows, thrust his head out, yelled back over his shoulder at his ancient mother, "*Putain! Ça mitraille!*" *Fuck! It's hammering!* He pulled the windows shut with a bang. Through the glass, he caught my eye.

He held my gaze, his mouth hanging open, then shook his head in despair and turned away. Roger had intervened in my life some time before, although he probably didn't know it was important. Our windows faced each other across the small courtyard, so we each had some vague notion of the other's habits, facial expressions, even moods. And one day, when my bedroom shutters didn't open by three in the afternoon, he phoned and let it ring and ring and ring, two hundred times he said, all the while staring out his windows at my closed, unmoving shutters, until I finally heard the sound of ringing, ringing, ringing down in the bottom of my sleep-deprived mind.

The thing is, what was bothering me, what was cutting into the joy of being alive in Paris was very real, and it wasn't going to go away with better eating habits or regular hours or a doctor's care.

I'd been sleepless for two or three weeks, worrying about a guy hounding me at work, where I was an international liaison on environmental issues. The guy bothering me was *un petit connard* of about twenty-five, with a shaved head, brown clothes and an aggressive attitude. No one could figure out what the kid was doing there, and no one intervened when he bullied me.

He and I had inevitably clashed. Specifically, we differed about strategy on an issue that was my responsibility. He shouldn't have had anything to say about it, but maybe it was naïve of me to think so, me being a foreigner in a French work setting. "You're mucking around where you shouldn't, you little punk," I finally shouted at him in a meeting, red-faced and sputtering. "*Tu n'es pas à ta place!*" he shouted back. *You don't belong here!* What arrogant contempt, I thought. But the next morning, I found my office ransacked, precious papers heaved out the window onto the street. A startling component of Parisian working conditions.

That night, late, I got a death threat over the telephone. There was heavy breathing, muffled words. I thought I recognized the voice and rhythm of a guy from the office. Another call came the following night, and I asked the phone company to monitor my line. There was never a third call. Whoever it was had been smart enough to figure out *I* might have been smart enough to call the phone company by then.

What my Roger had imagined, seeing my unopened shutters from across the courtyard, was something out of the ordinary. But he'd taken it in stride, which was reassuring and made me think I should do the same. Roger had grounded me. Just keep my head down, yeah. I only missed that one day of work.

I picked the mail up off the floor that wintry morning and saw a postcard full of sunshine. It was from Thailand, from Sansan! My heart leaped. I had to sit down. Sandra Sandra! Seeing her name on the card, I felt warm despite the cold, dark day. Despite all those years gone by, Sansan could still make me quake with wonderment and fear.

Fear I say. What alarmed me about Sansan was her unpredictable approach to situations I was involved in, and the change she often delivered. Her behavior propelled everyone around her into unknown territory, beyond the comfort zone. So getting a postcard from her out of the blue twenty years later when I was straining to hold steady against a storm front of confusion in my life made my heart pound. Before I could even gather my thoughts, the floodgates opened, and there was Sansan, a Siamese warrior fish in brilliant color, pulling me into the torrent. Would I drown this time?

It had been at least ten years since I'd seen Sansan when I got the postcard from her. Our communication in that period had been bits of gossip gleaned from shared acquaintances. The talk had placed her in Nepal with a rich, crooked Brit—a young Michael Caine type/all-around sexy beast she had told people she was sexually enthralled by and in love with, which would have been a first for Sansan. Falling in love, that is…or at least admitting it. She let it be known that the Brit was a dynamic man who took her to five-star hotels, provided her with servants and silver slippers, that sort of thing. It fit the unpredictable Sandra Sandra, but what wouldn't have?

This is what Sansan's Thai postcard to me in Paris said:

Darling, I'm sure you have heard I am living in Thailand. My old girl dog Kitcha and I are enjoying perfect health and happiness! I have found someone who loves me and finds me fascinating, a rich Thai businessman and landowner who brings me peace

and laughter and innocence. You must come visit me.
THE SOONER THE BETTER.

To this day, I have to sit down to read this postcard, it carries with it such a strange, spiked fruit punch of grandeur, followed by a mysterious, urgent straight shot in the form of a summons. The words in the beginning are literary, a joyful description of a happy new life in Thailand, words which did not alert me to the imperative request that followed. The whole thing might have warned other people off. But I did not think badly of her at all.

The first time I read the postcard, I went right on to wonder what had happened to her Brit in Nepal, her sexy beast. What happened to her sexual enthrallment with him—it came to a natural end? The old girl dog Kitcha—I remembered Sansan already had a dog named Kitcha all those years before in Portland. It could have been the same Kitcha. That dog would sit at the table and eat from a plate and slobber on the table, and San would eat the mess the dog left. "Why not?" she said. "We're all from the same planet." But Kitcha would be dead by now, or maybe it was a new dog with the same name, a possibility. Some dog owners do that—same name, new dog. I could imagine the beast drooling, sharing in Sandra Sandra's good fortune, perched on a plump silken cushion. The picture side of her postcard to me in Paris showed a golden Thai temple, a wat, angling

up into a deep blue sky. It was warm and composed
and powerful, reaching up, up as photographed from
below, two peaks piercing the sky as if by magic.

Portland, Oregon
Many Years Ago

Sansan made me eager to wear the strange rags she wore, those velvet vintage gowns. They were not unlike gowns I dressed up in as a child. But that's how she dressed now, when she was a star at the noisy Zanzibar poetry night, down in the semi-industrial zone. The Zanzibar was where I had first met my boyfriend, Sammy, who initially caught my eye because he kept looking at me like someone who wanted to talk. And it was at the Zanzibar where I watched Sansan talking with dramatic intensity about greed and danger and human deception. It was as if she were relaying news from the front, from Afghanistan that time. "The people there have no need for us. We are the ones in need. We need them," she asserted, both arms strangely in the air, her hands sculptural, fingers steepled as they pierced the sky like the dual peaks of a temple. Her tales brought the political story to the personal one, the metaphysical story lurking behind, and she included the bad parts, unlike people who edit them out. She wasn't afraid to reveal moments when she'd been naïve, or mistaken. This was impressive to me, and I struggled to figure out which side of her was the true one.

One dark wintry night, we were all packed in thick in the smoke-filled Zanzibar with its throbbing red walls and low ceiling, people slipping out into the alley to smoke joints. Jovial shouting exploded late in the evening when San got up onstage wearing skin-tight black clothes and a huge silver crucifix, her hair plastered onto her forehead.

"You must wonder about this crucifix," she said, eliciting a titter as she swept the room with an arch gaze. "It's from when I was a kid, in San Francisco. Sansan from San Fran, they called me. I ran with rough trade in the East Bay culture, and we all dressed in black, hair combed down to a point, knees tattooed, fist-fighting in wetlands that smelled like diarrhea."

People were rapt, hearing about San's East Bay past, or somebody's East Bay past. Whoever's it was, it was memorable. She tossed her long red hair, struck poses, shaped the space in front of her with flowing arms and clicking fingers...and everyone went with her into the muck. She held the crowd as she segued into how she married her first husband only to abandon their child, Eddy, to her husband's family of fundamentalist Christians. Rural Oregon was fundamentalist territory then, so her story was familiar and elicited common memories of escaping to the city. San's story was a chapter in her saga, and it was clear as she spoke that there were many, many chapters. Her brashness fascinated, but it also jolted, as she delivered judgments in a distinctly amoral voice. You had to suspend disbelief and follow her unreservedly or she'd leave you wallowing in a moral dilemma.

I had a surprise encounter with San at the public library in Portland, the elegant main branch. The Multnomah County Central Library is a handsome three-story Georgian structure built in 1913 of brick and sandstone, with marble floors, vast stacks and huge reading rooms inside. Portland was always a world of book groups and clubs, of public readings by all kinds of authors, a city inhabited by readers curled up indoors devouring book after book while the rains came down outdoors. That day, I was going in, and San was coming out carrying an armload of books. I was startled, seeing her hippie self in such a place, as if the books in her arms didn't really belong there. She saw in my expression that I was struggling to rearrange my understanding of who she was. Her eyes traveled back and forth between her books and my confused face until I finally met her gaze and her soft, gurgling laughter bubbled up. She got me laughing too, and we did a dance right there in the big revolving door entrance to the library.

"A library card and I use it, don't tell anyone," she sang out through the glass doors of the whirligig as she circled out and I circled in. "Nobody would believe it anyway, ha, ha," she echoed, taking a few more turns inside the merry-go-round. I stayed in too, and we circled round and round while other readers with books patiently waited, tolerating odd behavior.

We went for coffee after, and I realized that I hadn't really recognized Sandra's erudition before. It was so evident in her manner of speaking and range of interests. She said that her father was the reason for her intellectual curiosity, as he had introduced her to books. When she spoke of him as the owner of a bookstore in San Francisco, she radiated pride. Her mother, though, was someone she brushed off as absent, uninteresting and trashy—not in her father's class and certainly not an example for herself. She said she had lived mostly with her father, and his habit had been to seldom be there when she was growing up. San had apparently learned to make up what to do and be as she went along unsupervised. This casual upbringing attracted me, a contrast to my solid, middle-class childhood in provincial Portland, and I could easily imagine a smaller, younger Sansan motoring along under her own steam. She said her mother hadn't wanted to be married to her father and that she had left when San was very young. "I am a motherless child, and I am the better for it. I grew up fast after she took off. We would all be better off if our mothers left when they felt the urge instead of burdening us with their troubles." She sounded absolutely sure of what she was saying.

Paris, France
Many Years Later

It was unnerving those first days after getting San's postcard in Paris to think that a simple glossy card had traveled the distance between Asia and France precisely to scare the shit out of me, to untether me.

The writing on San's postcard was in old-fashioned, turquoise-blue ink, a color reminiscent of the turquoise ink for sale at Roy's Five and Dime in southeast Portland's outlying Montavilla neighborhood where I grew up. It was novelty ink, not acceptable for use at school, which made it all the more inviting. It was like art ink or gypsy ink; made you want to draw something exotic. And there it was on San's postcard, decades later.

Below the message, San had written a fax number and an address: c/o Tip Nohting, Rathani, Thailand. No, not Tip Nothing, *hah*, I only read it that way. Tip *Nohting*. To hear San talk about any man the way she did on that postcard—*someone who loves me and finds me fascinating...who brings me peace and laughter and innocence*—that wasn't how she had talked about her scary Brit beast. Different men. Different countries.

Sansan had broken away dramatically from the Portland community in the late seventies and gone to Asia, to Japan, to India and to Afghanistan where, according to her letters, the most beautiful green-eyed people lived. By the time she stopped to see me in my tiny studio in the sky in Paris, she was on her way to the Far East for a third time. There she planned to sell the quality vintage clothes and furs she'd been picking and trading in order to finance her adventure. She had letters of reference, stationery and calling cards, an old-fashioned classy lady at a time when other people were vanishing into their jobs and nuclear households, or into discovering America. It was the end of an era. But not for Sansan. Life in the USA could not hold her.

San had already met her Brit, Marty, by then and was going back to Asia to join him. "I love riding around with him in his Land Rover, drinking at his expensive hotel," she confided. "He has money, he has class—he's a good catch." To my ear, this sounded like someone concerned about her future, not like a bohemian looking for dinner. But she liked him, she told me, because he took charge of her, because he knew where to take her, knew what to offer her to eat and drink and read and smoke. Ironically, her independent, adventurer self wanted a man to take care of her, and somehow with Sansan it made sense. "I want to be with someone I can fall in love with," she said. "I want that."

Marty hadn't told her what he did for a living, but she'd guessed it wasn't legal. He showed her photos of his villa in Katmandu. He had animals—a tiger and giant raptors, she told me, purring, eyes flashing like an eagle's on its prey. Of course she was smitten. Marty sent her a one-way plane ticket from Portland to Nepal. She showed me the ticket and informed me she was joining him without knowing why—something about the way he had pushed her into the floorboards when they'd had sex in their Goa hotel room excited her, when in the past, she had always preferred tenderness. "I love his decisiveness, his self-confidence," she pronounced, and I didn't wonder or ask more about it at the time.

A few weeks after receiving Sansan's postcard in Paris, I faxed her from work at the number she had written on the card. I wrote that I'd been thinking about her, that I'd like to come to Thailand someday, but not right then. I would have liked to see her, if circumstances had been different, but visiting her at that moment would have been an irresponsible escape from my troubling work situation. That wasn't the way things had to go. If my job was crucial for me financially, which it was, then it was clear I couldn't leave work for any length of time for fear of further character assassination in my absence.

Even as an escape, I didn't have the money on my modest salary to go to Thailand, and I'm not just making up excuses for my hesitation. I really had no margin in terms of money. I admit I was rationalizing though when I came up with the idea that Sandra Sandra and I really didn't have much in common.

True, we both liked to read and talk about what we were reading. And she'd had a way of making me want things I wouldn't have wanted before she offered them—that cowgirl belt, for example. It had been like, "Here, put on this belt, show me what you got." I couldn't deny her power. I did put the belt on and wear it soulfully for years until it mildewed and rotted, the beads falling off one by one. I considered mentioning the fate of the cowgirl belt in my fax, telling her that it had finally disintegrated. But the machine signaled that my message had already been received at the number in Thailand.

I began to think about how there's a Sansan in every town. The mythical girl who is wilder, more beautifully exotic, who takes bigger risks (and who can ultimately be exasperating—like consistently ordering the most expensive thing on the menu when somebody else is paying). San was nevertheless a girl who looked me in the eye to see what I really wanted and then made me do it. She was clairvoyant. Those girls are often poets. With red hair. Who die young. At every stage of life, there's always some knowledge just out of reach, and there's always a Sansan who already knows it, or at least those of us who are less experienced think there's secret knowledge that others have already discovered. But still, Sansan wasn't selfish. She gave of her knowledge. She did not waste her time obsessed with her inner self but instead looked toward the horizon and the larger picture.

I decided to forget San, to let her be tough without me. Her dream in Asia was not mine. I left the fantasies and the fax machine and walked back through the gray office hallways to my outpost.

The story didn't end there though. I found a ten-page handwritten letter from Sansan in the mailbox when I came home that night, a letter written long before my lame fax was ever sent into the ether. Written in the same turquoise ink she'd used on the postcard, the letter luxuriated not only in heretical ink, but also in antique, gold-embossed writing paper. The kind only she could find, the kind found in the bottom of a moldy flea-market suitcase. The paper itself had been folded, maybe for years, in a different configuration from the one she had devised for mailing it to me in a too-small envelope. This one showed a different return address from the earlier postcard. Now, it was in care of someone named Ha. That was the name: Ha. A man or a woman? The long letter itself was a finely-wrought tale of stars shooting through a velvet sky at night on the beach with Kitcha her dog, and her man, the Thai, Tip Nohting. Her fluid voice spoke of adventures we would have when I came to see her, *of rain from the street splashing up onto our hot wrists, of rotting fruits I can identify one by one, because I now live where the strange stinking fruits grow and fall to earth to rot next to my window.*

Was she speaking to me in this allegorical voice or was she speaking to Tip as they walked the beach at night? Or was she speaking for posterity? Tip was described in her letter as her protector, her lover, *not an Occidental lover*. He had been her protector and lover, but all that was in the past. I could not understand San's verb tenses. She seemed to mix them up indiscriminately. Maybe what she was saying was that by the time I was reading this letter in Paris, Tip would no longer be her protector, her lover. The whole affair would be rotten fruit by now. I got the impression something important had changed. Maybe something was wrong. Re-reading the letter, it looked like she had written with a censor in mind. Or maybe she'd been gone so long from the United States that she spoke and wrote English as a foreign language:

Tip had to distance himself, because I improperly spoke to his wife in the street. I'm in love with a phantom, who I will likely never see again, though I live on the isle of his birth, I doubt he's often here. I feel it when he is—is it love? Or just my imagination?

The writing in San's letter changed dramatically in the last three pages. In this latter part, she wrote in a loose scrawl and told of coarse German businessmen who were showing up in the village to invest in property deals, men who strode noisily and drunkenly down the center of the main road singing in German. The police had stopped her one night as she swore at a swaggering band of men, assaulting one on the shoulder with her fists.

Fucking Krauts, she called them, and to me she said, *Next time I must hold back my anger or they will win and I will lose. Come now, my dear friend, before I lose sight of the delicious nighttime sky over the sand. You will find my tale hair-raising.*

It was intriguing that Sansan had put so much time into writing me ten pages when I hadn't even answered her postcard…until that very day. She had written the ten pages at least two weeks earlier and spent much energy doing so from the looks of the penmanship toward the end. But the measure of what was time- and energy-consuming or of value was different in a torpid Thailand from what it was in Paris. From Paris, I didn't know how easy or difficult it had been for her to devote a whole day to writing me a letter. On the other hand, San had written me twice, and she had made sure I knew she had access to a fax machine. Or at least she had access when she sent the postcard, so I concluded that her bivouac— island paradise or whatever it was—wasn't all that primitive. It wasn't the jungle. She wasn't down to her last piece of old, mildewed, folded-up paper. But still, I was beginning to see the recent postcard in a different light, not just a message of *peace and laughter and innocence,* but possibly more like a hint of real distress—*you must come visit me. THE SOONER THE BETTER.*

Southeast Asia was in my thoughts and dreams as my unconscious labored to flesh out the picture, seizing on scenarios far removed from stressful moments at work. I dreamed that all the Siamese cats I ever had were waiting for me in the Kingdom of Siam. I had only to go there to become whole again. Mornings when I woke up, it was obvious I was ripe for an escape, and Sansan's eyes were flashing green.

Plus, I love traveling alone, so that all the attention is focused on the adventure, not on a companion. Everything is unpredictable, like when you're a child. Traveling means being pulled in by everything, by what is happening on the sidewalk all around you, by what color the signs are, by the gestures people are making to each other, by the hats they are wearing, by the eye contact or lack of it. Nothing is that clear, because everything's unfamiliar.

I was beginning to see how to do it, how to go to Thailand. Why not? I was having trouble in a foreign land just like Sansan was. The coincidence was exciting.

At work, a fax arrived from San in response to mine:

Dearest, come now. I have not one soul now to whom I may speak freely and be understood. I miss making

love. I miss red wine and theatrics. You must come.
We'll eat together a putrid durian fruit. They are ripe
now and through May, and the air is heavy with their
foulness. I'm sure you'll eat one with me. I know this
about you.

Was she speaking through a putrid fruit? San
had always liked slime and smells—a finger suddenly
inserted into her vagina and then waved in front of
your nose, that sort of thing. It wasn't *nostalgie de la
boue*. She wasn't upper class pretending to be a peasant.
She was a peasant.

Lost in thought, I lingered in the mailroom and
watched a man and woman in the apartment opposite,
across the wide, busy Parisian avenue in the bourgeois
Trocadéro neighborhood, where our offices were
located. The man and woman were standing, fully
dressed, on opposite sides of a bed. They appeared to be
talking intently to each other, although at that distance
I couldn't really tell if it was a conversation or an
argument.

Dinner that night was in a musty loft up
Ménilmontant, the hill rising in the east of Paris. I
took the subway to the bottom of the hill then walked
up past the artists' squats, then went one street out of
my way to see the magical button store stuffed to the
ceiling with every color and style imaginable,
available wholesale or retail. The tiny proprietor,
with her crown of tight curls, was just about to close
the shop, but greeted me warmly regardless. Further

32

up were high-ceilinged industrial buildings now becoming lofts, in one of which lived a photographer named Ho Tay. She was French Vietnamese, worked for travel magazines and agencies, and was generous to her friends. I was just a friend of a friend of hers meeting Ho for the first time. She seemed to me very Parisian, the way she punctuated an ironic remark by reaching up, flipping a lock of her hair and ducking her head down, all the while smiling slyly. She was physically arresting. She said she was interested in hearing what I had to say because I was an American. But then she giggled, because what is that, an American? She said she had not known many and "after all, your country has such a baaaaad reputation." I said I was an example of an American haunted by America's wars. "Is that bad?" I asked. She didn't answer and our eyes locked and held for a long moment.

Later, seizing the opportunity, I asked her if she knew what kind of fruit the durian is. It was worth a try even though Ho Tay was born in France, not Vietnam. She had just been in Vietnam taking photos, so maybe she'd eaten a durian.

Ho Tay knew. "It's a fruit in the South," she whispered, "a smelly fruit. The odor rides on the breeze. The durian penetrates your nostrils, like scalding heat in a sauna." Here Ho Tay began twitching her nostrils separately—left, right, left, right. "If you eat the durian, it comes out your pores."

Nose still twitching—left, right, left, right—her eyes flashed from one end of the room to the other without moving her head at all, her hands poised in mid-air to show flight. An arch escape from a fatal smell. She was a living cartoon, so clever and funny, creating the illusion of being in two places at the same time. Everyone was watching her.

"What exactly does a durian smell like?" I finally asked, but Ho Tay only wiggled her eyes in their sockets. "Like a stinking amulet? A cross between vomit and shit? A diaper pail! A mango fart!" I could have come up with ten more stinks, but I stopped there.

"Why do you want to know about the durian?" she asked.

So I told her about Sandra Sandra writing me out of the blue from Asia. "Sansan knows many cultures, like you. She wants me to come to Thailand for something urgent, but it seems, uh, problematical." I stopped. I could have talked more about it or not talked more about it, with equal pleasure.

"So why is it she wants you to come and what's the problem?" Ho Tay said, eyes locked into my mystery as she swished her long, black hair into a clump. She held the clump in the air with one hand and with the other gestured me on.

"Is she in trouble?" she asked.

Her question hung in the air unanswered and returned to me later, during the short *métro* ride going home. Up to that point, I hadn't let myself get distracted from my own problems enough to think that San might really be in trouble. What if she was? If so, everything would change.

That night, I rummaged through boxes of papers under my bed and found a photo of San with her dog Kitcha and her servant in Nepal inside a chapbook of her writing from the Portland years. In the black and white photo, Kitcha wears a garland of flowers and sits on San's lap like a happy child. Both San and her Nepalese servant are wearing long embroidered silken dresses trimmed with jewels that catch the light. I had heard that San preferred DeeDee, the servant, to the sophisticated expats who came around the compound where she lived with Marty, and that Sansan and DeeDee spoke Nepalese together. In the photo, they look close. They both have painted nails, and San is wearing her trademark high-heeled strappy sandals.

It seems apparent in the photo that DeeDee's station in life (ambiguous, with San there, I imagined) is one San feels comfortable with. I heard she used her rich boyfriend's money to send DeeDee's family members to school. Sansan got herself a sister, is how it looked to me. On the back of the photo, San (I recognized her handwriting) had written, *DeeDee came in one morning with this marigold necklace for*

Kitcha. It was an offering, for Kukur Tihar, a holiday just for dogs. Marty took the photo.

How distant all this was, when considered from Paris—even though at the moment, I, like San, *had not one soul now to whom I might speak freely and be understood!* A frisson snaked down my back, and I felt lonely and small and very short. Did I really want to see San now? I asked myself. Was it just an escapade I wanted or was this something much more urgent?

As if an invisible rudder were steering events, Ho Tay telephoned the next evening and offered me a free plane ticket to Thailand, something she had gotten from one of her agency clients. She couldn't use the ticket, she said, and was giving it to me.

"I don't believe you. To...*Thailand?*" The information was hard to take in. I took the phone and lay down on my bed to study the ceiling. Ho Tay's offer seemed funny, so I laughed a good belly laugh, flat on my back. She didn't laugh with me, so I realized she was serious. "Ho Tay, you really think I need to go, don't you?"

"Yes, I do. Don't fight your intuition. It's your best trait." She laughed mysteriously, a laughing Buddha if there ever was one. "Ha, ha, you'll...ha, ha...you'll get the ticket in the mail," she said and then hung up. Ho Tay really did mail the ticket to me a couple of days later. Inside the envelope was a little folder with the free ticket: Paris/Bangkok/Paris. The inevitability of my departure took a huge leap forward.

At work, I faxed Sansan to tell her I had a ticket if I could get away to make use of it. She answered me by fax the same day:

You must come as soon as possible. I will try really really really hard to find a way to meet you at the airport on the island.

Peculiar, I thought. Why did she have to *try really really really hard to find a way* to meet me at the airport? There must have been something holding her back. It sounded adolescent, *try really really really hard.* She hadn't talked like that in the past. Was she without resources and unable to make her way? Was she busy doing something she couldn't tear herself from? Was she ill? At a loss to decipher San from afar, I left the course of events up to fate.

I was determined, however, to smooth things out at the office before taking off. I had to be self-healing since no one else was forthcoming. Hard work seemed the best solution, along with avoiding the nemesis. I would work at home or slip unseen into my office and close the door. It was winter in Paris, which made it easier to assume such rigor. The City of Light was dark, brooding and melancholy, a sequester. A shroud. I could think clearly under the covers of its large blanket. The productivity of the North!

As soon as possible, I went to the chic offices of Thai International on the Champs-Elysées, where the floor was made of polished, yellow-tinted concrete, the walls and furniture dark teak, the women in stiff red silk, the orchids in shades of purple. Several Buddhas were on display.

My documents got me a twelve-day round-trip ticket, Paris/Bangkok/Paris, with a boat trip to Sansan's island. The agency graciously agreed to fax Sansan with the date and time of my arrival on her island via boat from Bangkok.

In the *métro* I spent more time than usual looking at the Eiffel Tower as the train crossed over the Seine where the river veers south between Bir-Hakeim and Passy. The tower's lacy steel was reassuring, and reminiscent of the Thai temples piercing the sky. My mind was starting to dissociate the way it does when the sands I'm standing on begin to shift. Back at the office, I went directly to the fax machine to see if there was anything from Sansan. There was nothing. She hadn't answered the fax announcing my arrival in her paradise, which didn't seem right. I was now alert to every little lapse.

Three days later, I sent a second fax asking San to make reservations for me in a bungalow with hot water and air conditioning for no more than five hundred baht (about twenty dollars) a night. She didn't answer that fax either, and my departure date was only two weeks away. A week later, I tried a third time, and the next day got the following in response:

To Sansan's friend,

This reply is drafted by Rudy Zuur, Sansan's neighbor on behalf of Miss Ha, her landlady. Unfortunately, Sansan has gone out of her mind, literally mad. She is now in police custody (jail), awaiting transfer to a Songkhla hospital for examination which no doubt will confirm the condition. The landlady hopes you will arrive here soon and could possibly direct affairs. Please respond at your earliest convenience, supplying your address and telephone number. Poor Sansan is unable to help herself as she is incoherent and seems to know/understand precious little. As far as your accommodation request, there should be no problem, it being low season. Miss Ha will make an effort to get hot water/air conditioning for around that price.

Yours sincerely, Rudy Zuur

"I have accommodations, they're waiting for me to come 'direct affairs,' and Ha is a woman, not a man," I said that evening to Roger, my good Samaritan across the courtyard. I was seeking his amused perspective in order not to panic.

"Air-conditioned, that's good," Roger smiled.

He liked the way the story was developing. He liked the preposterous, the unexpected. He liked it even better when it was not his problem! Roger was himself a bit preposterous. He was a Frenchman born and raised in Algeria up until 1962, when the French government had to accept the loss of Algeria and thus repatriated the non-North African French—all the non-Algerians—so Roger was a *pied noir*. What this growing-up-in-Algeria business had meant, he had made me understand over an occasional supper, was that he had spent his youth going in and out of friends' homes, having people going in and out of his family's house, Arab-style, with everyone knowing a lot about everyone else's feelings and business. He had grown up poor, with six brothers and sisters crowded around the table. He told me his father would hang a single aromatic grilled sardine by a string from the ceiling beam above the table and swing it back and forth past each kid's nose for a whiff so they could all imagine they were eating grilled sardines with their bread.

I later encountered that story and that image elsewhere, but they nevertheless remained Roger's in my mind. Roger pretended to be able to predict the future, but he didn't use a crystal ball. Instead, he got a look in his eyes like he was getting a message and then blurted it out. "You won't stay on that island long," he announced, referring to Sansan's island. Roger had never gotten used to the distances maintained by most Parisians, and, like many *pieds noirs*, he didn't trust them. "In thirty years, no one in this entire building has ever said a word to me," he told me. "*C'est toi la première.*" *You're the first.* And you're not even French. So no one in this building has heard me predict the future. You're the first in that also."

"Did you predict Algerian independence?"

"Yes I did," he said, halfway between pride and loss.

Roger had Siamese cats. When his ancient dog died, someone offered him a Siamese cat, and he took it. She turned out to be pregnant, so Roger had six grown Siamese cats flying through the air, flinging themselves from one high perch to the next, licking themselves, sleeping in a pile on top of his ninety-four-year-old bedridden mother who saw and heard things no one else did, who wished she were still in Algeria. She wanted to die there, not in cold, humid Paris.

Roger listened to my tale of Sandra Sandra. "Show me your photo of her and her dog," was his response to the bad news fax from Rudy Zuur in Thailand.

"You want me to go get it right now?"

"*Oui.*"

I went downstairs across the stone courtyard and upstairs to my place, found the photo, went back and handed it to him.

He studied it. "Now that she's in jail," he said finally, squinting at me, "who's feeding her dog?" Realizing I was San's designated savior weighed heavily on me. With all the other things going on in the world, in my world, she had gone ahead and gone mad, as the fax from Rudy Zuur announced. San had gotten herself arrested while Tip Nohting and her friends in Portland were apparently unavailable, gotten herself thrown in prison and was on the way to something far worse. And it was my problem. But I was being ungenerous. It was also my chance for a venture into the unknown.

"I'm going to Thailand," I informed my elusive boss the next day when he was in his office for a change. He told me not to worry about anything, completely brushing off my concerns about the kid baiting me. "He's just an intern," he said, as if the whole problem were nothing.

"So I'm going to Thailand now," I repeated, relieved. "My friend Sansan needs me."

He stopped writing his signature on the stack of undoubtedly eloquent letters his secretary had typed, printed out and placed in a leather folder for him. He tilted his head to one side and swung his eyes up to look up at me in a boyish way. He considered me at length.

He finally spoke: "Sansan needs you, did you say? Is she in some kind of trouble?" he intoned paternally...or was it paternalistically? Did he care or did he not care? Not being able to distinguish was disturbing. I felt disoriented again, my earlier relief gone. It was raining like mad outside. The boss and I were on opposite sides of his desk in his gray-carpeted office, our eyes fixed on each other, and I couldn't tell if we were having a conversation or an argument. He was sitting down, and I, the supplicant, was standing up. There was palpable tension in the air. I was wondering what he was pondering with his detached gaze.

"I've got a free ticket, and I want to go," I offered, "and I'll make appointments at the ministries in Bangkok to talk. I'll give them copies of our work to date. It's an opportunity, don't you see?"

"You're going to sit on the beach and smoke hash," he smirked.

"You're jealous," I riposted, reaching up, flipping a lock of my hair and ducking my head down, more French than a French woman.

"*Bon voyage*," he said with a snicker, appreciating my gesture. "I'll try to calm things here at the office." Later, his secretary, Blondie, whose tiny face hid behind large black horn-rimmed glasses, came running to my office with a fax that had just arrived from Thailand. It said: *I am Ha. You can find Sansan. Ask for Class Lady 4. O.K. When you come you come to me. I tell you everything. Bye. Ha.*

Class Lady 4. Was that what they were calling San now? There was also a phone number at the bottom. I folded the fax and put it in my wallet. My hand shook, a strange spasm.

The next day, I left for Asia. As the plane took off for Bangkok, I saw there were empty seats. Stuck between two large people, I moved to a seat at the end of an empty row. I would be able to stretch out and sleep later on. At the other end of the row, a young woman appeared and sat down. She looked pregnant, was Thai, had a sweet face. I wasn't sure when it happened, but she stretched out over three seats and appeared to be sleeping. Suddenly she got up, left and came back with a little boy about three. She settled him down to sleep beside her, their arms around each other.

I was reading an article about arms trafficking in the ASEAN nations. The boy began to cry. Was quiet. I glanced over. The mother was kissing her son on the mouth. I was not sure if she was kissing him, or if he was kissing her. They were kissing hungrily, lushly. The boy went to sleep again, not a sound. I tried to continue reading, I no longer knew what. The boy woke up, whimpered and I looked over, wanting to see what was happening. The woman applied her magic again, and I looked away, hardly breathing.

How long did it last? I looked again. The mother moved her head slightly away from the boy's. The boy reached out his arm, his little fist grabbing his mother's hair to pull her mouth against his, and the kiss began again, lips moving, throats swallowing.

Then there was quiet. A long sleep. Then crying again. I turned to look and again saw a long, tender, loving kiss. The little boy stiffened, released, his legs and pelvis jerking spasmodically, his breath pouring into his mother's mouth. He came. His mother didn't react as if anything unusual had happened. The boy fell asleep again, woke up, and again pulled his mother's mouth toward his with his little hand which fell, as if by reflex always at the same place in her hair, just above her ear.

Aroused, I clenched my thighs together and reached for the lock of hair just above my ear, which felt loose, as if would come off in my hand.

Bangkok, Thailand

A gray pall hung over the Bangkok airport at five a.m., a seven-hour leap ahead in time from Paris. The heavy sky was a low ceiling, nearly at eye level outside the terminal. Being there was like standing on the earth with my head poking up into the sky, like Saint-Exupéry's Little Prince looming large on his own small planet, his head stuck up into the planet's atmosphere, red scarf wrapped around his neck.

In the taxi, the image of the Thai mother and her son lying together kissing came back. From the son's point of view, was their kissing a different sensation than when he sucked her tit? Had the child really climaxed? He visibly had experienced some kind of physical spasm, but I didn't know if a baby can ejaculate. I would have to add this to my list of subjects to research. It was certainly true that what might remain private sexuality in other cultures had been overt in this case. Or perhaps the experience had been an example of how you catch sight of a fair amount of sexuality on airplanes, even if you are not necessarily an active voyeur.

There were tiny garlands of white and violet frangipani hanging from the cab driver's rearview mirror. The garlands swung back and forth in rhythm with the taxi's movement. With each swing, a sickly-sweet perfume flooded the vehicle, and I recognized the smell. It was what I'd been smelling since we landed. It wasn't rot. It wasn't cum. It wasn't the durian fruit. It wasn't antiseptic. It was the flowers born of rot, Baudelaire's flower of evil: the frangipani.

"Frangipani?" I asked the driver, who shifted his eyes from the road to look at my reflection in his mirror. I pointed at the garlands.

"Yeah," the driver confirmed, gesturing toward a small picture of the Buddha taped above his mirror. He thought I was asking about the picture. "It is for…" he began and bobbed his head in lieu of words. Maybe he was miming praying. He caught my eye again as he found the word he was looking for. "It is for *luck*."

"Ah," I said. I had read that the Thai people are superstitious and tend to believe in demons, but you could say that about many Americans as well.

Moisture was gathering on the windshield now, and the driver turned on his wipers. Sweat was gathering in the hair on the back of his head, running down his neck, circling around his moles. My own upper lip and forehead were gathering moisture into rivulets.

"You want air conditioner?" he asked, and without waiting for an answer switched it on. The big old Mercedes was soon full of cold recycled air and for the next two hours was going to move slowly forward in dense traffic on a four-lane pike into central Bangkok. It was late in the evening, Paris time. I put my jacket back on, wound my red Little Prince scarf around my neck against the chill and dozed off.

My twenty-two-dollar-a-night, four-star hotel downtown on Suriwong Road was not far from the river. I had two days in Bangkok to get my bearings, recover from jetlag and do my arranged meeting at the ministry before heading down to Sansan's island. I checked in, went back outside to have a look around.

On Suriwong Road, noisy un-mufflered vehicles belched clouds of black diesel exhaust into the already thick street dust. The noise was deafening—diesel trucks, tuk-tuk taxis (motorcycles with open-air, two-seat compartments mounted on the back), honking cars. And the air was something unimaginable. Down Suriwong Road at the crossroads was a police officer directing traffic wearing an oxygen mask attached to a metal tank he carried on his back. I was already bored with the subjects of noise and bad air—subjects of interest from the world I had left behind. I stopped thinking about them immediately.

Next door to the hotel was a vacant lot filled with large hunks of corrugated sheet metal. The pieces of metal harbored puddles and three Siamese cats were lapping them up. They weren't pure Siamese, but scraggly ones, with striped points—"off-Siamese." How funny. All the stray cats in Thailand were going to be Siamese. Small, empty brown bottles were scattered everywhere in the vacant lot and along the sidewalk. There were thirty of them. I picked one up and examined it, a flat squarish thing, about four inches wide and five inches high, like a cough syrup bottle.

The next building was a large bungalow, an exquisite private dwelling built of wood painted dark green with gilt along the peaked roof, bamboo trim all around. The house was set back from the street with the garden out front, not sumptuous but prim. In front of the door was a celadon ceramic planter in which was growing a large orchid with multiple stems of white flowers. In the soil around the base of the orchid were three more square, flat, brown bottles, all empty. The contrast of beauty set against trash leapt out.

The little map in my guidebook told me the Oriental Hotel, the *grande dame* of Bangkok, was right down the street toward the Chao Phraya River. It would have been hard to resist seeing this mythical place. It was now eight o'clock in the morning in Bangkok, about one in the morning back in Paris. I made a plan to find the Oriental, have a coffee drink and use their phone to call the number Ha had faxed me in Paris.

My silk brown jersey sheath (with correct-for-Thailand long sleeves) looked good enough to merit gracious treatment from the Oriental's doorman. He appeared to have just come on duty:

fresh-looking, with hair sharply cut, his shirt crisp and dry. He bent toward me from the waist. He was wearing a clean, sharp tonic, something resembling Jil Sander eau de parfum. He gazed at me and tilted his head slightly to keep looking at me from his bent position. "Hello?" he murmured into my ear, surprising me. "You are *here?*" he whispered.

What was he saying? Did he know me? I didn't get it. "Yes" I said. "I am here." He gave me a sly look. I mimed using a phone, and his eyebrows shot up in collusion. No longer bent over but moving elegantly now, he eased me into the teak-paneled lobby and smiled all the way to the telephone booth. He didn't linger, left briskly. I was impressed with our communication, with its efficient scenario. San had alluded to the Thai smile in the ten-page letter she had sent me in Paris. I had the letter with me. It was like an anthropological road map. She had written it when she was acting strangely, cursing the German businessmen. Once inside the teak phone booth, I found the letter in my purse.

"The Thai people keep a cold heart and do not show their true emotions to foreigners, particularly anger, or sadness," she had written. "They want to appease and exploit foreigners and they know how. They joke and laugh and smile, but that's all you'll ever see. Watch out though if you see their eyes go hard."

Ha's number rang and rang down south on the

50

island, with no answer. I pocketed San's letter and went into the hotel's celebrated Authors' Lounge, sat down in one of the silk and bamboo chairs and when the waiter came, I ordered a vodka tonic plus an iced espresso, served with sweetened condensed milk. I wanted to take the edge off yet remain alert. Alone in the wicker-filled lounge, I waited for Somerset Maugham, or some other colonial in a pith helmet, to come by and try to pick me up, but no one did. There was no one there at all. It was too early in the morning, an off hour.

The iced espresso cleared my head, and the vodka tasted like a glacier. Refreshed, I was ready for some information about Bangkok. My guidebook was suddenly useful. It said that Bangkok, the jewel of modern Siam, has been the capital city since the eighteenth century, when the earlier capital, Ayutthaya, was sacked by the Burmese. Bangkok was just a group of islands in a marsh then, and was geographically never meant to be a metropolis with concrete roads bearing the constant traffic of automobiles, trucks and noisy tuk-tuks.

The book said that Siam has been called Thailand since 1936, almost yesterday in an ancient civilization that sprang up at least seven thousand years before Christ, when hunter-gatherer tribes stopped roaming to become the agricultural folk who still populate Thailand today; and that right outside the Oriental Hotel was the following mix of people:

hill tribes, farmers and craftsmen, Hindu and Buddhist sects, traders and bankers, street-dwellers, prostitutes, princes and kings. And lots of foreigners, the *farang*. There have always been foreigners in Thailand—Burmese, Portuguese, British, French, Americans and the original Thai tribes that had emigrated from China to become the first foreigners.

The empty Authors' Lounge had photographs with texts framed and mounted all around the room. A framed map had a text saying that Thailand, along with Japan, was never colonized by a Western nation (unlike most of Asia), and that Thailand modernized and westernized itself in order to compete, to protect itself and to earn respect. From the Oriental, it was a short walk to the pier to catch the river ferry north to the old royal kingdom and its palace, the Rattanakosin. On the map, the Chao Phraya River curved like a snake through Bangkok carrying heavy boat traffic up or downstream, or off into a side canal, one of the few that remain of the extensive canal system developed centuries before. The modern city of Bangkok was built on huge wooden piles driven into the swampy wetland. I was interested in the pilings and the structures built on top of them to form the city and the drainage systems going from above to below and eventually into the Chao Phraya. I'd already read somewhere that Bangkok was slowly sinking and would be one of the cities to go under when global waters rise. When I got to the river, I stared down into the rising waters. Some kind of jet-lag time warp almost overcame me, but I straightened up and saw that I was still standing on the pier waiting for the upstream ferry. The Chao Phraya was right there in front of me, fast-moving, rough and choppy, overflowing its banks, dangerous. I didn't know if the river was at flood stage, or just at its normal level. Maybe that was the way the river always looked. No one was there for me to ask.

Water splashed across the heaving wooden pier, wave upon wave, rocking the dock violently as the river swirled under and around and over it. A woman in a white blouse and pedal pushers stepped out of the ticket office and shouted at me in Thai, gesturing. I think she was saying, "Watch out! It's dangerous close to the edge." I retreated and moved in under the corrugated awning next to the ticket office just as the clouds burst, dumping more water onto the raging river. The pounding rain excited the woman, as well as a boy standing next to her. They had apparently been waiting for the rain and became animated, jumping up and down. The boy grabbed a fishing pole and sprinted to the end of the dock. He had a glistening hunk of bait on a hook at the end of about fifteen feet of loose line attached to his fishing rod. He dropped the baited line into the water and looked intently at the undulating surface which was breaking into patterns under the pounding rain. The boy must have known that fish are drawn to the surface by drumming rain.

In an instant, the rod bent in an arc. The woman ran out to hold onto the boy as he rode the bucking dock and fought with his fish. They rode the dock together on accordion knees. The boy rotated the rod in his hands, slowly winding the line around it to land his catch, which slipped up onto the dock at his feet. It was a giant carp about four feet long, red with touches of silver, its beautiful wing-like fins still trying to swim, its huge eyes and mouth open wide, gasping. The fish looked like Sansan used to look onstage in Portland, catching her breath in the middle of a poem.

"Sandra Sandra!"

The boy and the woman on the dock turned to look at me and smiled enthusiastically. They thought I was saying, "What a great fish."

I was seeing Sansan everywhere in my jet-lag psychosis. She was the gasping fish. She was on the heaving dock and in the flooding waters. She was standing on the ferry boat sidling up to the dock despite the danger, the boat and the dock rising and falling together. She was thinly disguised as the ferryman who grabbed my arms to lift me on board at just the right moment.

The rain stopped and the sun came out. Early morning and it was already hot. The ferry had chugged a mile or so upstream to the Rattanakosin, the royal enclave. Inside the famous temple, the Wat Phra Kaew, was the two-foot-tall Emerald Buddha, talisman of power and good fortune. I had read that lightning had struck an ancient tower hundreds of years earlier, revealing the Emerald Buddha hidden there. The Emerald Buddha had traveled far, the way icons do, across the North and into Laos, where the man who became the first king of modern Thailand found it and wrested it away to install it there in the Wat Phra Kaew. I took care, sitting inside the wat on the floor, not to point my feet disrespectfully in the direction of the Buddha, so as not to offend the Buddha—so as not to get knocked off the path I was on.

I felt shaky, so it was a relief to sit still for a while on the cool tile floor, out of the sunshine. But then I was thirsty, so I had to go out in the intense heat to look for water to drink. There were Western men everywhere—Americans mostly, it seemed…with Thai women. The men, all of them large, hulking even, gazed down fondly at the tiny, chiseled women with their perfect small bodies wrapped in ankle-length cheongsams slashed open to the thighs. The small women returned the large men's longing looks with huge-eyed, open-mouthed attention seeking to please, their small, tapered hands gently touching a massive shoulder here, a broad chest there, encircling a huge arm. All around me, tiny women's hands reached up to touch men's looming faces gazing down at such loving tenderness, the tenderness of a dying pet. A wave of fatigue washed over me. I bought a bottle of water at a street stand, drank it all, took a taxi back to my hotel.

In my room, I donned my nightshirt and slept fitfully, waking up hours later aboard the rollercoaster of disrupted circadian rhythms. I placed another call to Ha's number, which rang unanswered. Then I searched in my bag for the chapbook of San's writings, as if they might give me a clue about Sansan's current plight.

Portland, Oregon
Many Years Ago

My first time at a poetry reading at the Zanzibar, Sansan was performing and had chosen to wear a long, skin-tight, cobalt-blue, cut-velvet gown and strappy antique high-heeled sandals. She sat on a stool bathed in a warm pool of light, one lithe bare leg thrust out over the other to leverage herself on the stool's fulcrum as she pivoted, moving her bare arms like fins, her thighs exposed. She tossed her hair, and it glinted in the light. Her voice was the sound of a stream dragging pebbles across rocks. This was the poem she read:

Sometimes overwhelmingly
familiar, it gives one a sense of history;
(I've known her for years)
security, friends
to back you up, to bail you out.
Good friends, hundreds of them.
Protection, dedication, and a raft
of events to absorb years, for
now I want to cease the satiation,
to unbind scars long healed
to reach wisdom of others, not ingrown.
To listen.

Between poems. She had an arresting way of

directing remarks to an invisible person next to her on stage, a kind of phantom sidekick: "You think these people are understanding me?" she would ask the sidekick, pointing at the audience.

"Yes!" thundered her fans.

"You think I should tell them about getting the clap in Lahore?"

That got everyone's attention. "Yes!" came the reply.

So she told us. And it was funny.

Bangkok, Thailand

In my Bangkok hotel room, I relaxed. Things weren't going so badly. Sleep overcame me until I woke up famished at one a.m. My bodily needs demanded to be addressed. But first I called Ha again. This time someone answered. My heart fluttered.

"Hmmm?" the voice said, spurring rising expectations. "Ha? Is that you?"

"Yes," she said slowly, "I am Ha...who this?"

"This is Sandra's friend. Where is she? Can I talk to her?"

"Who?"

"Sansan."

"I think she better."

I waited for more, but a silence followed.

"Where is she?"

"You her friend?"

"Yes."

"You come Thailand?"

"Yes, yes, I here." Unwittingly, I was suddenly talking like her. "Where Sansan?" There followed another long silence. I could hear the sound of fish scuttling against the phone cable under the Gulf of Thailand. I was afraid I'd lost her, and my voice was sharp. "Ha!"

Silence.

Ha wasn't forthcoming. There was something going on that I didn't grasp.

"Where's Sansan, Ha?" That time I sounded accusing without meaning to. It was the wrong tone.

I heard her open her mouth and take a breath. Maybe Ha wasn't alone in the echoing room. "You come here?" she asked slowly, struggling to figure out where and who I was.

"Yes, Yes. I have ticket on boat."

"No."

"No?"

"No boat."

"There is no boat?"

"You no come boat."

"How come no come boat?" At this I snorted, but Ha didn't react.

"Come plane," she ordered.

"Plane?"

"Plane." After a beat, she went on, faster now, as if she had decided something, as if she were in charge. "When you come?" she demanded.

"In couple of days." I needed time to think, didn't want to rush into anything. And to sleep, I needed that too…if I wanted to have my wits about me. "I will change my ticket from the boat to a plane. This is possible?"

"Yes, yes. You call me…tomorrow night…same time, I give you…other telephone number…you call Sansan." Ha said this haltingly, stuttering, but I couldn't tell if it was discomfort with English or what. Perhaps she was talking guardedly because there was indeed someone listening. Was it Nohting who was listening? What had I gotten myself into? I couldn't tell, and it was finally starting to bother me. I needed to think things through. Call me tonight, was that what she said?

"Tonight?" I asked. It was already the middle of the night. So was it today or tomorrow we were talking about? It was the middle of tonight, but she was saying tomorrow night, same time: one a.m. I heard a machine start up on Ha's end. An electronic humming sound. Was Ha recording our conversation? What was this place where she answered the phone only in the middle of the night?

"Tomorrow. No, don't call same time..." Ha replied, covering the phone briefly, then added, "Call later, maybe two, three clock." And she hung up.

I was wide awake. And hungry. I'd never had dinner. It was one-thirty a.m., and I couldn't think anymore until I ate. I put my one dress back on, looked up the name of a restaurant in the guidebook and took the elevator to the lobby. Outside the hotel, idling against the curb, was a tuk-tuk with a driver who looked me over and said, "You hungry." He wasn't asking, didn't wait for an answer. "I take you to nice restaurant."

"The Busscaracum," I said.

"That's where I take you."

"You were taking me there even before I said it?" He looked straight at me. The matter was settled.

He probably took everyone there. "Twenty baht," I offered, and he looked away, disappointed. At that hour, he was hoping for better. Or maybe not, because he turned around and looked at me again and gave me what seemed like a genuine smile. I smiled back and decided to stop trying to interpret everyone's behavior. Everything would be simpler, and probably truer, if I didn't read anything into whatever was happening.

The onomatopoetic tuk-tuk was noisy, but the ride was short, just around the corner onto a thoroughfare called Silom Road and, from there, onto another road where we turned off into a *soi*—an alley-like, dead-end street. The ride was so speedy that everything flashed by. There were people everywhere—in the street, on the sidewalks, sitting at low tables on the sidewalks lit by dangling lightbulbs, in tuk-tuks and cars and on motorcycles. There was standing water a foot deep in the *soi*, but people were moving through the water, going about their business. The tuk-tuk made a wave moving through, and the driver let me off next to a concrete staircase leading up to a landing under an awning that read "Busscaracum." The *maître d'hôtel* smoothly lifted me up and inside, where he wooed me and won me and took me and left me in such swift succession I felt like writing a song.

The food began with a mango drink and cumin shrimp chips to think on. I looked around the room. It was two a.m., and there were dozens of people eating. On my left, three big Americans: one middle-aged, two young, accompanied by beautiful Thai girls. Another couple was sitting opposite me, ten feet away, just the right distance to watch them unobserved. The girl was very loving with a large blonde man from someplace like Ohio. She moved her hand up his arm, up, up to the neck. My hair stood on edge just watching, wondering if she was a whore or if they loved each other. I had no experience in the matter, so I didn't know how to think about it.

On the walk back to my hotel, there were portable metal kitchens and tables lining the sidewalks and hundreds of people sitting on low stools or on the sidewalk eating noodle soup with meat or fish on top. My next meal would be like that. It would be so simple.

There was heavy traffic, mostly tuk-tuks, and there was standing water everywhere from all the rain. No one seemed to care and walked right through it. Everything was more humanly noisy than during the day, more inviting.

Relaxed, then gliding, I listened to a guy who came alongside me describing the sexual performances you could see in the establishment whose name was printed on a little card he gave me. We were walking by Patpong 3, then Patpong 2, Bangkok's infamous sex industry streets, which had rampantly evolved during the Vietnam War. It happened that the American military's need for rest and recreation had coincided with the Thai desire to please and appease. And it had continued and grown into an enormous tourist attraction. How was it I had come across Patpong inadvertently while walking home from dinner? No answer for that. In the meantime, the young guy, only an adolescent, kept perfect pace with me, left, right, left, smiling all the while, touting animatedly in simple descriptive language: "Man fuck girl...girl suck man...girl fuck girl...girl suck girl...girl fuck man...man suck girl..." He stuck words together any which way, just as his performers would stick themselves together any which way you wanted. This rap of his went on for a block or two, and it was funny, me switching my gait repeatedly just to trick him, but he switched right along with me. Except it wasn't really funny, because I could see the guy's whole life after the first ten seconds, and it seemed harsh. It was the poorest people, often from the rural north of Thailand, who ended up working Patpong, or driving cabs and tuk-tuks. I started to say something personal to him when he stopped abruptly in his tracks, causing me to stop as well—we had become such a duo.

"Gotta go," he said suddenly, as if he had caught sight of somebody he wanted to avoid. He turned and headed back up the sidewalk toward the entrance to Patpong 2. We had probably come to the edge of his territory. Just ahead, two or three new guys were lurking, waiting, it looked like. Avoiding them, I pivoted into Patpong 1 and went into the first bar, which turned out to be one of those places where girls performed amazing tricks with their vaginas.

The planter just inside the door held a rubber tree surrounded at the base by the same little brown square bottles I had seen earlier. Further inside, in the dark room, I sat down at a table in the back. The place was nearly empty, only three or four men scattered up front, one to a table. Except for, I noticed, a tall, Caucasian man in a white linen suit sitting alone at the table right next to me. He was distinguished-looking: about fifty, thick white hair, very tan, svelte. European-Jewish, I thought. He gave me an intense, shit-eating grin. The waiter arrived then, allowing me to recoil from the wanton smile so I could order a bottled water and a Chinese beer.

"Don't worry," the man said to me after the waiter left. "I won't ask you a thing." He said this in French. He looked pleasant...probably because he wasn't grinning anymore. He wasn't moving. I wasn't moving. That was our little scene.

"But *you* can ask *me* anything you want," he added, with appealing eye contact this time.

The sing-songy Thai music changed and onstage, a beautifully made-up naked Thai girl danced while smoking a cigarette and blowing smoke rings. Then she leaned into a back-bend with her legs apart, took the lit cigarette from her mouth and inserted it in her vagina. She appeared to squeeze on the cigarette, contracting her muscles, took the cigarette out again with her hand and then she actually blew smoke rings from her crotch. It was impressive, like a magic show, or a *pétomane* performance, and it made me laugh. The Frenchman laughed too, and when I looked, he was watching me laughing, not looking at the show.

"Thai whores are the best there are," he said, leaning slightly toward me then, drawing on his cigar, exhaling the smoke. He chuckled. I looked at the woman onstage again for a minute and then turned to him and asked him what he meant about Thai whores being the best.

He took a puff, exhaled.

"French whores are mechanical, like the Americans. They draw you in by flirting with their eyes. Once in the room, they'll give you a good three-minute blow job, fuck…and that's that. Latin American whores," he went on, "are passive. They wait for you to come on to them. Inevitably they wear bras, and are often reluctant to let you feel their tits during the groping process. Once in the room, they tend to lie passively on their backs and wait for it to be done. No fellatio, no cunnilingus, no foreplay."

He stopped and reflectively puffed on his cigar again for a few moments. He went on, "The Asian whore is different…she is the aggressor. In Hanoi, for instance, a street whore approached me one night as I was returning on foot to my hotel. She pressed her body against mine, grasped my cock, kissed me on the mouth and, while massaging me to a full erection, begged that I join her for our mutual pleasure."

"Okay..." I said, wondering why he was sharing his knowledge with me, but also wanting to know about Thai whores. So I asked him for more detail.

"The Thai whore will do everything within her power to entice you. They're the only ones I've ever known who'll expose their tits and pussies to attract a man, which of course is precisely what a man desires from a whore...raw sex. The Thai whore will immediately announce that she is anxious to suck your cock, which, of course, is most every man's greatest wish, especially if he is of a certain age, when hard-ons are less than certain. For the period that you hire a Thai whore, she is your greatest lover, ready to do most anything you desire, for as long as you are inclined to pay her...a whole lifetime, if you wish."

Pop! came the sound of a ping-pong ball onstage being forcefully shot across the room from the girl's vagina. A man at a table up front lunged to catch it, as if it were a home run ball sailing into the stands. The first "pop-fly" was followed by a second one, then a third, then a fourth. The girl had had four ping-pong balls in there and had hit four homers, batting a thousand. I turned back to my white-suited friend. He was watching me intently, but without any apparent expectations, more like a mentor.

"So the Thai whore makes sex inevitable?" I asked him.

"Yes," he confirmed. "It is a wonderful disconnect."

A French intellectual no less. "Tell me," I entreated, not quite believing the way things were unfolding, "are you talking about the *whores* in each country, or about the *women* in each country?" We stared at one another for a long while then. I had no idea what he was thinking. Suddenly he stood up, reached inside his jacket, withdrew a calling card and handed it to me.

"Thailand's a dangerous place you know... I'm tired now, but call me another time if you wish." He bowed, bid me *au revoir* and departed. I suddenly felt bereft. His card, which I could barely make out in the darkness, said Docteur Dominique Renard. Well yes, the doctor was a bit of a fox, nice to look at, careful, then not careful, flashy. Perhaps he had become uncomfortable, finding himself talking to me the way he was. He was intriguing yet off-putting, perhaps because he seemed so analytical, so practiced. I find the analytical approach to sex to be a turn-off, but I am perhaps hopelessly romantic. Maybe he thought I was a lesbian coming in there to watch naked women. And what had he meant about Thailand being a dangerous place? That was definitely the most important thing he had said. I finished my beer and got up to leave, pocketing his card.

Outside in Patpong 1, I walked by a brightly lit shoe store near Silom Road. It was open at that hour—the middle of the night—serving its clientele. There in the window was a pair of luminescent green platform high heels, open-toed, with an ankle strap. Sansan shoes! They were snakeskin, the sign said in English, only four hundred baht, or about sixteen dollars.

I had to have them. I went in, tried them on and bought them with no words exchanged between me and the salesgirl. Fantastic shoes. She agreed. It was five a.m., and she and I were in sync. I wore the shoes out to the street, and there was a tuk-tuk right there waiting for me. The driver looked at my shoes, smiled, then took me to my hotel, which was only two blocks away. I hadn't even left the neighborhood. When I walked through the hotel lobby to the elevator, the girls at the desk noticed my new whore shoes and smiled. I felt capricious, free of constraint, for better or for worse.

Back in the room, I found some of those small, flat brown bottles in the fridge, and these bottles were full. "Lipovan," the labels said in English. The brownish liquid inside smelled unfamiliar. I called down to the front desk and inquired, "What is Lipovan?"

The girl who answered said, "Hmmmmmm"

and giggled and passed me to another girl who also said, "Hmmmmmm" and giggled, and then there was a stream of talk in Thai amongst the personnel down there—a whole crowd of them it sounded like, no doubt talking about the woman who had just walked through the lobby in green, luminescent snakeskin platform high-heeled whore shoes and now wanted to know about Lipovan.

Finally, a man came on the line and said, "What you want?"

"What is Lipovan?"

"You going out?" the man asked.

"No, why?"

"You going to sleep?"

"Yes. I'm going to sleep."

"You going out tomorrow?"

"Yes."

"Drink Lipovan when you go out," the man explained. "Okay?"

So Lipovan was betel nut in a bottle, Asia's answer to lethargy, to hunger and malaise, to living at night but getting up the next day. It wasn't like Red Bull, which is caffeine. It was speed, a kind of amphetamine. This was the East, where you had to speed up to counter the natural slow down on the curve. This is different from the West, where you slow down on the curve, mostly with alcohol, to counter flying off the edge. The patterns aren't the same at all. Slowly dropping off the curve into sleep, I was seeing the patterns at play and hoping for a time sooner rather than later when they would move in tandem long enough for me to find Sansan.

The next day, the taxi driver agreed to wait while I went inside the Thai government ministry, which was housed away from the center of Bangkok. The place felt remote, as if it would be hard to find transport back to the hotel without a taxi, although we were still in Bangkok according to the map. A vast city it is. The drive had taken three hours, but the traffic was so dense it would have been tricky to measure how far we had traveled. Maybe only ten miles. I'd been thinking about my meeting, writing notes, but had still noticed that we negotiated several cloverleaf exchanges as we shifted from one crowded freeway to another.

What am I doing here? I scrawled across the top of a page as we inched along the elevated concrete roadways. I was in Bangkok imagining I could do something for Sansan, a woman who had lived in Asia for years without my help. When I'd first met her, I felt bourgeois in comparison. Maybe I still felt that way, even though I had ended up bolting from that earlier bourgeois life thanks somewhat to her influence. But in Paris, I was a person with a job again, in an office—superficially secure if not bourgeois. But compared to Sansan, who was in jail, very secure. San had remained true to type, living at risk. And now, curiously, as if on cue, she had reappeared to…what?

To liberate me again? But this time, *she* was the one who needed liberating.

The taxi driver had kept his cab un-airconditioned, even though it was the hottest part of the day. "I like true temperature," he announced, pointing at his cab's open windows. During our long drive, the flood waters from the night before had been evaporating in undulating waves above the paved surfaces. There was no apparent drainage system. The idling cars had been adrift in standing lakes. There was a point when the car was immobile long enough for me to watch a nearby pool evaporate to nothing as the sun beat down on it.

From where the taxi parked, the two-story concrete-block ministry building was hidden behind a lush fringe of palm trees and hibiscus. Plant life was pushing out through every crack in the building as the jungle reclaimed the site.

The cab driver turned to me and, in English, said, "I drink ice coffee." He wanted two hundred baht as an advance on the seven hundred we had agreed to for the round trip. I gave him the money and watched him angle toward a metal cart set up under the trees across the street from the ministry. It would have been fun to join him rather than go inside—I was having a hard time focusing on what was supposed to happen in the ministry. My work and my job in Paris were far away. I was intently watching the taxi driver, who stopped walking toward the food cart and turned back to find me looking at him. Still looking at me, he walked backwards across the street. Then he pointed at me and gestured that I should cross over too. I didn't hesitate.

Once I was across the street, he commanded, "Wait here. I bring coffee and crescent." I stood in the shade of a palm tree and waited. What I really needed was a Lipovan. The driver came back carrying fish-filled potstickers on pieces of rice paper and glasses of sweet, creamy iced coffee for both of us. It was perfect. We stood together eating and drinking, not talking. When he finished, he lay down on the grass under a palm with his hand behind his head. "You go now. I wait."

The conversation at the ministry had been arranged to justify my coming to Asia when there was work to be done in Paris. But it might also be useful. So I was on task in Thailand. My agenda there was to establish future contacts and learn something about Thai government environmental policy. I tried to get my mojo working.

Inside the ministry, the corridors overflowed with paper and folders and cartons, as in ministries worldwide. I found the right office and, after a good exchange with a very knowledgeable official, she handed me over to her young male deputy, who then took me to his cubicle. He was nervous, sweating even, quite frenetic, and I struggled to follow his heavily-accented English.

"Saucepan! Saucepan! Saucepan!" the young man shouted at me in frustration when I stopped him for some clarification.

"Saucepan?" I was hoping to intuit his meaning. I needed another iced coffee and a potsticker to illuminate me, but they weren't forthcoming. Furious, the young man jumped up, knocking over a stack of folders, and ran out of the cubicle to fetch his superior, who arrived with a disappointed expression on her face.

"It is a technical phrase," she explained condescendingly.

"What is he saying? I can't understand."

"Source point," she enunciated politely.

"Oh, of course. I'm so sorry." Of course that's what he'd been saying. I wanted to hear more of their thoughts on the issue, but the conversation ended, the talk ceased. I did regret not having understood the deputy's English, but let myself off the hook because of jet lag and dehydration. I hadn't done anything terribly wrong. Just traveled some distance and got off-kilter. And then there had been no display of photos, no slideshow on their part. The ministry was not a large operation and probably had a small budget. It was the 90s, and perhaps environmental issues, which had long been part of the country's historically sustainable agricultural practices, were becoming problematical. The government was now pressing for vast, intensive single-crop development, so the rural population was flooding into urban areas. There was so much I would have liked to ask, but I stood up to go and gave them a copy of what we had written in Paris so far. The meeting had lasted an hour and a half. Long enough. Don't look back.

The taxi driver, who had slept, was now fresh and ready to take charge again. He seemed happy to see his fare show up and turned around to smile at me in the back seat as he pulled into the slow-moving traffic. It was my turn to fall asleep.

Craaaack, came the sound of metal against metal, as the taxi driver slammed his door, waking me with a start. His face peered in the back window at me. I'd been dreaming some psychedelic out-of-focus thing, but now what I was seeing was the taxi driver's face framed by the window, and beyond him was Bangkok, and the taxi was parked on a busy commercial street with traffic grinding all around. Concrete buildings with steel front gates lined both sides of the street, an overpass loomed just above. The driver opened my door, and I lurched out. We were not at the hotel.

"What's this?" I demanded rapidly and took a step back.

"Come," he said, taking me by the wrist, smiling. "You go tailor, you buy clothes, you like."

"Like *what?*" I growled as if I were an animal,

digging in my heels, feeling dizzy. The driver was lavishing winsome sidelong glances on me as we stood on the sidewalk. He was still holding me familiarly by the wrist. In fact, he had the fingers of both his hands laced around my wrist. He drew my palm up toward his chest coyly. I noticed that he was wearing shorts and had long black hairs on his thighs.

"What...?" I shook my hand loose from his grip and tried to ask what was going on, but no sound came out of my mouth. The driver moved his smiling face closer to mine and said something, but I couldn't hear what he was saying. I had gone deaf and dumb. My vision was narrowing, closing to a point. It was a tunnel with light only at the end, the famous view that people back from near-death describe.

Later—how much later?—I woke up. The time—how much time?—was gone forever. I had fainted dead away. We were indoors, inside the tailor shop now. Shelves all around the room were filled with bolts of fabric. Tall mirrors lined the wall at one end. Outside, the traffic, the tuk-tuks, the honking continued.

"Water?" I said, not knowing if anyone was there. I was stretched out like a bolt of cloth on a row of hard wooden chairs lined up underneath the shelves filled with cloth. There was someone standing behind me. I craned around trying to see who it was, but the effort made me dizzy. The smell of charred cigar tobacco hung in the air.

A cup of water was placed at my lips. I grasped the hand holding the cup, drank the water and clung to the hand, which let itself be clung to. There was a salty fog over my eyes. I blinked several times trying to see. The hand was gentle and firm at the same time and certainly didn't belong to the taxi driver.

"More water." Water was all that mattered. The man with the cigar loosened my grip and placed my hand on my chest. He walked off, the heels of his shoes clattering across the wooden floor.

"She's all right, it's all right, she fainted, I'll take care of it," he said to someone, and I recognized the voice, which seemed impossible. I strained to look in the direction the man had gone, knowing he would return, and I would see him. I heard the sound of water running from down the hall, and then the man came back into view. It was Dominique Renard, from the Patpong bar. Docteur Dominique Renard smiled his huge grin when he saw me peering at him from my position flat on my back on several chairs. He executed a series of expressions with his face and shoulders in the controlled way a Parisian might, as if his arms were held to his sides with an elastic string, so the shoulders and head were forced to display their virtuosity. He looked caught, found out, guilty, but then genuinely surprised to see me; innocent, almost vulnerable, eyes casting about, then cool, detached, ironic. All this without a single word. Where was the truth in what he was doing, wriggling around like that? What was he doing in that tailor shop? So many questions.

I started with: "How is it you're in the same place as me twice in two days?"

"Oh, these taxi drivers are paid to bring people to the same places," he answered easily, brushing me off. Very cool.

"Did a taxi driver bring you here just now?"

"No, two years ago." He laughed and relit his cigar with a wooden match he struck on a matchbook. He puffed on his cigar. "But now I get to come here on my own." He laughed again, enjoying himself. He was still the Dominique Renard from the night before, only he wasn't wearing the white linen jacket. Now he was wearing a red cotton shirt, sleeves rolled up to the elbows, and white linen trousers, probably the ones from the night before. They were rumpled, as if he had slept in them.

"We lost you there for a moment," he said and handed me another cup of water. We looked at each other. I remembered he was a doctor. The dusky perfume of the polished wooden floor just below my head floated in the air. Over the top of the cup, I saw Renard take a small foil packet from his pocket, open it and hold out a hard white wafer for me. With his other hand, he took hold of my wrist.

"Suck on it, it's glucose. You probably have low blood sugar. And heat exhaustion. You're dehydrated.

Your blood pressure seems low, and your heart is slow and irregular. This is a shocking climate until you're used to it. It's the worst time of year, just before the monsoons. Have you been drinking lots of liquids?" he asked as he moved around beside me so I didn't have to peer down my chest at him.

It was still unfathomable that Renard was there. Time passed. The traffic was heavy outside in the street, horns honking. I sucked on the wafer. Finally, I pulled myself up on one elbow and looked closely at Renard. "What are you doing here?" My arm wobbled. I felt weak and reclined again. I thought about our situation. We were in a tailor's shop, with traffic crawling by outside, night falling. It seemed safe enough. Renard felt like a reliable guy. As if on cue, he moved closer to me so I could really see him. He was slow to answer. He shrugged his shoulders in a restrained way, like someone taught to be less flamboyant than was his impulse.

"What am I doing here? I'm buying a suit," he pronounced, bowing his head toward mine slightly.

"And you?" He smiled that smile again, nice teeth in a tan face. Pale brown eyes focused on mine. He was funny. Seductive.

I gave him a weak smile. "Do you think I fainted hysterically?"

Renard stood straight up, laughed with delight and clapped his hands. I held out the cup for more water. Off he clicked in his loafers across the polished teak parquet floor, still laughing. I closed my eyes.

After the fourth or fifth cup of water, Renard going back and forth, I pushed myself upright and saw an elegant chocolate point Siamese cat sitting on its haunches in front of the shop's counter gazing at the whole scene. The cat had been there the entire time. Then I saw there was another person there as well, a man leaning against the counter who hadn't made a sound, not a word as he'd witnessed the scene between Renard and me. It was the tailor.

He had a tape measure around his neck, a pin-cushion bracelet on one wrist. His hair was shiny black, his handsome face subcontinental. He was wearing a blue and white striped shirt, the sleeves rolled up to his elbows. When he spoke, I knew he was from India. "I can make you any suit you want," he announced—a merchant first and foremost.

He walked across the space between us, his hand outstretched to shake mine. "I am Apache John."

I got up and shook his hand.

Thus began a period of comfort because of the tailor's presence, which gave me a purpose. And because of the cat's presence too, which brought familiarity. I ended up ordering a shirt just like Apache John's for myself—blue and white striped, crafted of heavy cotton with a band collar, extra-large...for sleeping in. Renard and I stepped out into the evening air together, and he offered to take me to my hotel or perhaps to dinner. It was nine in the evening. I said I would like to have dinner with him, but that I had to be back at my hotel by one-thirty a.m. for an important phone call.

"One-thirty is good with me," he said. "*Moi*, I must also telephone to Paris tonight." Had I said Paris? I was feeling more on edge about the situation now that we were no longer in the shop. Renard noticed my tenseness and put his arm around my shoulder firmly. There followed an intimate awkwardness as we bumped along together in the direction of a taxi. Once in the cab, I saw that the tailor shop was right down the street from Patpong, just around the corner from my hotel, where a taxi had picked me up that morning. I still hadn't left the neighborhood, except for going to the ministry of course, but it felt like I already had a neighborhood to come home to. Renard looked at me, tilted his head, flicked his eyes away and cleared his throat.

"What are you doing all alone in Bangkok?" he asked finally. "I mean, look at you."

I didn't answer. I didn't feel like telling him. Not yet anyway.

We went to a little Indian place just two blocks away. Nothing fancy. Strange decor: wagon wheel chandeliers, like an American Western cafe. We drank beer. There was a dish of rice and meat that came with little plates of condiments. Had I been drugged? I wondered, trying to account for my erratic behavior, fainting and all. I wolfed down the food, drank beer, sighed, inadvertently burped. I felt uncool, clumsy, silly, unsophisticated—like an American slob.

Renard gazed at me, an amused smile playing about his lips. "You have a lover who is younger than you, don't you? I can tell by your mouth."

Paris now seemed even farther away. As it was, I didn't have a younger lover just then, but I didn't answer. Renard continued studying me.

I felt one of those Mona Lisa smiles sneak onto my lips, the kind of smile women frequently give when a man is embarrassing them…or when a man is hard to resist. I blushed. If I was flirting with Renard, it was involuntary. He seemed to have an interest in me, or perhaps it was I who had an interest in him.

"What is your political background?" I demanded, inwardly questioning if he was in Bangkok just for the whores. After all, that was what he had talked about in the Patpong bar.

"I don't see what that's got to do with anything?" he replied, making a face.

"What did you come to Bangkok for?" I pressed.

Renard paused, leaned back against the red vinyl banquette. "I came here as a doctor. Some time ago. In 1980."

He was surprised at my eager reaction, and then

intrigued, then dubious, then cynical—in that order. He shook his head dismissively. "It's an old story." He didn't go on, had apparently decided not to talk about it, but his body was tense: head poised, eyes torn, hands restless on the table. He picked up a book of matches and, with a flip of the wrist, pitched it violently at a glass a few inches away. The glass wobbled and fell over.

"There's nothing to talk about," he asserted, righting the glass. Then he started talking after all. "It was something people I knew were doing," he explained. "We practice emergency medicine, basic things, over and over. There's a lot of dehydration." At that, he chuckled at me pointedly. "That's the part you remember, the dehydration?"

I didn't reply.

Renard smiled tightly, lips together. He tilted his head. "It's a way of feeling you're doing something that matters…" He shrugged again, pocketing the book of matches from the table.

"But it does matter to the people you've treated," I insisted.

"Yes, but we are just borrowing their melancholy." He got up to leave.

In my hotel room later, the expression resonated: *borrowing their melancholy*. I wrote it down in my journal. I also wrote down that Renard had thought of himself as borrowing the melancholy of the suffering since he described his doctoring that way. Perhaps he'd had that thought fleetingly at that moment but also felt many different things about his work depending on the circumstances.

Suffice it to say, I didn't know the man at all, so trying to figure him out was pointless.

I went on to think about Sansan and myself and took a few notes. It was true that Sansan had come into my life at a time when I might have been looking for the shock of the real, which is one kind of melancholy. So if Dominique Renard was right, this sort of attraction was just a middle-class flirtation with danger, a self-indulgence.

Whatever. In any case, I didn't regret having met the doctor without borders, not at all...although he could easily have been a liar, for all I knew.

My mind was beginning to slip sideways. It was two o'clock in the morning and almost time to call Ha, though I would have preferred to sleep. I opened the mini fridge, selected a bottle of Lipovan and took a swig.

The phone rang twice before Ha answered, and the sound of her voice echoed in an empty room just as it had done the night before.

"Ha?"

"Yes, I am Ha," she said evenly, then fell silent.

My heart sped up. Was it the Lipovan? Ha had been urgent and mysterious the day before, but now she sounded calm. I tried looking at the situation from her point of view. Maybe her silence was simply a struggle with the English language. No one had told me how well she spoke English. We had eventually communicated clearly the night before, however.

"Ha?" I said.

"Yes, I am Ha."

I was relieved by her familiar answer. "Ha, I changed my ticket from the boat to a plane."

Silence on the other end.

"Hello?"

"Yes." She was still there.

"Listen, Ha, I arrive tomorrow at two-thirty." Recalling the hour of the day at which I had now reached Ha twice, I added "In the afternoon. Two thirty *in the afternoon*."

More silence.

"On the plane," I said gravely.

"Yes." Her voice was flat, noncommittal. Was she uncomprehending or uninterested?

Suddenly she burst out, rat-a-tat-tat: "I call Sandra today, she wait for you to call now. You call her now. Eight, three, three..."

"*Wait!* Ha, stop..."

"Yes?"

"Will you wait until I find a pen?"

"Okay."

I fumbled around on the dresser top, found a pen and sat down again, phone pressed to ear. "What's the number?"

Ha said the telephone number slowly this time. "Ask for Class Lady 4," she instructed mysteriously, and then, "Bye."

"Ha, wait!" There was silence again. "Ha, are you there?"

"Yes," she said impatiently. The connection with her was fragile.

"You say I should call her now, in the middle of the night?"

"Yes. Now. She awake. Or they wake her."

"Where is she?"

"She in hospital."

"Yes, but *where*?"

"In prison."

"Where?"

"South from Songkhla. You call there now. Class Lady 4. Bye."

"Ha, wait, what's Class Lady 4?"

"That her name there, she in bed number 4," she snapped sharply, as if I were slow.

"Okay, but one more thing, how do I find you when I come tomorrow?"

Ha was silent again. I was thinking about my accommodations. In the fax Rudy Zuur had sent me, he mentioned that Ha would get accommodations for me. My neighbor, Roger, had been so pleased to learn there would be air conditioning. I wanted to be able to tell Roger about my air-conditioned beachside bungalow paradise.

Ha was still silent. Was the reason for her silence that she didn't want to have anything to do with me? She wanted me to go directly to where San was? She had thought she would never lay eyes on me? There was no reason I would ever need to visit Ha's location. But that was not what I wanted. I wanted to go to the place where San had been living, at least for a day or two, in order to discover what had happened to her, to track her. I wanted to pursue her slowly, cautiously, to understand what had occurred, so that I didn't screw up. I was a novice collecting information to prepare for what turned up later on. Start at the scene of the crime, they say.

"Ha?"

"You wanna find me? Ask for Ha, everybody know where I am." She hung up. She wanted out, it was clear. She wanted me to "direct affairs," as Rudy Zuur had phrased it in his fax to me. I felt alone and small again, like a little girl in over her head. And the hotel room was so colorless, anonymous, so anywhere and nowhere. It offered no particular identifying characteristics. It could have been a Best Western in Topeka. I went to the window. Outside, the locale was more identifiable—the signs, the concrete fronts, the people. There were real Thai people down on the streets bent on real missions. There were lights moving by, transactions being made, words being shouted. I needed to ground myself again, go downstairs, outside. But I had to stay in the room and call Sansan. I regretted not having connected at all with Ha. Was it my fault? Was I dim-witted, a dolt in culture shock?

Portland, Oregon
Many Years Ago

I heard that Sandra was back in Portland from her latest Asian adventure, all aflame with success according to rumors, lapping up the pleasures of Stumptown before she left again. I was making a film at the time about the afterglow of the counterculture in Portland, and I wanted Sansan to be in the film. She agreed to play herself.

We were filming a scene where Sandra was saying she was going to Asia. I asked her to say, "I'm going to Asia" over and over, trying to get the perfect take. She wasn't a natural actress, but she was a natural star, her face simultaneously sucking in and emitting light. The cameraman noticed the way her face played with that light. "She's got some kind of electrical field," he told me. He wanted to capture her magnetic field on film.

"I'm going to *Asia*," she flirted, green eyes flashing as the camera rolled. "I *am* going to Asia," she insisted demoniacally. "I am going to Asia," she confided, conspiratorial. "I'm going to...*Asia*," she whispered, like Auntie Mame tapping on your breastbone to punctuate the mysteries you might discover in the Far East. It got richer each time she repeated the line. We played it for satire, for comedy, for real, and it became clear it was much more than a simple line for her. "I thought she was going to melt the lens," the cameraman said lustfully between takes. "I thought her eyes were going to catch fire, and it wasn't just the long shaft from my side key light! She's hot!"

I wanted to keep going. I knew there were a dozen more possibilities in her. San wanted to stop. She wanted a drink of something stronger than water. I said keep going, but she rebelled. She stopped and walked out, calling me a few choice names, taking all the other actors with her.

That night when Sammy came over very late, I was already asleep in bed. I woke up to weep on his shoulder about what Sansan had done. He listened and then told me what had happened after San and all the others had left me and the cameraman standing there. They had gone to the Zanzibar where Sammy was having a drink, and they took a table together. San told her side of the story, defensively, he said. The others began to say that she shouldn't have done what she did.

Eventually, San said that she'd made a mistake, that she'd been selfish, self-conscious maybe, but really selfish. She felt bad and began to tell everyone what a good thing our little film was, how important it was to record the moment in Portland's history, when life was no longer so easy, so cheap. She wanted to come tell me that very instant how sorry she was. She was my greatest fan, Sammy pronounced.

"She saved you," Sammy said. "She burnished your image more than anyone else could possibly have done. She saved you. She saved your film."

Bangkok, Thailand

With that memory from the past fresh in my mind, I took another look at the facts, always a good idea. This is what I knew: Sansan had been associated somehow with Tip Nohting, a well-off Thai businessman, but she had made a mistake, had insulted Tip's wife, and then something bad had happened. That was all I knew. Plus, I knew that San's mailing address had changed, and Ha had become her landlady. I was probably expecting too much involvement from Ha, who was only San's landlady after all. I wouldn't want my life to depend on my landlady in Paris. But Sansan had taken things to the limit. She had become a police problem. Now she was another kind of problem.

Perhaps Renard had gotten me off track more than I realized. He had drawn me into intellectual and moral considerations, like whether it's appropriate to try to save people. I had lost my white-knuckle grip on reality. I was also attracted to Renard, which fogged my thinking. I resolved to avoid further distractions.

I was ready to speak with Sansan. I settled back in the chair, took a deep breath, looked around the nondescript hotel room, picked up the phone and dialed the number Ha had given me for the hospital. It rang only once. The woman who answered spoke in Thai. She remained silent when I asked if she spoke

English, or perhaps French. Nothing, no answer. Then I said, "Class Lady 4" three times, three different ways.

Declarative, like an announcer at the horse races: "CLASS LADY 4."

No response.

Like a hotel desk clerk, calling out a name in a lobby. "Class Lady 4?"

Silence.

"*Class Lady 4.*" Like a scientist identifying a bug.

The woman on the other end hung up. I waited a minute then called back. This time, either the first woman had gotten some new information, or I had a different woman, or I said what I had to say in a clearer manner. Once I uttered the words, "Class lady in bed 4?" my new interlocutor emitted a syllable that sounded positive. She did not hang up, but set the phone down, *clunk*, on a hard surface.

It was painfully regrettable that I hadn't learned a few words of Thai, at least "yes," "no," "wait" or "help." I had gone into this adventure too hastily, shabbily. What I'd been intrigued about doing when I'd contemplated coming to Thailand was not at all what I was doing. I had wanted to compare stories with San in order to see my own life more clearly, and so far what I was doing was like a game, or a test. I was not well-prepared in other ways either, having sought no information or legal advice from anyone, from the American embassy in Paris, for instance, about the rights of an American citizen in custody in Thailand. That was pretty stupid. Really stupid. But instead, I'd been preoccupied with my own precarious work situation, with that arrogant little punk at the office hounding me.

I went to the little fridge, plucked out a Heineken, twisted the top off and drank.

Sansan's voice came on the line, and it was a strong jolt. I was thrilled. "You came!" she whispered throatily, sexily. It was the familiar sound of pebbles tumbling along in a stream. "I knew you would come, I knew I could count on you to come," she was saying and it really was San's voice. She sounded great. She sounded fine. She sounded normal. Maybe slightly hysterical. Maybe her voice cracked a little, was somewhat broken. But it was San. I definitely recognized her voice and couldn't believe I was hearing it. I was relieved. Maybe this wasn't going to be so bad after all.

A moment went by while those thoughts raced, and then her gravelly voice said, "Hello? Are we cut off?" She coughed with a horrifying violence and spat out what sounded like a huge volume of phlegm, then said, "Hello? Hello?"

"I'm here. I'm just stunned."

"You're stoned?"

"No, *stunned.* You're coughing so violently…"

"I knew I could count on you, you're one of those people you can count on," she said flatly. Very flatly.

"I don't know," I returned, cautious. "I guess you were right to count on me, because I did come." I chuckled and waited for her comment. None came, as if my statement had gone right by her, as if she hadn't heard it, as if there were no humor to be found in our situation. "Did you know I was coming? Did someone tell you?"

"I didn't know until Ha called today. I was thinking...I would die today," she remarked in a terrible monotone. "I have diarrhea real bad. I'm emaciated. They fill me with drugs. I have no food."

Her voice was suddenly faded, used up. She was speaking with great effort, operating on adrenaline no doubt, trying to rise to the occasion. Die today? Did she say that? Untreated diarrhea is a fast way to die. She went on rasping, gravel on dry pavement now, the stream dried up. The words themselves came out like diarrhea, in spurts, with pauses in between while the organs drained deeper into the bad shit. "They wait for me to die...the other women...the other inmates...they're Muslim...I'm one of them...Muslim women...less than dogs...treated badly by the nurses who are Buddhist, the nurses are, supposedly, Buddhist...I'm left to die...they hate Muslims, it's a religious war...they think I'm a Muslim who came here from another country to make trouble…I beg food from the Muslim ladies…they give it to me…even if I'm not a Muslim…it's part of their culture to share food…otherwise no food…the point of being here is to die, the nurses want me to die. Like Eddy…Eddy's dead…my son is dead…the voices told me…you don't have to tell me, I know already…Eddy's dead." She sucked in air, coughed explosively.

"What are you talking about?" I asked as soon as she started breathing.

"I know everything already," she said, starting up again, her voice scraping against the raw sides of her throat. "Did you bring my grandson, the boy you had with Eddy?"

"I don't have a son."

"You had a child, you and Eddy. Doesn't he live with you in Paris?"

She was speaking out of her nightmare, linking unrelated things together. She frightened me as never before. Eddy. I hadn't seen Sansan's son in fifteen years or more, and at that time he was a marginal, nervous kid, edgy, very good-looking, with San's marvelous facial bone structure, her Asian eyes even. I remembered him wanting to be a musician or an actor, but he had no discipline, no preparation for fulfilling his dreams. He was an attractive young man short-changed by life, not to put too fine a point on it. San had never had the means to provide for Eddy properly. Providing for herself had taken everything she had. She had left her son with relatives more than once, and then turned him over to Eddy's father's fundamentalist Christian family and run off. When Eddy turned thirteen, San had decided she owed it to her son to rescue him from his redneck life, so she kidnapped him and ran with him to Mexico. This shanghaiing of her own child sealed her reputation as a wild woman. Everyone in the poetry crowd was impressed when they talked about the episode. It was life lived to the hilt. It was a story that lent itself to repeated telling and had no doubt been embroidered as it was passed along.

In Mexico, the adolescent Eddy became a hippie, thanks to San's knack for finding her kind of people wherever she went. It was a different life entirely for Eddy, and the people were very unlike the rigid fundamentalists he'd been living with before she kidnapped him. Sandra Sandra, by then a kidnapper wanted by the authorities, took the risk of coming back to the States with her son, because she wanted him to go to school. She envisioned everything turning out favorably. As testament to the prevailing progressive Portland zeitgeist, as well as to San's own originality, Eddy's legal custody was granted to a community of her friends, intellectuals mostly—the very household that had originally chipped in to bring San back from Hawaii. She didn't choose to live with them anymore, but Eddy liked the arrangement. San was happy to have her son raised by her friends, and they all saw it as a sort of socio-political experiment and were happy to do it. Grown up, Eddy did all right for a while, got by on his good looks, but he always remained on society's scruffy edge, not somebody you could count on to rescue you in Thailand.

So was he *dead*? I glanced around the hotel room wildly. The alienating quality of that beige room was again looming close, as compared to Eddy's strung-out mother dangling on the far end of the telephone connection.

She made my hair stand on end. She had always been so far out there, standing on the ledge, so to speak, and ready to jump at the greatest possible risk. And it was so like Sansan to go so far out she would have to muster her forces beyond all resourcefulness to make her way back. She would rise to the occasion, no question, I was sure of it. Past experience made me sure of it. I decided I didn't think Eddy was dead. I would have heard about it if he were dead.

"San," I said into the phone, "I don't think that Eddy is dead. Who told you he was dead?"

"Oh, I know they killed him. They turned on me and killed Eddy, just to hurt me, and now they're killing me here..."

"Who told you Eddy is dead?" I wanted to take hold of her and shake some sense into her, but she was clear across the Gulf of Thailand.

"The voices told me, it's a long story, that's why

Tip Nohting threw me out." She stopped to cough violently again, tried to clear her passages, to breathe, and during that effort, she went from manic to earnest, a heartbreaking leap. "Is it true?" she whispered, her voice now pleading, pathetic. "Is Eddy dead? Is my son Eddy dead?"

Her whispering freaked me out. I could hardly speak, and the most distressing thing was that I didn't know if her son Eddy was dead or not. I only knew that San was at the nadir, in some kind of prison or asylum. Why couldn't I just say her son Eddy was alive even if I didn't know? Did the truth matter at that moment?

"San. Eddy isn't dead. He's not dead."

"I think he's dead," she pressed on, not listening, caught up in her own words, unrelieved by my assertion. "I think they might have killed him. And what about your son with Eddy? My grandson? You two had a son. Is he dead too?"

This idea that I'd had a son with her own son was coming from somewhere deep in her psyche, and it had more to do with Eddy than with me, I was certain.

"San, I have no son," I said quietly. When she didn't respond, I added, "I never slept with Eddy."

"I think you had a son," she insisted.

I stood my ground. "I have no son, San." Did she think she and I were somehow related? I cleared my throat loudly to create some space, but San launched into another coughing fit. She wasn't trying to get my attention. She was trying to get her breath. She was trying to end what must have been a painful spasm. She was trying not to expire. I got ready with pen and paper and held my breath until she stopped coughing.

"How will I find you?" I asked her when she stopped, and she unexpectedly turned lucid, making me think I had misunderstood everything about the conversation so far. It was as if she had already figured everything out, if sketchily, and was waiting for me to catch up and understand. San spelled out her scheme: "Get Ha to take you to my little house near her shop. I am naked. I just have a strapless bra, but it falls off I am so skinny. They gave me a huge pajama bottom I hold up with one hand, but it falls off, so I just leave it around my ankles. Bring me some shoes. I have no shoes. Go to the police and get my passport. Bring money. You will have to bribe them to get me out."

This was very reassuring, these instructions. The details were missing, for me to discover, but it was a way forward. San was now exhausted by the physical effort it had cost her to get her information across to me. "I knew…you would…come," were her last words before she hung up.

I was bombarded with doubts. The urgency of the exchange was too much to take in. What had happened to Sansan to reduce her to her abject state was a harrowing question. I hated to admit exactly how much ambiguity I was feeling about what I was doing. And resentment, yes, resentment. Such resentment is not attractive. It seethes out of your guts like steamy bile. It is the mother of murder.

I was shocked at myself. What a jerk I was. But at the same time, I was thinking San was a jerk, a manipulative jerk. If that was what I was thinking, why not acknowledge it? Everything was part of the mix, and there was no separating out any part of it. I got up out of the chair and hysterically ran around the hotel room screaming. I caught sight of myself in the mirror on the wall above the dresser as I lunged past it and didn't recognize my face, which was flushed red, with sweat beading up on my upper lip and cheeks, my dark brown hair curling into tight corkscrews in the humidity. I cursed Sandra, wanted to tell her off, wanted to lecture her about the way she amused herself playing with other people's lives while she lived her own life on the edge and then called for help.

A cold shower calmed me down. The water felt good pounding on my head. After the shower, I looked at myself in the mirror over the basin and wondered if I was the same person in Thailand as I was in France. My hair was never in corkscrews in France. Superficial changes happen first in a new country, and then come the deeper changes. Such as speeding up, or slowing down. The person in the bathroom mirror in Bangkok was not yet fixed in a new place. I would have to stay in Thailand for a while before any extreme changes would take effect. My eyes would gravitate further apart and take on a slant like Sansan's if I stayed in Asia long enough. I'd read that it takes seven years to replace all the cells in your lungs after you stop smoking, so how long would it take to replace all the thoughts in my head? How long would it take me to do that in Thailand if I started right then?

I hesitated about turning the air conditioner on in the room. I wanted to be hot in order to know what climate I was in. In bed, I sobbed for a few minutes, then stopped. The anguish had passed. I had already gotten over my feeling of resenting San. At least she wasn't dead, was what I was thinking now. Or dead *yet*. That was the kind of thought I needed to egg me on to find her. I had to get to her before she was dead.

I didn't want Sansan to be dead. I wanted her to be alive, for herself, but mostly, I admit, for me. I wanted her to be alive for me. I wasn't through with her. She was an unfinished story in my life. I hadn't forgotten that she was an avatar, a myth to follow, and now she was Class Lady 4, a new myth, and I would have regretted it for the rest of my life if I had decided not to come to Thailand and Class Lady 4 had died there, had died just before I arrived. I was sure she would be heroic again, evading death at the last moment, just as she had always done. There would be no death this time either.

The Island, Thailand

The small island-hopping plane dropped from the sky to a tiny black tarmac, taxied to the terminal and stopped. The light was blinding outside, the heat dry and still, an absolute contrast to the gray dampness of Paris. The situation in Paris had lost its force, it seemed so trivial. It had shrunk to an amusing puzzle, the kid's villainous effort to get rid of me was reduced to a French melodrama.

The other passengers on our little plane were on a group tour and not in a foreign land at all as they walked together toward their Swedish tour bus joking and laughing in their native tongue. Inside the terminal, there was a simple stand advertising resort accommodations, including brochures showing bungalows and tourists sitting on white beaches under thatched awnings. Behind the counter, a bright-eyed Thai girl in a tight yellow dress, big fake pearls and bright lipstick was waiting to please, a half-smile painted on her lips.

"How much are your bungalows?" I asked her.

"Five hundred baht for two," she answered sweetly in English, leaning out of the stand with a map of a round island. She pointed out her resort near a volcano peak, the dominant feature in the island's geography. Next to the peak was a photo of a temple—a wat—which was the exact image that had appeared on Sansan's postcard; the card that had ridden a gust of wind under my door in Paris. The girl's map showed a road circling the island's edge, with the airport and villages represented by dots alongside all the beaches. The road circling the small island got my attention. It was a road I wanted to get on and take all the way around. Small islands say to me, "Come circumambulate me, go all the way around, and like magic you'll arrive back at this very spot." It is primitive, the sensation I get from small islands. I got it from circling Ross Island in Portland with my father for sure. That first circumambulation with him had intrigued me, and since then I had circumambulated many other small islands. Now, seeing that map of Sansan's small island in Thailand, I wanted to do it again.

My thoughts had strayed from the girl in the bright yellow dress behind the counter in the resort stand, who I now saw was staring at me, waiting for some kind of answer. Her eyes suddenly jerked from one side to the other and back again, as if she were alarmed. Her mask dropped away and revealed an emotional confusion which vanished rapidly when I finally smiled at her. Her bright-eyed face came rushing back.

It must have been one hundred degrees outdoors. It was less humid than in Bangkok, and the air was definitely cleaner. The tour bus pulled away leaving only me and a boy dressed in an ironed t-shirt, baggy pants and Air Jordans. He was standing near a new red Toyota sports utility vehicle and appeared to be waiting for someone. He studied me as I approached him but didn't speak.

"You take me to Ha?" I asked him in English.

He looked bemused but nodded his head violently, yes. He looked around for my luggage, but I had none, only my roomy purse into which I had stuffed my jacket, bathing suit and cosmetics. I had thrown away my old nightshirt in Bangkok in anticipation of the big shirt from Apache John the tailor, and at the Bangkok hotel I had checked my nylon bag with my scarf and the fluorescent green snakeskin high-heeled sandals inside.

The boy gestured for me to get into his SUV. It was clear he had been sent by Ha to look for me, his actions were so crisp. He was so controlling it occurred to me Sansan might have been telling the truth on the phone, that somebody really did have a plan to kill her, and I had walked right into the situation simply by showing up. I glanced quickly at the boy's face, at his eyes. He didn't look like someone I should fear.

Soon enough, we were zooming down a two-lane highway through paradise. "This is a nice car," I noted, wanting the boy to talk. I fantasized that the Toyota would veer off the highway onto a rutted, washed-out road, powering straight up the mountain's flank to a hideout. The boy looked over at me disdainfully. "The car's not so hot," he said in American English. "We're gonna get a Jeep Cherokee…much more power."

We passed a roadside billboard advertising Monkey Training School, with a picture of a monkey halfway up a coconut palm tree.

"What's that?"

"They train 'em to pick coconuts," he uttered reluctantly. His arrogance began to seem like universal adolescent behavior. He didn't have the smiling Thai facade I'd seen so far, was instead coldly efficient, an excellent driver in any case, but he already had hard eyes, and he was only a kid. I didn't know what to make of him.

We drove through an old-fashioned resort town, like something out of the fifties. The buildings were scattered and shabby. It was the legendary South Pacific, from the musical of the same name, with a smattering of one-story concrete boxes topped by corrugated tin roofs outside of which women could have taken showers and sung about washing men out of their hair. The Toyota stopped in front of a tiny, concrete block of a shop facing the highway. A black motorbike was parked in front. I gave the boy two hundred and fifty baht (ten dollars) which he looked at, then stuffed in his pocket.

"That's Ha," he pointed with a jerk of his head toward the front window of the squat, whitewashed building. Inside, a woman stood behind a counter. My heart leapt. There she was. I'd come halfway around the world to get to this place, to this woman who was going to have the answers to all my questions. She looked to be about thirty, quite beautiful, clad in a simple white blouse, her black hair long and straight, her eyes cast down toward something on the countertop. She shifted her shoulders as she stood, turning her upper body like a dancer.

Ha looked up then, having felt our presence. She probably couldn't see me looking at her from inside the car. She was not smiling, was instead hard-eyed. I turned back to the boy, thanked him, got out. He said nothing.

"Hello," I greeted Ha inside the shop as I reached over the counter to shake her hand. She took it, her grip firm. She smiled at me ever so slightly, with the tiniest possible movement of her full lips. She was wearing long white pants with her white blouse. She eyed me impassively, or was it carefully? I couldn't tell. There was no one else in the tiny shop, which had only the counter, behind which Ha was still standing, and a telephone.

After we stared at each other for an eternity, waves of anticipation washing from me to her only to dissipate on her passive shore, Ha suddenly swung into action, jerked her head to one side and said "Sansan need you. We call her now?" She already had the telephone in her hand.

Ha, slow down, I was thinking, wanting to ask

a few questions before I talked to San. Just then, a fax machine behind the counter went into action, pumping out a page, and I was saved as Ha shifted her attention from the phone in her hand to the arriving fax. The sound of the machine pumping out a page was the sound I had heard in the background during my phone conversations with Ha but hadn't identified before. How silly. I'd made it into something important. And of course the shop we were standing in was the empty-sounding room where Ha passed the wee hours and received perplexed phone calls from me. The shop was probably a rental office, an essentially empty one, except for the counter, the telephone and the fax machine. And now, I noticed, there was also a bulletin board where small notices written in ornate Thai script were posted. While Ha was occupied with the fax machine, I stepped over and looked at the notices. Thai words—*sooksomboon, matchimawat, prachathipat*—looked sumptuously royal when written in gilded curlicue script on little pages with gilt borders.

I looked back toward Ha, who was eyeing me and may well have been doing so for some time. There was a silence while we contemplated each other again. "Did you get me a place to stay?" I asked, a wave crashing onto her dock.

She looked surprised. "Oh," she said, as if this were news to her, "you want place? Okay, you wait

outside...two, three hours. The person come back."
She really hadn't believed I was going to stay
overnight there in her village, regardless of what we
had said on the phone.

"What person?"

"Person with key to bungalow. Nice
bathroom, air conditioning." Ha picked up the fax
that had just arrived. She was apparently resigned to
the fact that I was staying overnight. She studied the
fax in her hand and dashed outside with it as if she
had forgotten me and climbed on the motorbike that
was parked out front. Only then did she turn and look
back at me still standing in the shop. She hadn't
forgotten me. She was waiting for me to leave the
shop. I trailed outside after her. Impetuously, like a
child, I inquired, "Where am I going to eat?"

"Shut door," she instructed. She pointed with
her head down a path and rode off, efficient like the
boy had been. They had to be related. It turned out
the path Ha indicated ran down to the beach.
Following it, I was not so disoriented as to not notice
the beauty of the lush, exotic plants, the
bougainvillea, the hibiscus, the rakish palm trees, the
sweet smell of the light trade wind, the rustic
thatched-roof bungalows, the turquoise sea just
beyond—paradise, in a word. Midway, the path was
blocked by a little cement mixer. A man was
smoothing out a freshly-poured patio in front of one
of the bungalows. Hands together as if praying, we

110

bowed heads to each other, and I went around him toward the sights beckoning just beyond.

The path opened out onto luxurious white sand. People were scattered around the beach in chaise lounges or on towels under the palm trees. In the middle of the beach stood an open-air shack, with a tin roof pitched over a wooden deck filled with wooden tables and chairs. There was a handwritten sign in English tacked onto one of the beams holding up the tin roof: "Fish Noodle Soup or Pork Noodle Soup."

A barefoot boy crossed the floor to take my order and was back in no time with the food. The pork noodle soup was excellent, very spicy and topped with cut-up green onions and carrots. The pork morsels were good, and the Thai beer perfect for cutting the fat. Sansan had no doubt draped her lithe limbs across the very same chair I was sitting in, only she would have eaten with one hand, a cigarette in the other, and she would have tossed tidbits to her dog Kitcha. Which reminded me, where *was* Kitcha?

It was four in the afternoon—siesta time for anyone in Thailand already in sync with the local culture, which probably explained the long wait for the key to my bungalow. The person with the key would be asleep in the bungalow. It was easy to understand why the Thais sleep during the heat of the day and live by night. Following suit, I fell asleep in my chair, woke up with a start, ordered a tall glass of sweet, creamy iced coffee to keep going. It was going to be iced coffee or Lipovan, as I wanted to stay awake.

Ha had the key to the bungalow when I went looking for her after a couple of hours. She gestured down the path (my bungalow turned out to be the one with the newly poured concrete patio) and waited for me to leave the office, but I didn't leave. I lingered to ask her if she would tell me what exactly had happened to Sansan that led to her being taken away from the village.

"She crazy," Ha said, relaxing her guard and letting slip a few pieces of information. "She in jail for month, nearly die, no food, I take food, two, three times, but too far away. Now she in crazy jail, very far away."

"You're her friend, yes?" I asked. "Sansan wrote me that you helped her get a house here. You're her friend. She wrote me about you."

It was true what I was saying. In her ten-page letter, San had written that Ha had helped her when she needed it. She had also noted that Ha was independent, or separate, or some other word like that, but San had underlined it and added in the margin, "This behavior is *unusual for a Thai woman.*" I hadn't paid much attention to the description of Ha when I'd read it, but now it seemed very important, and I wished I'd reread that part of the letter before meeting her.

"Yes, I a friend," Ha replied coldly, as if she weren't a friend at all. She gave no indication she cared a whit about San. But she had just said that she took food to her in jail a couple of times. Why would she have taken food if she didn't consider San a friend? Was there some other motivation? Such as not wanting Sandra's death on her hands?

"Can we go to San's house?" Going together to San's place might give us some time away from the shop to communicate. I wanted her to confide in me.

"Tomorrow," Ha answered curtly. "I can no leave now. I call Rudy Zuur. He come here tonight. You talk him tonight. He tell you what you want." The conversation ended there, as Ha turned her back on me and picked up the phone, giving me a look and a head gesture that screamed: *leave!* I had no choice but to wait for a day.

At my bungalow, I leapt across the patio to avoid leaving my foot in the fresh concrete. The bungalow was a simple structure sheathed in dark brown, weather-beaten siding—T-111, it's called in the States, the kind of siding you see on cheap, weather-tortured cottages next to oceans all around the world. The room was an oven, the interior walls stained dark brown as well. I turned on the dim light and the air conditioning, fished a bottle of water out of the little refrigerator and watched the geckos scurrying to hide from the new light.

The darkness required some getting used to after

the stunning light outside. The bed was a thin piece of foam rubber laid over sagging springs, but the room had a cool tile floor which made the room clean and refreshing. It seemed about right for five hundred baht (twenty dollars), the price I had mentioned in my fax sent from Paris. The fancy resort accommodations advertised at the airport had been five hundred baht (for two!), plus I had seen signs on the highway for bungalows at two hundred and fifty baht. I wondered what Ha would ask me to pay, and I also wondered who was buried under the new concrete patio outside. I put on my bathing suit under my dress and set off down the path to the beach.

Everything written in the guidebooks about the limpid Southeast Asian light is true. Everything written about what happens on Thai beaches is also true and happened within five minutes of my settling down on the skimpy bungalow towel. A man came by and sold me a cold drink, a Fanta. A kid came by and offered to sell me dope. A middle-aged woman appeared and massaged my shoulders perfunctorily. She offered to put my hair in tiny braids, but I said no. Next, a nervous young woman suggested I come make love with her husband, who, she said, was nearby in their room with their baby daughter. If I wanted, I could have sex with the two of them, husband and wife together or separately. Before she offered me sex with her baby daughter, I gave her twenty baht and told her I needed nothing. She left but returned with a beautiful dark blue cotton batik scarf. "A gift, a gift," she insisted, but didn't refuse an additional one hundred baht. I didn't want to keep spending money. I had only a few hundred dollars in my budget so didn't want any more vendors. I had eventual bribes to plan for. The next person who approached I waved off.

Night fell like a curtain. There was no dusk. It was light and then, abruptly, it was dark. Why that happens is obvious if you give it any thought: the closer you are to the equator, the more rapid it becomes dark after sunset, because the equatorial sections of the Earth are traveling faster than the surfaces in the northern or southern hemispheres, where the slower turning of the Earth allows you to experience the twilight, the magic hour after sunset.

Later that evening after dinner, in the same open-air restaurant on the beach (the fish noodle soup was also excellent), I went up to the office to find Ha. I waited for an hour but then went back down to the restaurant for a beer, and then another. Just when I was thinking of going back to the office again to look for Ha, she materialized, like a ninja accompanied by a young man who might have been her boyfriend. They stood close together, if that meant anything. He acted like a lover who'd been recruited into being a bit player, whereas she acted like someone on a mission, her eyes boring into me. What a powerful woman she was, or did I think that just because she knew things I wanted to know? As for the boyfriend, he was very good looking, too. He had his black hair pulled back into a ponytail and was wearing a gray zipper-front sweatshirt and jeans, plus one gold earring. He looked more Japanese to me than Thai, features angular rather than rounded. He looked angry. He was very direct with his dislike for me, not elusive or vague, like Ha.

"You know Sansan crazy, she the devil," he said, putting his face right up next to mine in a threatening way. He punctuated his words by spitting, not at me but next to me, as if he were spitting on her, on the devil. I froze. He froze. Ha slowly looked from him to me and back again.

"Come on," she told her friend in English, pulling him by the arm, changing into harsh-sounding Thai. After that, he shut up, but his eyes stayed hard. While he was direct, Ha might have been difficult to read, but she was in charge. San had written in her long letter about the power Thai women have over their men, how women hold onto their control, which is a counterweight to the power of the king, the strong male model that permeates Thai society. This was important in regard to what was happening with me and Ha. She expected I would "direct affairs," because that was the sort of thing she would do, if it were in her interest. She wouldn't mess around with unnecessary details, such as whether she and Sandra were friends or not. *Managing* or *manipulating* is what women do in the Thai culture, San had written. Sansan's descriptions of Thai people's general behavior were suddenly very pertinent. But her descriptions of people in her storytelling had always been deeply observed. Why, then, hadn't she been able to use her keen sense of observation and make a story out of her precarious situation instead of getting in trouble? Her luck, which had always carried her in the past, might have been running out. And maybe her abundant charms had lessened as she got older.

The three of us walked silently up the path to the office, single file, Ha first, me next, her man bringing up the rear—his hostility masked but still palpable. I was uncomfortable having him behind me as we walked. None too soon, we approached the office, where there was a Caucasian man waiting inside. I looked at him with relief—with the asinine expectation of being able to communicate better with him simply because he was white like me, an expectation exacerbated in this case by fear.

The man was very white indeed. And tall, with bushy red hair, freckles, spectacles, big teeth. Rudy Zuur turned out to be Dutch. He was fifty-five, a writer and a twenty-year resident of the island, he told me. At first, he spoke as if I were an investigating officer or someone from the American embassy, even though I hadn't implied anything of the kind. Twenty years might have brought him to an appreciation of the Thai female authority figure, so he now transferred those feelings onto me. Nevertheless, it was odd behavior, as Rudy Zuur knew how and when I had innocently come into the story. He had read my faxes to San announcing my arrival. He had been the one to answer me. It was Zuur who had faxed me the day before I'd left Paris explaining what had happened to San.

I asked Zuur what he did for a living, and he told me he was a novelist...not a great one, he said, and I recognized a certain professional distortion in his behavior: He had turned me into a detective and made himself the guilty suspect. He and I sat in the rental office facing each other on two folding chairs that had materialized since earlier that day. Our exchange was monotonous: *question, short answer, question, short answer, question, short answer.* He didn't enter emotionally into the exchange, but I did learn that he had lived next door to San the last few months, before the "incident," as he called it. He didn't really know her, he claimed, didn't know where she had come from, had spoken to her at length only once. He had nevertheless noticed her becoming more and more erratic.

"In what way was she erratic?"

"She was talking to herself, having some kind of exchange with herself," Zuur explained, sucking on his big teeth. He held himself stiffly on the uncomfortable chair, looked at me sideways through his spectacles, didn't relax at all. His freckles stood out like spots of blood on white skin.

"What was she talking to herself about?" I leaned back in my folding chair, trying to appear casual as I delved deeper into my gumshoe role.

He dismissed San with a hand gesture. "She was incoherent."

"Oh? What else was she doing that was erratic?"

"She shouted angrily at whoever walked by."

"What was she shouting?"

"She was incoherent, made no sense at all. She assaulted some Germans in town, and then, a week later, she was outside my house, drunk, shouting my name. When I went out to my car, she came running at me and attacked me with a butcher knife. She wanted to kill me. She *would have* killed me, but I put up my hand to stop her." Zuur raised his hand against the invisible knife, then put it back in his lap. "She cut my hand and arm...deeply. I got in my car, she stabbed at the car, scratched the paint, knocked the rearview mirror off. She kept stabbing at the car, she was acting cra—" he started to say, then stopped himself, deciding to wait for the next question. I reached out my hand toward his, the one he claimed he had held up against the assault, but he pulled his whole body away from me, didn't show me any evidence of his wound. Why was that? I felt ambivalent about demanding to see proof. I wasn't a cop after all. But why hadn't he shown me his scar? If there was one… It's not like I didn't believe him, but his description of Sansan seemed out of proportion to anything I'd ever seen or heard of her, so I kind of needed to see the wound as evidence. There was a moment of silence. I let it pass and casually went on with the questions, like a village gossip wanting all the dirt.

"So why was she so angry? Why did she attack you with a butcher knife?"

He *almost* answered spontaneously then paused to reflect, or edit himself, finally settling on responding with irritation. "I don't know. She called me a thief, which was ridiculous. She said I stole her soul. She is clearly schizophrenic. I didn't expect…" Zuur was shaking his head now, warding off further questions. Color was rising in his cheeks. He reached for his cigarette case in his shirt pocket, opened it, took a cigarette, lit it, puffed, picked a bit of tobacco off his tongue, exhaled, got control of himself.

"So how did she end up in jail?" I queried, ignoring his remark about San being schizophrenic. "Did you call the police?"

"No, no, no," Zuur said *quickly*. Too quickly, I noticed. Which seemed, to me, an indication of guilt. He hunched his head down into his shoulders, as if to avoid a parental blow, body language speaking across years of exile.

"No, no, no, I was in the hospital…for my hand,

I had forty stitches," he insisted, holding it out but again drawing it back too rapidly for me to see much of anything beyond a redness. "I absolutely did *not* contact the authorities." He took off his glasses, which were on a chain around his neck, dropped them to his chest, rubbed his eyes vigorously, shrugged and sighed heavily. "I did *not* call the police. I didn't *have to* call the police. Her Thai neighbors were terrified of her. They all talked about her. They thought she was possessed by a devil. To them, her delirium suggested possession by evil spirits. They were frightened. *They* went for the police. I'm sure they did. They must have."

Zuur sighed, mopped his brow with his handkerchief, put his glasses back on and puffed steadily on his cigarette. We stared silently at each other for a long while. How long would it take before he went on without my prodding? It wasn't long before he finally blurted out, "You know they give you nothing at all to eat or drink in jail in this country. That's the way it's done. Prisoners get no food, it has to be brought in by your family. Sansan had no family, so I took her plates of food for a week after I got out of the hospital, but the guard told me she didn't want it after she found out it was from *me*. She hated me."

Zuur shrugged, through with the subject, through with the interrogation, through with me. He stood up. Unexpectedly, he sat down and began again, speeding on to the real finish. "I had a business trip, so

I left the island for a while…I don't know what happened to her after that, they took her somewhere in the South, to the psychiatric facility, the asylum, the hospital, the jail, whatever it is…" He darted his eyes over toward Ha, seeking her concurrence. Ha had been standing quietly all this time by the fax machine next to her tense boyfriend. In the short time it took me to glance at Ha and her boyfriend, the latter's eyes pierced me like a knife.

"I took Sansan food, too," Ha asserted, repeating what she had told me earlier in the day. Her boyfriend grimaced. He unnerved me, so I looked at Zuur.

"Why was Sandra angry at you?" I asked again. "What did she mean, that you had stolen her soul? Is that what you meant by her being schizophrenic?"

He snorted dismissively. "I think she was envious of me as a writer."

"Oh? Why do you think that? What did she say? She's a published poet, you know."

He raised his eyebrows in surprise. "She accused me of stealing her ideas, which is ridiculous. She was crazy, just ranting. She'd apparently been in the hospital to have some kind of tumor removed, and her dog died while she was gone, and she was just crazy after that."

Her dog *had* died! Tumor! Zuur *did* know a few things about San. I didn't know anything about any tumor or operation, and I certainly didn't know San's dog had died.

"Kitcha *died?*"

"Yes," Zuur confirmed, edging toward the door, turning toward me to offer to take me to the people who had been caring for Kitcha when she passed on. The conversation was over, and I was left with the impression Rudy Zuur felt he had failed San when she was in need. He felt responsible for the horrible mess she was in now, and maybe he *was* responsible, but he was relieved to have somebody else in charge of the problem. Perhaps I was wrong about all of that, and instead he was thinking this was all a waste of time and that it was best to be done with it.

It was midnight, the shank of the evening in Thailand. I thanked Ha, who gave me a look of approval, the first bit of empathy she had conceded. Zuur said something about getting home for dinner, and we left in his car. I got nothing more out of him as we drove two hundred yards down the main street, two hundred more uphill on a smaller, unpaved road.

My thoughts turned to Roger, my neighbor across the courtyard in Paris. Roger had looked at the photo of Sansan and Kitcha taken in Nepal and had asked me who was caring for her dog now that San was in jail. Roger had seen the story unfolding way back then. He really was clairvoyant. Or at least empathic. He had looked at my closed shutters across the Paris courtyard and intuited that all was not well, that I needed help. He had intervened—the opposite of Zuur's behavior. Some people are aware of what is happening to another person and are willing to take action, whereas others see nothing they want to get involved in and slam the door. Roger suddenly felt dear.

"Here it is," Zuur announced, bringing me back to the hot, humid night as he stopped his car and pointed at something in the dark, something I couldn't make out. "There." Then I saw he was pointing past my nose at an open-air, one-story structure. A concrete block. It was a short distance off the road surrounded by palms. The place was lit up with flashing lights like a disco filled not with dancers, but with body building machines.

"Manley's Gym," Zuur said, looking me in the eye for the first time. "Ask for Manley."

I got out of the car, slammed the door and bent forward to say something to him through the open window, but he took off quickly, the sorry mess between us—between him and San—concluded. I felt foolish, my body still curved like a question mark.

Inside the gym, there was a man leaning against the wall in the far corner talking loudly on the phone in what sounded like Scots. I could hear him ordering his dinner, but I couldn't wrap my head around his accent. Not right away at least. There was also a naked male customer bench-pressing weights, but he vanished just as I noticed him. I saw only his taut buttocks bathed in sweat. Maybe he simply evaporated. It must have been ninety degrees even late at night, with one hundred percent humidity. The Scot pushed himself away from the wall, hung up the phone, then jumped in genuine alarm when he saw me.

"Manley?" I asked, and his face made an exaggerated expression of shock. He was tall, lean, with an agile Mick Jagger body, large mouth, bony face. He had tousled, longish bleached blond hair. He was a fit fifty-five or sixty, and he was wearing a pair of orange shorts. He narrowed his eyes, peered incomprehensibly, shook his head slowly from side to side.

"Whazzat?" he replied at last.

I told him I was trying to find Sansan.

"Oww, she's inna nuthoose, dinna you know?"

"Yes, I know. I want to find out what happened to her before that. Do you know where I can find Tip Nohting?"

Manley gave me a suspicious look. "You her sister?"

"No, a friend."

"Whadja sigh your name woz?" Without waiting for an answer, he turned and walked toward the back of the building, looking back over his shoulder to instruct, "Come awn out here, luv." Then he shouted, "Jimmy!" and a man outside in the dark came into view. Jimmy had been there all along, but my eyes were just now adjusting to the dark. There were four chairs lined up outside facing the inside, so people sitting in them could watch from out there what was going on inside in the gym. "Ay ordered Chaynese," Manley announced to Jimmy, then to me: "Oww, you hungry, luv? Ay c'n cawl back." He half turned to go back inside, but I said no to Chinese…and then yes to a beer. Jimmy was also long and lean like Mick Jagger—it must have been a cult. Jimmy was clad only in turquoise shorts, with an earring and shaved head, a look which added a certain chicness to a man as weatherworn as this one. He was Australian. Yet another exile.

"Sandra? That lunatic wit' red 'air?" Jimmy blared. "She always walked by 'ere talking to 'erself, lived back up in there." He gestured up the dirt road, rolled his eyes and reached over to put a Rolling Stones cassette into a tape machine. How could I have been so right? The tape was at the midpoint in "Brown Sugar." Jimmy turned up the volume and dropped out of the conversation. Just then, a Thai kid showed up with two plates of rice and veggies which he placed on the ground, one in front of Manley, one in front of Jimmy. Manley stepped over his (from what I could make out in the darkness) refrigerator, held shut with a padlock on the handle. He came back with three Thai beers and handed me one.

Manley and I had to shout over the Stones grinding away. He shoveled huge forkfuls of food into his mouth. I had no time to gather my thoughts before Manley was finished and saying "'Hat dawg o' hers, Kitcha, he up an' died, ay knew he were goin' to, ay begged him, ay sez, don't die awn me. Just wait a little longer, ay sez, Sandra'll be back, but then ay looked an' he were just dead."

"The dog was a female," I said. "Kitcha was a girl dog." Manley stared at me as If I made no sense. "When *was* this anyway?" I asked. My thoughts were leaping around. Manley didn't seem like such a bad guy, the way he talked about Kitcha.

Manley succeeded in telling me a few things whether he meant to or not. He told me San had come to live in the jungle farther up their dirt road about three months before, after she'd gotten into some kind of trouble somewhere else, another island maybe. She was living in a hut, not really a house. "'Hat's all 'ere is up 'ere, just huts excepting Rudy Zuur's place, it's a real hoose actually."

That was interesting. Rudy Zuur was the king of the hill up their dirt road. According to Manley, Sansan had started coming into the gym every day to talk when she passed by on the road. He was pretty sure she'd been living "awn some other ayland" before but she hadn't talked much about it; she'd been secretive. He said the word secretive with a twitch of the shoulders and arms that looked like it meant she'd been putting on airs. He was actually quite entertaining. Then he looked hard at me. When he saw I was very interested in what he was saying, he grew wary and insisted he knew nothing more. Then he got up and walked into the gym. A light went on in a room, and I could hear him pissing and then flushing. He came back outside, sat down in his chair and started to talk again.

At first, Sansan had wanted to use the gym machines without paying, and he let her, but she didn't do it right, and she hurt her foot. Later she told Manley she had to go to the mainland to have an operation. "A tumor, she sez, but ay think she were preggers—she were huge."

Manley was an incredible source, a great gossip.

"Sansan was pregnant?" It didn't seem possible. She would have been over fifty by then.

Manley looked at his watch, bored. "It's two o'clock." He yawned so wide I could see he had few teeth. "Ay dunno if she were preggers, she looked it."

"So when she went to the mainland for an operation, that was when you took care of her dog Kitcha and she died?"

"She died?"

"Yes, the dog died. Not Sandra."

"Oh, ay thot you 'ere saying Sandra died…hey Jimmy, you hear 'hat, ay thot she 'ere saying Sandra were dead too…" Jimmy looked over in our direction, made no change of expression and said, "Royt." He couldn't have cared less.

"So," I started up again with Manley, "what happened next?"

"She dinna believe me, when she came back," Manley replied, his voice rising. "She thot ay killed 'hat Kitcha. She hit me and cursed me out. She wanted to know where we buried the dawg so she could dig him up, ay dinna know what for. She went round here looking for a fresh grave. Ay dinna even remember what we did wi' the dead dawg. Maybe threw him in the rubbish? What difference do it make? She come by here an' cursed me every day after 'hat. 'Hat Sandra were crazy after she come back. 'Hat's when she started talkin' to herself."

"She were a lunatic," chimed in Jimmy.

"Jimmy's a deejay at the disco," Manley said conversationally.

"Is he really?" Silence. I had to pull his attention back to the main thread. "So how long was Sandra here after she came back from the mainland and before the police took her away?"

"Gawd, ay dinna know!" Manley was impatient now. A bit angry. "Why you askin', girl? A month? Two? Ay didna pay 'hat much attention for Chrissake."

He fixed me with his best stare now and held on longer than I could. I looked away first.

Manley had described a woman not at all like

the Sandra I'd known in Portland, the golden girl always able to land on her feet, always self-sufficient, goal-oriented. Alone that night in my bungalow bed, I was stricken by disbelief, outrage, nostalgia, melancholy, resentment. Sleep did not come easily.

Portland, Oregon
Many Years Ago

Sansan wrote a little masterpiece of a story that evoked extreme emotions in various people. It was a piece written in Nepal and sent to Portland to be published in the main local literary mag. The story told of San giving birth to a baby in Nepal—a shriveled old man, she called it in the story. She had gotten pregnant by her Brit, Marty, was living in precarious circumstances and had refused when her friends had begged her to come back to the States to have the baby. She did not go back. She had not judged the situation to be that risky. The infant was premature, and delivered in wretched surroundings. San and Marty watched helplessly as the baby died, and San nearly died herself. Then she buried the dead child, digging a hole in the ground with her bare hands.

Only Sansan could be that candid, that direct about something so harrowing. The story gave San's fans in Portland a jolt when it was published. People were disturbed by it; not just by what it recounted, but more so by the way she said it: unforgiving and unforgivably. Advocates discussed the pros and cons of her behavior, as if they were on a jury. It was an era of great debates about moral issues. Sammy told me the brouhaha over Sansan had been like the earlier debate in his circle, the one where they'd been deciding whether or not to bring Sansan back from Hawaii and support her as a group.

Then, one night, there was a scene in the Zanzibar. The bar owner had read San's story and pointedly wouldn't serve a drink to the guy who had published the piece in his magazine. The bar owner actually refused to serve him. He shook his head and said, "No." A scandal! Something dramatic had happened. When I asked the bartender what was going on, he said that San's story went too far for his taste.

"She has no moral compass," he told me, but somebody else heard him and repeated the judgment in a loud voice. "No moral compass!"

This set off an animated and prolonged bar altercation about San's animal-like behavior and her willingness to share it in print with the public. It was astonishing how she set people at odds. She proved herself to be a woman capable of generating instant polemics about her behavior from thousands of miles away. In the olden days, duels would have been fought because of her.

The Island, Thailand

Remembering Sansan's story from inside my island bungalow, I plunged into the slough of despondency. I smelled my own self-pity.

That's what life comes down to: our souls are carried away a piece at a time. I sobbed myself to sleep.

When I awoke, my watch said eight o'clock. I was suffocating in the brown box I was in, that cave, a daytime refuge from the fierce heat outside, not really meant for being awake in. There was no air. I burst out, crazed and starving.

Outside, though, it was still paradise. The breeze in the palms and the bougainvillea helped to soften and smooth the kinks as I walked out to the main road and headed for the other end of town to find a place to eat. There on a bluff above the shimmering turquoise sea sat an open-air restaurant-bar where I ordered an iced coffee, a croissant and an orange. There was no one around but the tall, willowy boy who waited on me. And then he, too, vanished.

My driver from the airport sailed by in his Toyota, giving me an idea. I would go see the Buddhist wat upcountry that San had written me about, the serene image on her picture postcard. I would salvage my spirits and perhaps learn something. Besides, Ha mentioned she wouldn't be around until late afternoon, so I had all day.

133

When my former driver whizzed past, I saw that he had a Caucasian couple—tourists probably—in his car, which he parked in front of the restaurant where I was eating my orange. The tourists got out and walked away, down the road. I jumped off my bar stool and ran out of the restaurant toward the sullen driver.

"Can you drive me somewhere?"

"Sure," he said, unsurprised, blank.

"Wait here." I went back to leave money for the barman for my breakfast. He had reappeared, maybe because he saw me running out without paying. My breakfast cost twenty-one baht (eighty-four cents). I gave him a five-baht tip. He took it with no expression.

Back outside, I asked the boy if he would drive me up to the wat. He looked at me sharply and appeared to measure something—what was it? Was I unpredictable and dangerous like Sansan? He decided to do what I asked, and I got in the Toyota. The ride was short and fast, inland and uphill on a rutted road, just the way I'd fantasized. We kicked up clouds of pre-monsoon-season dust as we climbed through the dense palm forest and raced further up through a mixed understory of bougainvillea, frangipani, banana trees, guava trees, lime trees, giant Ficus and some kind of vine clinging to everything. We passed a few locals, women and children walking downhill with baskets of fruit. Abruptly, the boy slammed on the brakes when he saw that the road ahead was blocked by a parked car serving as a roadblock. The parked car's driver was hunched down at the wheel, his face hidden behind dark glasses.

"You can walk," my driver declared, reaching over me to open the car door. I climbed out hastily, and he threw the vehicle into reverse, roared downhill into a wide opening where he backed in, then peeled out in a fast-forward motion that left behind a thick haze of dust. He hadn't waited to be paid. He had seemed nervous, anxious to get away from the roadblock and the man in dark glasses, and maybe even from me. Had he done something wrong, bringing me up to the wat? And if so, wrong in whose eyes? Who was in charge here?

The golden wat soared up behind the roadblock into the blue heavens. It was a welcome sight, its pointed stone spires thrusting up above the jungle canopy into the brilliant sky.

A number of locals were coming out one by one from behind the wat onto the road, turning up the hill or down, carrying baskets of huge mangos and what looked like sweet potatoes. I knew that monks in Thailand grew produce to give away to the poor. Buddhist benevolence. San had written me in her long letter about getting fresh vegetables and fruits for free upcountry, up the side of the extinct volcano behind the wat, so now I could imagine her with these people, wearing the same draped cotton clothes, lugging home a basket of fruit...a smelly durian perhaps.

A monk in orange saffron robes, almost hidden in a miniature gatehouse, caught my attention. He sat with his legs crossed beneath him. The gatehouse he was sitting in was part of the wall surrounding the wat, and he blended into the scene as if he weren't actually alive, just a splotch of orange.

The monk appeared to take no notice of the car blocking the road, or of its gangster-like driver sitting fifty feet from the gatehouse. I followed the monk's example and took no notice either as I walked around the car toward the gatehouse. The driver didn't move a muscle. The monk became aware of my presence without really looking at me. He reached for his begging bowl and held it in my direction. He looked at me, but it wasn't a gaze that engaged. It was a blind man's gaze. His pungent odor, redolent of palm oil, washed over me as I drew closer. I opened my purse and found a five-baht note for his begging bowl. He lowered the bowl and his head at the same time as I dropped it in.

Steam rose all around us from the hot sun's rays penetrating the jungle, perfumed by frangipani and palm oil. I turned and left the monk, entering the wat through an open doorway. Inside was a marble floor with a path worn into it. Up ahead was a stunning sight, all in gold, a staircase-like altar, drawing the eye up and up and up. At the top, high above, was a gilded sitting Buddha. The ceiling was made of dark wood, intricately carved into swirls and flowers. The room was silent—I heard only my own breathing. I sat down on the marble floor and waited for clarity. It came in the form of two orange-clad monks who entered the wat laughing quietly together, their laughter like the gentle nickering of two playful colts. I smiled at them and they smiled back before settling down to pray.

I returned to the outside world and walked toward the roadblock, where the man sitting in the car was still there, hunched down. From behind his dark glasses, he seemed to be looking directly at me. I stopped and looked back at him. We stared at each other for a long moment and then, when nothing happened, when there was no change of expression from him, I walked back down the dusty road toward town wondering what kind of life that guy had, sitting in his car all day—kind of a dull job—preventing the passage of a line of cars that couldn't cross anyway, even though some of the locals carrying baskets of fruit had gone on up past the roadblock. It wasn't that the guy in the car had gestured at them, allowing them to pass—not at all. They seemed to know it was okay, without him needing to do anything.

In due course, the downhill road I was on went right by Manley's Gym, so I seized the opportunity to pay yet another visit to Manley. I had a new question for him: why was there a roadblock up at the wat? There were also other things he'd said the night before that I wanted to clarify— for example, that Sansan was in trouble before she came to their little enclave. The trouble, whatever it was, must have corresponded to her change of address— from c/o Tip Nohting to c/o Ha. So was Tip Nohting the father of the child San aborted? Is that what this whole mystery was about?

Manley was startled when he caught sight of me in front of him, just the way he'd been the night before. This time, though, he'd been asleep, and he leapt up like Mick Jagger himself, Jumping Jack Flash. We were well into the heat of the day, and Manley had inserted his skinny, nearly naked self into a string hammock hung like a cobweb in the corner of the darkened gym. When he opened his eyes and saw me standing there, he scrambled out like a daddy longlegs spider, hopping to and fro.

"Ay th-th-thot you woz S-S-Sandra," he stuttered like someone who'd seen an apparition. Manley and I were alone. There was no one on the machines, no one around anywhere. He seemed vexed by my reappearance, as if it meant trouble for him.

"Well, it's me again. Perhaps I should have made an appointment?"

"Whadja want?" Manley said, bunching his face up into pleats. He looked flummoxed, shook his head and shoulders forcefully as if to indicate "no" before I said a word.

"Sandra really is my sister," I lied. "You were right."

His eyebrows shot up. "Ow, ay thot she were your sister, royt." He calmed down, becoming conversational. "Yeeeeees, royt, your sister." He took a step back—the better to see me head to toe. "Royt," he said again, and he smiled. "Ay thot you woz Sandra when ay see you standin' 'ere. Royt."

"You're her sister." Manley's shoulders relaxed; his demeanor became fluid instead of jerky. I guessed he had decided I wasn't a cop. He bent toward me and whispered confidentially: "Sandra woz scared oot o' 'er fuckin' wits woz wat she woz."

"What was she was scared out of her wits about?" I whispered back.

Pleating up his face again, Manley put his finger to his lips for me to shut up. He gestured vaguely toward the walls and ceiling to say they had ears, then ushered me outside into the hot sun, away from the building to a spot under a palm tree.

"'Hat chap she 'ad, in Katmandu..." he began, still whispering.

"Marty?" I interrupted, racing ahead. "But she was in love with Marty. Why was she scared of him?"

Manley shook his head. He paused and considered me for a long moment. What was he thinking? Deciding which story to tell? I decided I should shut up.

"'Ee beat her," he admitted finally. "Dinna you know?" There was a tinge of sarcasm on his voice.

"I thought he was some well-educated, Sandhurst-type rich guy," I said earnestly. "That school in England where royalty and rich people go."

"Exactly. Royt. Sandhurst…royt. 'Hat gangster Marty, 'e went to Sandhurst just layk the King of Thailand Bhumibol hisself. But Marty were into big stuff, big-time big. 'E were big all over Asia. Sandra wanted oot, you didna know 'hat? She wanted to be rid o' 'hat arse'ole. She left 'em she did! She escaped! E's in prison now 'e is! Ay think, it were me, ay'd send somebody ta get 'er, wouldna you? 'Hat's why she were scared ootta 'er bloody wits. Ay woulda sent somebody ta kill 'er it were me. You see wot ay mean?"

"I see what you mean…" I replied. But I didn't really. Something was missing. "Was she pregnant by Marty?"

Manley shrugged, gave me a look like I was really stupid. For him it was unimportant who had gotten Sandra pregnant, and he couldn't imagine why I cared. He found me hopeless. I risked completely losing his confidence but rushed ahead anyway, wanting to get more information before he clammed up again.

"Could the father of her child have been Tip Nohting? You know who Tip Nohting is, don't you Manley?"

At the mention of Tip, Manley's eyeballs nearly popped out of his head. His mouth stretched wide into a rictus out of which came a silent scream. He withdrew his tall head into his shoulders. He looked like a turtle, bug eyes flitting around.

I went on. "Sandra was living with Tip Nohting before she came to live up the road, you know. Do you know Tip?"

Manley regarded me intently, incredulous. He could not believe how big a chump he had right in front of him. He bent toward me and mouthed, "Tip owns everything, doncha know? 'E *owns* 'is 'ere ayland."

"Tip owns everything on this island? Is that Tip's roadblock up by the wat? Does Tip Nohting own *you*, Manley?" I demanded melodramatically, way out of my depth, casting about, going too far. "You, too? Does he own you, too?"

The expression on Manley's face made it clear the conversation had ended then, but it also ended because someone came into the gym. Manley brushed me aside, left me standing there in the noonday sun. I was left wondering how exactly Manley fit into San's story. How did he know the things he told me? He must have known San better than he let on.

From outside Manley's Gym in the torrid heat, I could see into the darkness inside where the new customer was flat on his back on a machine, pulling on chains with weights attached, moving in a steady rhythm. He was another tall, skinny Mick Jagger-type, this one in crimson shorts. Music came on over a loudspeaker. Manley must have put in a tape. It wasn't Jagger though; it was Elvis Presley, or perhaps an Elvis imitator, singing "Love Me Tender." I slipped around the outside of the building like a burglar escaping.

Back down in the village was a storefront shop in a building painted turquoise with a sign in English out front that read: "Faxes Sent and Received." The place was full of people. Fax machines were clearly a necessary and popular service on the island, the means for fast and relatively cheap communication with the outside world. This used to be the role of American Express, or the post office, but there was no sign of either anywhere in sight. There was no cybercafé either, as email technology hadn't yet arrived in paradise. Nor had cell phones. The fax was *the* operational technology.

Outside the busy shop was a bulletin board full of faxes flapping in the breeze—one from Germany, one from England, one from Sweden. A fax addressed to Sansan caught my eye. It was from me. How strange it was to see my own signature on a piece of paper in that foreign place. I was spooked again and snatched it down. It was the one telling San that my arrival was on such and such a date by boat. The first fax number I'd had for her was evidently this shop, not Ha's—or maybe it was the reverse. But San had never picked up this fax. No one had read this message. Except everyone who had walked past and read it. The last time San faxed me was weeks before the message in my hand had been sent, when I faxed her about getting the plane ticket, to which she had replied that she would try *really really really hard* to meet me at the airport. I was beginning to understand why she might have had to try so hard. She had been hanging on by a thread. She had no doubt I'd be there in a few days. She had hoped she could hold out that long. She had been arrested for assaulting Rudy Zuur right after her last message to me, and a lot of time had passed since then. Rudy Zuur's hand and arm had completely healed, if, indeed, he had really been injured. In those six to eight weeks, San had been in jail a month, and now the asylum.

The clincher was realizing she had been counting on me to come the whole time. I had concentrated on other matters in Paris, donning my north-country shroud, sacrificing myself to work. The focus had been the little punk spreading rumors about me. Now, that other life in Paris was a mirage. It seemed certain to me, standing there in the road on the island, fax from myself in hand, that I would lose my job in Paris. From afar, I could see it coming, whereas I hadn't seen it clearly from there. I had left my fate in indifferent hands. That was exactly what San had done, gone off and left her fate in indifferent hands. And it had turned out badly for her. It was probably going to go badly for me as well, and I was far away and unable to do much of anything about it.

I went into the fax shop. Would it do any good to send a fax to my boss? Try to stay in his good graces? Make reference to our common purpose? Tell him the facts picked up at the ministry in Bangkok? I bought a postcard and a stamp in the next shop and wrote cheerful greetings to my boss and his wife, then gave it to the clerk. She dropped it in a tray full of outgoing postcards and smiled.

The Island, Thailand

Ha was in her shop at one o'clock in the afternoon. She stared daggers at me when I walked in, like she'd been waiting for me to show up, like she was there in the middle of the day only because of me. My timing was still off—late when I should have been early, too fast when the tempo was relaxed. Or perhaps Ha was trying to adapt to my hours while I was trying to adapt to hers, so we remained out of sync.

"Where you go?" She knit her smooth brow, showing her undeniable authority.

"I went up to the wat."

She looked hard-eyed, disapproving, dark. What was it about going up to the wat? What was going on up there? I would have thought it was the safest, most serene place to go, but Ha's eyes were as menacing as I had seen them so far. My going to look at a religious temple was supposed to have been a neutral act, a tourist act, but it was true there had been clues that going there hadn't been neutral at all—first the driver had practically bolted and then there'd been that character blocking the road.

"Why is the road to the wat blocked?" I asked. At that, Ha's face became withering. She made me feel small even though she was smaller than me. Our communication was at risk and, although I would have liked to just shout at her, I feigned guilelessness.

She decided in my favor, and I sensed it was because she had a practical streak as well as a mean facade. She was goal-oriented, is what it was. "Come on, we go Sansan's house," she said, back on task.

"Good idea. When I talked on the phone to San, she said to bring shoes and clothes for her. She's just wearing a bedsheet or something…" I faltered, as Ha wasn't listening and had reached down to pick up a plastic shopping bag from behind the counter. She moved toward the door with the bag, head-gesturing for me to follow. She was picking up the pace.

I followed Ha outside, watching as she mounted her motorbike and ordered me to get on behind her. At first, I didn't hold on, but she gunned the bike to give me a scare, so I gingerly took hold of her waist. She nodded her approval, and we shot out onto the main road.

Just past Manley's Gym, we turned onto a bumpy dirt path that zigzagged through the jungle. Little wooden huts on stilts materialized in the dense foliage, kids and dogs leapt and bounded in the green undergrowth, adult voices rang out, orange chickens scattered as we passed. Ha stopped the bike, gave me a kick on the leg accompanied by a head gesture and got off. We halted next to the one real house in the vicinity, a deluxe architect's version of the smaller boxes on stilts. The house was the king of the huts.

"Is this Rudy Zuur's house?"

"Yes, stay here." Holding up the plastic sack she

had brought with her, she added, "This for him." What was in it? Even a plastic sack was a mystery to be solved. Ha padded lightly across the grassy area in front of the house and up the wooden staircase to the veranda. She turned to look back at me to see if I had stayed put. I had. Satisfied, she moved across the veranda to the front door of the house. The door itself was interesting: It was painted Delft blue, Rudy Zuur's Holland brought to the tropics. Ha knocked on the blue door and someone opened it—not Rudy. A Thai woman reached out, bowing and scraping. She took the bag from Ha, said some words in Thai, retreated, shut the door. Ha turned and fixed me in place with her laser eyes, glided back down to where I was standing.

"We walk," she commanded, and we sliced silently through the undergrowth, snaking a path past one, two, three, four little weather-beaten plywood huts. A man looked out from one of them, said some words of greeting or homage in Thai to Ha, who replied without looking at him. Perhaps Ha owned or at least managed these huts, which were certainly all rental units. But the placement of the big house with the blue door in relation to the little houses suggested a big boss and little people, so maybe Rudy Zuur owned the whole lot, which Ha managed for him. Or maybe Tip Nohting owned it all and Ha was his sister.

We stopped next to a hut. This was it then: Sansan's hideaway in paradise, a humble dwelling.

Ha stepped up onto a plank resting on concrete blocks in front of the entrance and pushed open the plywood door, which had no lock or even a knob. Another step, up and over the hut's threshold, and she disappeared down through the doorway into the interior space, a box about two meters by two meters. I followed her. Despite the open door, it was dark inside the box until Ha lifted the boards away from a large window opening, and light flooded the interior. There was another boarded-up window on the opposite wall. When I lifted the boards off the second window, the smell of frangipani poured in from a tree growing right outside. Just beyond was a little girl with thatched hair and big, round, webbed eyes looking at me. She leapt out of the undergrowth like a frog. She ducked down half out of sight, running bent over. A short-legged dog flew after her, its large ears like wings straight out in the wind. The little girl stopped suddenly, stood upright, then turned slowly and looked back at me. We stared at each other. I made a gesture for her to come back. She took a few cautious steps in my direction, then stopped. She looked intently at me with an unspoken question in her eyes. Had Sansan made friends with this little girl? I wondered. Had she invited the child into her hut to share a treat? I made another gesture for her to come closer, but it was too much. She turned and ran away, the dog flying after her.

Down below the window bloomed white gardenias, the famous flower used in Western teenagers' corsages in the fifties, with that familiar heavy fragrance. The gardenias were at home there, strewn lewdly across the foliage, not mounted primly on some D.A.R. woman's bosom with a curly ribbon. San must have loved the fragrant odors wafting in the windows to perfume her nights. Perhaps she had worn flowers in her hair the way people do in Hawaii, or in Tahiti, on one side if they're in love, the other side if they're not. Or, on the other hand, she might have grown oblivious to the flora long ago and no longer floated on its scented waves. She'd been in the tropics a long time. How she might have evolved or devolved spending time in a place like this was something I was hoping to discover.

Inside the tiny room, Ha was picking up things from the floor and looking at them as if they were dead mice. She lifted up a torn pink rayon slip by its tail, peered at it, wrinkled her nose and tossed it in the corner. "I come back later and throw out trash," she said, her nose twitching left, right, left, right, just the way Ho Tay's nose had done in Paris when speaking about the durian.

I examined San's things myself, wanting to take inventory before Ha tossed everything. None of it smelled bad to me, or even of anything in particular—San's own perfume of choice, for example, whatever that might have been in her reduced condition. The stuff on the floor was just rags and pieces of junk not even the poorest neighbor would have wanted: a battered pot, one spoon, a ratty basket, a low wooden table or stool, an ancient, broken typewriter. Or maybe the neighbors had already taken the good stuff, and this was what was left. The place might well have been decorated with treasures San had come across the way she always did, but everything of value had disappeared.

To clothe San when I eventually found her, there was a torn Chinese silk wrap and a kind of a jacket in green, which would match her eyes. There was also a pair of blue silk Chinese trousers still pretty much intact. Four shoes were scattered about, two of them a pair, but they were spike-heeled sandals. How like Sansan to have high heels for the jungle. The other two shoes were unmatched flip-flops. They were both blue, one larger than an Edith Wharton novel. But it wouldn't matter if her shoes were the same size when she made her escape.

The wooden stool was the only piece of furniture in the hut, and I sat down on it now, wanting to go slow, to drink in the efflorescence, to listen for sounds outside, to wait for the little girl and her dog to pop into view again. Ha did not slow down. She was in a hurry. I took my time and continued looking around the tiny space. There were candle stubs in a broken brass candleholder, an ink bottle. There was very little paper lying around for someone who used to write a lot—just a folded-up packet of paper, the outside page of which appeared to be a map drawn by hand in the familiar turquoise ink. The other side of the page was yet another fax from me, the earlier one where I'd said I was thinking about her, that I'd like to come to Thailand but wasn't going to. The fax plunged me into a time/space warp, wondering if my faxes from Paris were the only accounting of time and the only paper San had had access to.

The hand-drawn map on the reverse side of the fax was a map of the village, an arrow pointing the way to her house, a dotted line leading to her hut. It was essentially the route Ha and I had just taken. I guessed the map had been for me.

What had been the chronology of events? She had apparently gotten a later fax saying I was coming to Thailand after all, because she had answered. Those last few days she had spent there in the hut, she must have thought I would soon join her in her jungle. I would have happily joined her under normal circumstances. I would have liked it there with her for a few days, smoking hash, laughing over our woes, looking at things she'd discovered, eating smelly fruit and especially listening to her talk about her life and this place she'd been living in. I wondered if she'd ever been there in monsoon season when the whole area was likely a wetland, which was why all the little houses were on stilts. They would be surrounded by water. There would be crocodiles floating by outside when it flooded. I had seen a photo in a newspaper in Paris showing crocodiles liberated from their chicken-wire enclosures by heavy flooding in Thailand during the monsoons. The photo featured laughing kids poking at the escaping crocodiles with long sticks.

The second page in the packet I'd found on the floor was a letter to me. A nicely typed letter, a letter never sent:

Darling friend,

I have no idea when I wrote you. I went from an elegant lifestyle to 120 days without bread. Kitcha is dead. She bought the farm before I returned from the free government hospital where I had a twenty-centimeter-long tumor removed from my ovary. It was so huge everyone thought I was pregnant including myself. Before the hospital, we'd been thrown out by Tip's wife Song—she called me a bitch. Kitcha gave birth in a cave where we had made a home. Magnificent Kitcha, the best sport of my whole life. I must dig up her skull. I am fit, more fit than in years, have been using the steel machines at the gym. My neighbor lent me this typewriter. I am cozy in my tiny hut high on stilts, an adorable gypsy joint I've pieced together. Aura, Kitcha's daughter, is a mischief—short legs, one lame, floppy-eared, tick-

ridden, golden. I am so active, turning any adversity to an advantage. I have sent a package of my writing to the States. The realities, they are certainly not Kansas, Toto. The best stuff I've ever written. People think I've become a spaced-out junkie. Fact is, I'm in better form than ever. This is my dream and I am living it. Send tape recorder, send a care package. A long letter?

Yourself?

Got myself in a whole lot of trouble, falling in love with another woman's husband. I could use your brilliant company.

Sandra

"We have to go," Ha barked, breaking into my shocked reading. She was done sifting through bits of this and that and wanted to leave.

I wanted more time, time to fit together the story, to weigh what to do next. The idea came to me to get Ha to introduce me to Tip Nohting. Why not? Taking the chance, I said, "Ha, I want to meet Tip."

Ha lifted her head and lowered her shoulders at the same time, like someone getting ready to spit, or to declaim, or like an animal preparing to attack. Her eyes were on fire. She sank back quickly, got control of her face and body, said nothing at all. She and I stared at each other, breathing in tandem in the silence of the hut.

"Do you know...Tip?" I whispered in a sacrificial voice. We were both standing, and I wished we were sitting down; it would have been more intimate. Ha narrowed her gaze on me, measuring me again, finally deciding in my favor once more.

"I know Tip," she began, looking deep into my eyes as if to control how I heard her. "Tip Sansan problem. She want to steal him. She very classy, very beautiful."

"Yes?"

"Sansan had to leave Tip house. She come here. I help her, but she sick."

"Yes?"

But that was all. Ha didn't give more details, and the look on her face showed she regretted having spoken at all. She turned abruptly to leave. I glanced around one last time and followed Ha with the two pieces of clothing, the two flip-flops, the fountain pen with turquoise ink, the packet of papers containing the letter to me. Ha hadn't answered me about meeting Tip. She wasn't going to answer. I wanted to meet Tip in order to see what he was like, to have a picture of the rich businessman and landowner who had booted San out, who had banished her to that hut, who had essentially condemned her to death. What about the laughter and peace and innocence between them? Everything was lost because she spoke inappropriately to his wife Song on the street? There had to be more to it than that. Tip must have been a jerk. San hadn't been pregnant after all, let alone by Tip, so Song must have wanted to get rid of her. But why had Tip let the police, whoever, put San in prison? And now he was leaving her to die in a madhouse. In Ha's fax to me in Paris, she had said she would tell me everything when I came to the island, but in fact she hadn't told me much at all. Promising to tell me everything was a ruse to get me to come for Sandra.

Making our way back to where the motorbike was parked, I held out hope that Ha was taking me to see Nohting even though by then it was ridiculous to expect such a thing. We traipsed through the understory, there was nobody around, or else there were hundreds of people around, all of them hidden from my unseeing glance. Once on the motorbike, Ha drove even faster than on the way in. She gave off an angry body odor. Back at her storefront office, we dismounted in a flash.

"Get things from bungalow," she ordered.

"Am I leaving?"

"Yes, my brother take you." Brooding, I shuffled down the path to my homely bungalow with its new concrete patio (now dry and solid), gathered up my belongings and returned to the office. Ha's brother was of course the petulant boy with the Toyota SUV. I'd been right about them being related.

The brother was waiting for me in the office with Ha, the SUV parked out front.

"His name Tung," Ha said when I came in.

I smiled at Tung. I wanted to break through his mask all the more for having failed to penetrate Ha's. Tung was wearing a freshly pressed black t-shirt and shorts. He looked healthy and strong; young and international. This should be like talking to an adolescent anywhere, I thought, as if that were a promising prospect. Tung sent a fake smile back at me.

"He take you for Sansan passport," explained Ha. "Here name prison where she is, south from Songkhla." She handed me a small piece of paper with one very long unpronounceable word written on it in Thai script. She was already pushing Tung and me out the door. I stood my ground. "So, is it a hospital or is it a prison?"

Ha gave me a smile which read like humiliation. With that strange smile, she seemed to acknowledge some responsibility for San's plight or embarrassment about not telling me more.

"How much do I owe you for the bungalow?" I asked her, but Ha was shaking her head and gesturing no, nothing at all. She was not asking me to pay because I was doing her a favor, taking San off her hands. In her long letter to me in Paris, San had written that, for the Thais, all favors must be repaid. Ha was repaying me for getting San out of the picture, and it wasn't really costing her very much, all things considered.

"Thank you, Ha. So it's goodbye?"

"Yes, goodbye." She bobbed her head and pressed her palms together under her chin. I followed suit.

"You have any message for Sansan?" Ha's body language said I was asking too much, didn't I understand it was over? "Do you want me to call you when I get to...wherever Sansan is? She felt close to you. Would you like to know how San is?"

No answer from Ha. If she wanted to know what happened she could hear about it on the coconut telegraph.

Her eyes were glued to the floor, and her brother's face was expressionless. This noncommunication was of a different sort than any misunderstanding I had felt in Paris, when I hadn't always comprehended the Gallic follies. This reticence felt smothered, muzzled, brutal.

Out on the highway in the Toyota with Tung, I told him I was hungry. He made no objection, so apparently it struck him as a reasonable request. He was nicer now than before. He stopped in the next village, a fishing community arrayed around a lagoon, with boats of all sizes tied up at wooden docks lining two sides of the shimmering turquoise inlet. Small boats were mixed in with motorized longboats alongside the boardwalk, and diesel exhaust hung in the air, a sour odor mixed with the smell of overripe fruit coming from sagging tables near where Tung had parked.

My nose had begun to differentiate varieties of overripeness, rot and decay.

I ate standing up near the water's edge at a metal cart on wheels from which an old man in a white t-shirt and white apron served up noodles and broth with pieces of dark tuna and hot peppers scattered on top. Tung waited in the Toyota, listening to a CD through headphones, eyeing me now and then. I smiled and waved at him once, and he returned my smile. I could hardly believe it. Back on the road, he seemed content, and I decided to be content too, as I was finally fulfilling my wish to circle the island.

The tiny isle in the Gulf of Siam was part of the archipelago east of the isthmus between Thailand and the bulge of Malaysia to the south. The island was not ruined by tourism, but was marked by attempts at development on a small scale, foreshadowing a possible future. In her letter to me, Sansan had described Tip Nohting as a landowner. If Tip really owned the whole island, it would have been interesting to know how that had happened. An ancestral holding, for example, or perhaps the result of criminal activity. The unfinished development on the island gave the impression of having been sporadic, and we drove by several wood-framed or concrete-block ventures that looked abandoned. There was a small-scale intentionality to everything we passed by, as in a tiny kingdom, a sense of proportionality.

Zen-like, we drove without talking toward an unknown destination for perhaps twenty kilometers as Tung kept his headphones on and listened to an ABBA CD, then a Thai one...according to their covers. He didn't keep time to the music.

We passed a pristine, white-sand beach with its fringe of palm trees, the stunning blue- green sea sparkling just beyond. With an island that size, there was the feeling of gradually turning, always in the same direction, circling around. As we rounded a bend, there was a sense of the land having been made by an eruption, magma pushing up from a vent deep in the ocean floor, black lava building up over hundreds of thousands of years. What I couldn't viscerally feel was how, when the tectonic plate under the archipelago had shifted, as it must have done, later eruptions from the same vent would have become part of the next island in the chain. This tectonic shift would have had to be sudden, marking a clean break between one eruption and the next, between one island and the next.

As it turned out, I didn't get to come full-circle on that particular island, to hold it in the palm of my hand. Too soon, we arrived at the island's main town, a busy place full of cars, motorbikes and songthaews—tiny pickup trucks whose open backs held wooden benches full of people. The town was a little metropolis, the capital of the island, with banks and travel agencies, a Kentucky Fried Chicken and a police station with a sign that said "Police" in several languages.

Tung pulled into the station and stopped. My heart was pounding. Unceremoniously he reached across me, opened my door, pushed me out and drove off without saying anything. He did not look back, and I never saw him again. Alone in the parking lot in the blazing sun, I shrugged off my disappointment. I went up to the door of the police station and struggled to get it open. Eventually, I saw there was a doorbell and understood that the door was locked. It seemed like a joke that the entrance to the police station was locked. I laughed out loud.

It was good to laugh. My plight was at once familiar, weird and sobering. Sobering because police stations are not the safest place to be in many countries, and I had an impulse to get the hell out of there.

Yet how could I? There was no one but me to carry on with my mission, no one but me to get Sandra Sandra's passport from the police, and so on. I rang the doorbell.

The young man in uniform who answered the bell looked at me blankly, like a monk, until I said San's name, whereupon he took me by the arm and pulled me inside. He half-dragged me to another man in a more elaborate uniform, obviously his superior. The first man let go of my arm and stepped back. The second man was sitting behind a desk below a portrait of King Bhumibol, who went to Sandhurst, according to Manley. The official behind the desk wore the same expression of solemn authority as the king in the frame above him. The official, who looked about forty, stood up suddenly, smiled unexpectedly and came around the desk to greet me, his hand outstretched to clasp mine in what seemed like warm hospitality.

"Hello," I chirped in an ingenuous way, like a high school girl. You never know what part of you will come to the fore when you're running on nerves. My voice wasn't phony, just hijacked by terror. The officer tilted his head and lifted his chin in the direction of the subordinate policeman and then watched until the younger man exited and shut the door behind him. The older man then dramatically pushed a button on his desk. It made a loud buzz in another room.

The door to that room opened, and an even older officer of about fifty joined us. A very handsome man with an intelligent, long face, limpid eyes and coal black hair styled in finger waves across his forehead. He was garbed in an elaborate, colonial-era uniform of courtly decadence. He was beautiful—not handsome, but beautiful. He bowed and fixed his gaze on me, then parted his lips slightly to elicit my story. An air-conditioner hummed in the background, competing with the slight squeaking noise of the ceiling fan that rotated overhead.

"Water?" he asked.

I had cotton mouth and couldn't answer.

Taking my silence as a yes, he poured me a glassful from a pitcher of ice water. He was overwhelming me with his beauty, his courtly behavior. His appearance and gallantry were somehow familiar (from the movies?). But why couldn't we sit down? We were all three standing and remained so throughout the exchange that followed.

"We do a photo?" the beautiful official implored, reaching toward my face to tilt my chin like a lover wanting to photograph me in perfect light. I blocked him half-heartedly. The younger man picked up a Polaroid camera from the desktop.

"No…" I was saying, but the official was deftly at my side. He leaned his face flirtatiously toward mine and pointed at his younger colleague. "Look there, look at him, look there. Look, he make our picture together." Reflexively, I did look there. The flash went off, and soon there was a Polaroid of me and this beautiful Thai police commissioner leaning close together. The two men were laughing at my expense. My own laughter was strained. *A photo op! Better that than something else!* My mouth was dry. I drank the ice water. We were all standing. They were still smiling.

"What can I do for you?" the man in charge said to me purposefully now that photo was out of the way. He took a handkerchief from his pocket to pat his brow. He had a gold eyetooth, which struck me as a sexual touch. I put my empty water glass on the desk.

"I'm here for my friend's passport and purse." My voice was wispy. I cleared my throat and took a deep breath. "You know her, yes?"

"Let me see your passport," the officer commanded. I handed over the document, and he read the vital statistics page slowly, glancing up at me once or twice, smiling, holding the passport next to my face to compare me to the photo. He chuckled, picked up the fresh Polaroid of us and took my chin in his hand once again, this time to gaze at me and compare—all the while smiling. I breathed deeply. My heart slowed as the officer's hand still held my chin. I smelled his fruity cologne. His hand on my chin had gone on too long, I was thinking. What could I do about it? He said something in Thai to the younger man, who opened his desk drawer and took out a vintage lizard-skin shoulder bag. He handed the purse to his superior, who finally removed his hand from my cheek to take the bag. I took another deep breath. We were still standing, which had become very strange and hard to maintain. I would rather have been sitting in order not to fall over. The superior held the lizard bag in front of himself like an art object, looked at it quizzically. "Is this the bag?"

I didn't know, although the vintage bag certainly *looked* like something San might choose. "I don't know," I breathed. "Her passport should be in it, and some money…I do know that."

"How much money, do you think?" He was being clever now, trying to find out what I really knew. He held the lizard bag up to gaze at it, as if to guess the contents from its appearance.

"I don't know."

Finally, he opened the purse and pulled three objects out—one by one—and set them down on the desk, his little finger held aloft each time. It was the picking-up-dead-mice gesture that Ha had used, a purposeful demonstration of repugnance. On the desk there was now an American passport, a small, flat wallet with nothing inside and a cardboard booklet that turned out to be a bankbook. The officer opened the latter, and with his manicured index finger showed me Sandra's name and the last sum in the column. She had 1,900 baht in a local bank, it said. It wasn't clear to me if he was pointing out that this was a very large sum or a ridiculously small sum. I said nothing.

Everything went back into the vintage bag, and we were all three still standing, perched at odd angles in an impossible tension. I opened my own purse and took out a folded one-hundred baht note I had prepared for baksheesh. San, in her brief lucidity on the phone, had told me to bring money for bribes, and I had trusted her to know. This seemed like the moment.

"Can I have the purse please?" I whispered, motioning to it with my head as I reached to place the folded-up bill in the senior officer's manicured hand. His hand moved to meet mine. He took the money without looking at it, pocketed it without losing eye contact with me. Still looking at me, he took the purse and dramatically turned it upside down and shook it. The contents fell out on the desk.

"All?" he said, holding my gaze, his head tilted while his hand gestured toward the bag and the three separate objects we had already seen. His eyes raced from mine to the bag and back again in the same mimicry of being in two places at once that Ho Tay had used to convey escape from a smelly durian. I gasped at the similarity. The officer looked at me sharply.

"All of it," I confirmed, and gave him another hundred baht. He reached for the empty wallet, the least interesting item, but relief flushed through me. The transaction looked doable now. I gave him another hundred baht, and he gave me the empty lizard bag. We continued on that way. The bankbook cost me five hundred baht, the passport one thousand. In the end, after I had everything, I tried to smile, but that phase of the exchange had ended. The handsome colonial officer with his melting eyes and soft curls on his pensive forehead was now indifferent.

There was just one more thing. I asked if he could arrange for me to meet Tip Nohting. I was prepared to pay, but I didn't get to finish what I was saying as he ignored me now and talked rapidly in Thai to the other man. Should I have offered baksheesh as I asked the question, or...? The beautiful officer turned and left abruptly, closing the door behind him. When they're through with you, they're through with you. He hadn't liked hearing me say Tip Nohting's name any more than Ha had liked hearing it. Or Manley. Tip had everyone terrified, me included. Just saying his name was enough to set the world on edge. The prevailing social structure on the island appeared to be submissive human relations in a small, contained system overseen by one powerful figure. Like in a royal palace. Or the mafia.

Once I was in the parking lot, the younger man gestured me into a police car. I was scared shitless. Neither of us spoke as we drove a few blocks, then veered onto a dock. I had no hope of being introduced to Tip Nohting by then and was not surprised to find myself ordered out of the car into the blazing sun.

"Take ferry to Songkhla," the lieutenant commanded and then drove away, leaving me standing there not quite understanding what he had said. I did for sure understand that all doors on the island were now closed to me. I was supposed to get on a ferry that would take me to Songkhla. I looked in my guidebook and saw that Songkhla was a port city across the Gulf of Thailand, on the eastern side of the southernmost part of the country. Farther south was Malaysia. It was only when I got to Songkhla that someone might be able to tell me how to get to the place whose name Ha had written out on a scrap of paper. The whole operation was iffy, a fool's errand, a goose chase. What the fuck? I couldn't go back to the island where I was no longer welcome, but what could I do instead?

Standing there on the dock in the unforgiving sun was intolerable. After fifteen minutes in the heat, handkerchief covering my head, I felt faint and sought shelter. On the road above the pier was a telephone booth that offered some shade. I took a long drink from my bottle of water and decided to phone Dominique Renard. Why not? At least one person on Earth would know where I was, just in case. Maybe he would have an idea for me.

The modern telephone attached to the wall of the phone booth had a slot for credit cards. Three o'clock on a hot Bangkok afternoon, what would Renard be doing? Sleeping, if he had taken on the local habits, and he surely had. Rummaging in my bag I found the calling card he had given me at the Patpong nightclub when he'd made his exit. He had made an exit when we dined together as well. An escape artist, I concluded. I inserted my Visa card in the phone slot.

Renard answered on the first ring, and by the gravelly sound of his voice, he had been asleep. I envied him his comforts and his acculturation. He wasn't surprised to hear from me and asked why it took me so long.

"How long has it been since we had dinner?" I asked.

"Three days."

"Three days?"

"You haven't fainted again, I hope?" He was awake now and sounded concerned. His response was ingrained, he couldn't help himself. Or perhaps he thought the only reason I might call was if I needed help.

"No, I haven't fainted. I'm getting used to the heat." It was true I was getting used to it. I had stopped sweating, had become like a lizard or a camel, a cactus, retaining water.

"Yes, well it takes a few days. You drinking lots of fluids?"

"Dominique?"

"Yes?"

"Is it okay if I call you Dominique?"

"Yes, of course." He was pleased. I could almost see him smiling his big grin, which made me smile.

"I wish we could talk, but I'm not in Bangkok anymore."

"Oh?" I could hear him lighting a cigar, probably an old butt he'd fished out of the ashtray. If he wasn't alone, he was being discreet. He exhaled cigar smoke and said, "Where are you?"

"Hmmm, on an island in the south." I was beginning to regret my phone call. Why had I really called him? What did I want from him?

"If I were dying, would you come save me?"

He didn't laugh. "Are you in trouble?"

"I don't know. Maybe. I'm waiting for a ferry to take me to Songkhla. To get a friend out of prison, or out of the hospital, I don't know which it is." I spelled out for Renard the name of the place I was going to. "If you don't hear from me in a few days, would you, would you consider coming after me?"

There was a pause, followed by a sigh. "We shouldn't have talked about my work the other night."

He had completely misunderstood. "No, I'm not talking about that, really I'm not. I had your phone number, and I thought I would just call you. And you answered your phone. You were right there and you answered."

He listened, said nothing.

"It makes me feel better knowing you are there."

"Hmmm. And that's why you called?"

"Yes. Thanks. Yes, really, thanks. I'm going to that place I just spelled out. Maybe you would be able to find it?" There was a silence.

Dominique puffed on his cigar. Then he spoke. "Yes, I could find it."

"Thank you. I'll call again soon. Thank you." I hung up.

I felt better after I hung up, despite the awkwardness of our exchange. Renard was very cool, he would be able to make sense of what I was saying. And now, with that under my belt, it seemed to me that things hadn't gone so badly at the police station either. I'd been empty-handed before going there. I spent seventy-two dollars and retrieved Sandra Sandra's passport so she could go back to the United States. A passport had to be worth more than seventy-two dollars on the black market, so it was a fair price. What difference does that make, anyway? I had San's bankbook as well, so she could withdraw her money. And my first bribe hadn't been too small, too insulting. What extraordinary good luck. Who would have ever known if I'd made a dumb move and disappeared into the police hole? No one would have ever known where I'd vanished to. It probably happens to thousands of people around the world every day, but it didn't happen to me. I didn't vanish. What good luck. The police station transaction had been more or less a success. I decided to think about it as a success. So I felt good enough to leave the telephone booth and see what was farther down the dock.

I came upon a sign in multiple languages, one of which was English. It said the next boat to Songkhla would leave at five o'clock, an hour and ten minutes away according to my watch. More good luck! And there was a food stand farther down the dock where I bought a bottle of water, a cookie and a Coke from the middle-aged-looking woman operating the shabby wooden structure that sold only those three items. I had noticed by then that food stands in Thailand sold only two or three items. The dock had few other distractions for the small crowd of people waiting for the ferry. I sat down on a Coke crate to eat my cookie. Three mangy dogs came out of nowhere—begging, breathing their stinking, starving breath from open, panting mouths. They cowered as soon as I stood up though. The cowering was startling. They were obviously accustomed to being beaten. I threw the cookie down the dock as far away as possible. The dogs took off after it and left me alone.

A wooden ferry appeared in the distance and sailed toward the dock. It stood tall in the azure water. It was no doubt the ferry to Songkhla.

The ferry boat had an unpainted wooden hold—steerage—featuring a narrow aisle between platforms on each side holding rows of benches facing forward. I climbed onto the platform on my hands and knees and, once up there, I was at eye-level with windows that ran the length of the boat, forward to aft. The view was spectacular. The other passengers were young and not so young backpackers. I heard German, Scandinavian and Australian voices. There were also Thai people, and Malaysians, a handful of Indians or Pakistanis. Backpacks and baskets were strewn everywhere. There were Thai women traveling with children, and one very elderly Thai couple, their faces worn and shiny. Most people had brought food with them and took it out to eat once we got underway. Down the aisle and aft was a food stand, where I could buy another bottle of water, a banana and some Reese's Peanut Butter Cups (the only thing with protein in it). I was looking forward to a good dinner somewhere.

Once away from the island, we sailed past isle after isle, most of them tiny, not on my map. The Gulf of Thailand waters were deep blue, but became deep green near each island, as if each tiny dot of land were wearing a dark green skirt. The islands were covered by jungle, the lighter green foliage coming down to meet the dark green sea in what were mangrove swamps, one of nature's busiest, most fragile ecosystems. As we sailed by one of the larger islands, I could see a lagoon, the kind where pirates lurk, even in modern times.

I had a whole bench to myself. In front of me was a Thai woman with two young children, a boy and a girl. She gave them something to eat, and they washed it down with swallows of brownish liquid out of a bottle she had brought with her. When they were through eating, she spread a blanket on their bench and the boy and girl lay down together for a nap. They had their arms around each other and were cheek to cheek. They slept. Rocked gently by the boat, I fell asleep, head propped against the window. When I awoke, my watch showed that a half hour had gone by. Standing up to stretch, I saw that the boy was no longer napping at his sister's side. He was now with his mother, the two of them stretched out together on the far end of their bench, right in front of my own resting place. They were so close, so entwined that they breathed in and out as one. She was holding him in her arms as they engaged in a sucking kiss. His hands were on her breasts, the fingers moving rhythmically.

It was his hands that held me. They were like a kitten's paws, kneading, as if the boy were nursing. His tiny hands took hold and released, squeezing the flesh. The scene was suffused in goodness. Seeing this act between mother and son for the second time, I recalled something else San had written in her ten-page letter to me in Paris: "A Thai mother's sensual love for her children is unrelated to intellectual notions of right and wrong, but is like an animal mother's treatment of her babies. You can see all kinds of things between mothers and their babies in Thailand."

Back in Paris, where I had first read her letter, I thought she had meant protective behavior. I hadn't really imagined this sensuality, this earthiness of a cat with her kittens. It was impossible not to reflect on how inevitable it would have been for opportunists to have commercially exploited the intense sensuality that was so readily exploitable in Thailand. The Thais would have wanted to please and manipulate and earn a living, and, thanks to the arrival of the American military next door in Vietnam, a booming sex industry had taken hold.

I imagined this little boy in front of me would have early sexual memories as he grew up. Did that mean he would be a great lover as an adult? What I wanted just then was for someone to take hold of *my* flesh, *my* breasts, *my* shoulders, the curve of my hip, as if they were so much plaster.

Songkhla, Thailand

There was a mad rush out of the ferryboat as passengers swarmed onto the deck and across a flimsy gangplank with no railings. Everyone was shouting. Rickshaws and tuk-tuks and songthaews maneuvered close, their drivers hollering and honking to hawk their services. It felt like Asia in the most clichéd, bustling sense.

The first offer came from a tuk-tuk driver who hauled me up onto the rear bench of his open vehicle.

"An expensive hotel," I suggested, but he shook his head.

"Rohng raem phaeng khâ?" I tried next, saying what I had just read in my guidebook, the words that mean "expensive hotel" in Thai, but I had no idea how to pronounce them. The driver lit up brightly and twice repeated what I had said.

"Khâ," I answered, meaning yes. The driver, who was maybe sixteen, jumped onto the motorbike part of the tuk-tuk, tossed me a glowing smile over his shoulder and took off. He stopped soon after for an exchange with another tuk-tuk driver. It looked like they were continuing something they hadn't finished before the ferry arrived and probably wouldn't finish now either. The two were very animated. There was no hurry, really. I couldn't leave for the hospital prison that day anyway. Night's curtain was about to fall.

We passed through a town that appeared to have no hotels at all and continued on to what a sign informed me was the Ho Wang Hotel, located on the far outskirts of the town—the only Western-looking building I had seen as we passed through the city. The concrete structure was twelve stories high, its architecture similar to Parisian public housing built in the seventies. The hotel could, in fact, have been almost anywhere except that its windows looked out onto swirling waters filled with floating lotus blossoms, and the hotel grounds were surrounded by a hibiscus hedge in full bloom. I gave the tuk-tuk driver one of those folded-up one hundred-baht bills I hadn't used as baksheesh at the police station back on the island. My room on the tenth floor cost me six hundred baht (twenty-four dollars) in advance for one night. I didn't know if I would be staying longer.

I ordered tiger prawns from room service, turned on the television set and found CNN out of Hong Kong. There had been a terrorist bombing in the United States, in Oklahoma, the anchorwoman said. She went on to say somebody had driven a truck with a bomb next to a federal building in Oklahoma City and blown up part of the building. Many people had been killed. There was a day care center on the ground floor, so children had died. The anchorwoman said that American investigators thought Islamist terrorists were responsible for the bombing. Nothing like that had ever happened in the States except for the World Trade Center garage bombing two years before, in 1993, but that had been in New York, not in a town in the Midwest. The Islamist terrorist line sounded bizarre to me.

Where I was at that moment was in the Islamic part of Thailand, the far south, not far from Malaysia. From my hotel room, it was hard to believe that a federal building in Oklahoma could have attracted the attention of Islamist terrorists. Who had said the bombing was carried out by Islamist terrorists anyway? The FBI? The anchor had stated only that "American authorities said Islamist terrorists are thought to be responsible."

The story was frustrating with its shards of information. My meal arrived just after. Immense prawns served with coriander and a timbale of sticky rice, a feast after famine, but I'd been distracted by the Oklahoma story and had lost my appetite. The next story on the newscast was about Thailand. Human rights advocates in Thailand were outraged because there had been dozens of shooting deaths due to a government campaign to bring an end to Thailand's epidemic of drug use, methamphetamines in particular. According to the news report, the Thai government spokesman insisted that the drug runners were killing each other. They were not being killed by the police. The news anchor said that human rights advocates were convinced it was the police shooting the drug runners in order to meet a government quota. Most of this activity was taking place in the south of Thailand near where I was, the anchor remarked, and the story ended.

I turned off the television, having eaten none of my giant prawns. I was thinking about the shootings taking place nearby, and I thought about the gangster at the roadblock near the wat back on the island, and these thoughts wiped out any interest in eating.

Late the next morning, after a bad night's sleep, I talked to a travel agent in the hotel lobby who enlightened me about where I was in relation to where I wanted to go. He told me there was no taxi or any other kind of car available to take me south to the asylum, or the prison, whatever the hell it was. "This not popular tourist area," the travel agent noted, a casual way to explain the lack of transport. The agent was dressed in khaki, a nice-looking young man who knew smatterings of several languages and studied the piece of paper on which Ha had written the name of the prison hospital where San was incarcerated. Earlier, I had shown the paper to the clerks at the Ho Wang desk, and they had looked at me with sharp disapproving eyes and then ignored me, shunned me as if I were a pariah, which contributed to my disorientation after a very bad night.

Maybe he would be more helpful—like Manley had been—if he knew it was my sister I was trying to retrieve. So I lied, "It's my sister…don't you know anyone with a car I can hire for a day?"

He shook his head, frowning. "No…there nobody."

"You mean there are no cars, or do you mean there's no one who would take me there?" I pointed at the name of the place on the paper. The man looked up and half smiled at me, an acknowledgement the asylum was the problem.

"No, there nobody," he repeated.

"Is it because it's too far?"

He contemplated me silently for a moment.

"How far is it?" I pressed.

He paused, then said, "Why your sister there?"

I had lied about San being my sister in case blood mattered, so now she was mine. "My sister had some trouble, and I will get her and bring her back here and then take her home."

"Where is home?"

"The States."

This seemed to satisfy the man, who apparently now had the right information to take an interest in helping me. There was no predicting whether mentioning the States would have a positive or a negative effect, but that time it was a winner. Maybe he was imagining money would come his way if he helped me. The agent consulted his watch, a map and a schedule, and then wrote "6" and "43" on a small piece of paper, which he handed me. He showed me the point on the map where, if I understood what he was explaining, I would get off the six bus and change to the forty-three. The map was in Thai, so I got only the vaguest notion of how the two bus routes intersected.

"Driver, you show this." He meant show him my piece of paper with the name of the hospital on it. And hope for an open-minded bus driver, one who wouldn't spit on me and throw me off the bus.

"Number six bus right outside hotel, come in two hours, you ride ten minutes, change. Travel there take maybe three, four hours." He seemed pleased with himself now that he was in travel agent mode, and he maintained steady, easy eye contact. His manner suggested he was telling me how to get to a popular resort hidden in the jungle. He was very clear and detailed in what I might expect, what I might look for along the way, the scenic views to watch out for. It was a relief to have somebody act like what I was doing was just fine, a good thing to be doing—not like I was messing with the devil. The agent was smiling, bobbing his head, pumping out welcoming energy. When I was leaving, I turned and made a quick movement with my head and my hands and an expression that was meant to ask if I should pay him. He moved his eyes and shrugged to say what looked to me like he thought I was very nice and no money was necessary. Or maybe that was just my interpretation.

Stashed in my bag for the trip were a big bottle of water, mosquito repellent, chewing gum, cookies and a Mars candy bar...pretty much all that what was available at the shop in the hotel lobby. On the number six bus, I showed the driver the paper on which the travel agent had written the number forty-three, and he nodded. The six was a local, with frequent stops along the water's edge. After only five minutes, the driver craned his head back to me and said something, pointing at the exit. I got off, easily found the stop for the forty-three and sat down on a convenient bench. The panoramic view was of a gorgeous, broad, swirling river carrying tangled, floating islands of lotuses down toward the sea. I recognized it as a sight the travel agent had told me to look for and he was right to have told me. It was invigorating.

On the forty-three, it was a wild, dusty ride farther into provincial Thailand, south toward Malaysia. The bus served the rural poor, many of whom had their belongings in immense parcels, or they had livestock—chickens, ducks, one small calf. The bus driver never stopped his vehicle, just slowed enough for passengers to leap on or off. At the back door, there was a driver's assistant dressed in white clothes now darkened by dust. He shouted continuously, instructing passengers how to jump off the bus at just the right moment when the bus had slowed as much as it was going to and just before it sped up again. When they hesitated too long, he pushed them off. He also caught hold of new passengers running alongside and reaching up to be pulled onto the bus just before the driver accelerated again.

After about an hour watching this athletic routine, I made my way up to the bus driver to show him the paper with the name of the hospital on it. He looked at it and then at me with distrust (or perhaps disgust), but nodded his head sharply and pointed me toward an empty seat close to him. A couple of hours after that, he stopped the bus and got off to relieve himself in the tall grasses. We were near a pond where a laughing child was splashing water up onto a water buffalo. Underway again, the rough, noisy ride continued less chaotically, as there were fewer people and fewer pauses and longer, more peaceful hauls between stops through the watery, sometimes jungly countryside. Suddenly, the driver shouted at his assistant, who came forward, took me by the arm and hustled me toward the back door of the vehicle where, when it slowed and the door opened, he pushed me out onto the dusty shoulder. I fell rolling and ended up, unhurt, on my back. My little brown silk dress was torn across the left hip. Too bad.

Right in front of me was a large sign, a billboard, with a long word in elaborate Thai script that matched the one on my piece of paper. I had arrived. Fifty meters into the jungle on a paved path was a gatehouse, a simple concrete building with three people behind the glass window. The uniformed man who came to the window didn't know what I was talking about when I said, "Class Lady 4" or "Sandra Sandra." The woman behind him, clearly in charge, stepped up to the window and, even though we didn't speak any languages in common, understood why I was there. She'd been informed. I was in luck again. Or she was an enlightened being. She turned to a third person (the flunky)—a husky man in a white shirt and dark blue pants—and gave him orders. He then made his way outside the booth, and we got on his motorbike and headed down a paved asphalt road into the jungle.

The man drove slowly, so I didn't have to hang onto him. I realized I hadn't paid any bribe back at the gatehouse. I'd forgotten. Was it important or not? Maybe the whole baksheesh issue was of less importance than rumored. Soon, I was overtaken by the fantastic place we were riding through. It was very dark on each side of the road, with shapes and forms suddenly visible in the wall of jungle, and overwhelming fragrances of frangipani and sweat. The man's sweet body odor washed over me as we moved forward. It was unfamiliar, like none other I'd ever smelled.

The slowness of our plunge into the jungle was marked by the steady *putt-putt* of the motorbike. My heart began pounding in sync with the bike's pulse. A wave of perspiration washed down my forehead, carrying the dust of the road into my eyes and mouth. I was drowning in my own sweat, in the heavy perfumes of flowers, sweet body odor and diesel exhaust.

We passed a gardenia tree. Its white flowers vibrated like specters, and they looked like spirits in the darkness. Just off the path, there suddenly appeared and disappeared an open-air tin-roofed building where the people inside of it were separated from each other by nothing more than hanging fabric. Had I really seen that, or was I imagining things? As soon as I had noticed the building it was gone, in a blink. But I could still hear the sound of voices. Had there been voices? Did I hear music?

The sudden shriek of birdsong was followed by what could only have been monkeys chattering. I could see we were coming up on another open-air building, but slower this time, not flying right past it. We entered the dirt driveway and stopped. We were in darkness. Night had fallen.

Before I saw her, I heard San's voice. And she was close by. "Oh!" she sighed, and then, after a few seconds, "Oh!" And then again after a pause. "Oh," again and again. No one moved and no one else made a sound. I had stopped breathing. It was like a performance in the dark.

But it was real, it wasn't a performance. As my eyes adjusted to the dark, I saw San, or the ghost of her. I got off the motorbike and moved toward her. She was sitting on a bench outside; other people in the building behind her were now visible. San tried to stand up but fell sideways, gracefully, then pushed herself upright again. "Oh!" she sighed like before, then she tried again to stand, falling back. "Oh!" Trying to stand, falling back. "Oh! Oh! Oh!" She looked like a puppet. A marionette with jerking movements.

"Sandra!" I shouted. San's head jerked toward me, as though on a string. Her long, red hair was shorn and calico-colored. She was so thin, her cheekbones stood out like tent posts. Her shoulders and arms were skin and bones. She looked like she was starving to death. Her hands were like claws, one a clutched fist straining to hold up her fluttering pajama bottom. I stepped forward and reached for her and we came closer in the darkness. Her rib cage was square like a box, covered with a red satin bra.

We reached for each other in the palpable, warm evening haze. I wanted to get hold of her, to seize her and run away. Up close, I could see that she was drooling heavily and jerking her face to one side in a horrible spasmodic tic. I hugged her hard, probably too hard, and it made her let go of her pajama bottom to hug me. We lurched and fell over into the underbrush. She sprawled on her back laughing and coughing. Then she looked down at her skinny, naked, still-red bush—embarrassed by it, perhaps—all the while drooling and mopping at her drool with the back of one stiffened, claw-like hand. Our eyes finally met, and her animal, pale-green gaze glowed in the dark.

I rose to my feet and pulled her up, but she buckled. Bending to help again, I was startled by a uniformed female form exiting the low wooden building. I stiffened and let go of Sandra. I didn't know what to expect. The woman grabbed San by the arm, pulled her upright with a grunt, yanked up her pajama bottom and gave her an order I couldn't hear. Sansan obediently clamped her claw onto the pajama. The attendant, or whatever she was, wasn't gentle. She was harsh, a jailer. The two of them jerked along inside under the building's corrugated roof.

I followed, but I tripped on the step that led into the building and found myself sprawled out on the concrete floor. Luckily, I wasn't hurt. I got up again, looked around. The space we were in was vast, whitewashed, low-ceilinged, barely lit. Down the center were two rows of mats with people on them— all women it appeared. The mats were spaced about a yard apart, maybe forty mats in all, each occupied by an inert human shape. The sides of the room were lined with tall windows with screening, no glass. From inside, in the dim light, the building had a colonial feeling, fans rotating slowly above. Outside, jungle creatures could have been looking in on the humans, who had begun grunting and whispering and cooing like birds.

The attendant took San to a nurse's station, a bamboo counter with shelves in an open area away from the other prisoners, or patients, who were now making a mewling whine, like puppies in a dog pound. The fans hummed overhead, going *thump, thump, thump*. The smell was moist and thick and human…oddly intoxicating.

Under the fluorescent lights, San was yellow and shiny. I looked hard at her, all lit up that way. She had dried out, like a lizard, and must have weighed no more than seventy-five pounds. I could have scooped her up and carried her away. I could have folded her and put her in my pocket. Her body moved constantly, feet shuffling, hands jerking, face twitching, jaw grinding. She was like someone stricken with Tourette syndrome. I wondered what kind of drugs they'd been giving her. They had destroyed her. I was struggling not to start bawling hysterically and lose my nerve.

"I'm Sansan's sister," I announced to the uniformed attendant in a fairly smooth voice.

San's eyes fixed on me, studying me while her body continued its grotesque dance. She was studying me as much as I was studying her. She smiled ever so slightly with a genuine look of lucidity.

"She doesn't…understand…I'll tell her…" San

said, displaying her intelligence was still intact. But she could barely squeeze out her words, with little control over her mouth, spit flying, head jerking. Seeing her deteriorated state, someone who didn't know her might indeed have thought she would know precious little of what was happening around her, which was what Rudy Zuur had written me in his fax on behalf of Ha, but he had been wrong. There was no elegance left in Sansan's gyrations, but she had her wits about her. She was still in there, I could see that.

San spoke to the attendant in Thai, taking hold of my arm, pointing at me, probably to indicate I was there to take her away. She showed great authority for someone on the verge of collapse, a performer drawing upon her last resources.

The woman suddenly grabbed San, spoke harsh words to her, and San lost her authority and once again became a passive rag doll in the attendant's hands. I had never seen San cower like that, and I wondered if it was genuine. It looked like she didn't want to get hit, so I knew that they had been beating her in this place. It was submissive survival behavior. The same kind that I saw in the dogs on the dock before coming here.

"No, no, no, no, you not going anywhere," the attendant barked at her. The male flunky stepped forward aggressively, his arms extended to bar me from San, as if I were going to snatch her. Maybe I would have if I could have, but I stopped dead, frightened and submissive, just like San. It was instinctive. No one moved. Without even thinking about it, I'd lowered my head, slumped my shoulders, shifted my pelvis forward and bent my knees.

The attendant arrived at her station and released San, who remained slumped over. "San," I whispered.

"What's happening? Are we leaving?" She snuffled breath in through her nose, freed her tongue from her clenched mouth, then snarled, "Doctor…must sign to…release me, I can't go without it…"

This was preposterous. I tore myself out of submission, pushed aside the flunky—a small Thai man no taller than me. He let himself be pushed. I started talking to the attendant via San, who perked up again.

"Tell this person, this attendant, this nurse, that I've been sent by the government to take you, that I'm here to 'direct affairs.' Tell her I'm your sister. Tell her I have your passport."

San translated what I'd said and the attendant listened. I was amazed at myself. Amazed at Sansan. Our dual performance under extreme pressure was like two friends on some escapade together, which was what we had been and done a few times in the past, so there was some history there. An easy rapport to fall back into.

I took San's passport out of my bag, along with the mismatched rubber flip-flops I'd brought for her. She grabbed jerkily for the sandals and struggled to put them on without losing her trousers again. She stood and brushed herself off, as if she were now dressed, a credible person with shoes on. She addressed the nurse again in what sounded to me like competent Thai. The nurse listened and barked an order at the man, who by then was wearing an expression of bewilderment, the most unguarded expression I would ever see on a Thai person. He stayed where he was, didn't move, remained confused. The nurse repeated her order, and the guy snapped to attention. Further proof that in Thailand, the women are definitely in charge.

Hesitantly, carefully, the nurse reached for the passport I was holding in front of me. She took it to the lamp on the counter, and we all followed like moths drawn to the one bright spot in the ward. She held San's passport in the lamp's glow and turned the pages.

San's passport photo was a glamor shot, a far cry from her present self. The nurse and I, two mimes in a silent movie, looked slowly back and forth from San to her photo, both of us expressing doubt but for different reasons. I took out my own passport, and we repeated the process. The nurse studied my photo and then my face and nodded, deciding that I was the same person as the person in my passport photo...even if Sansan might not have been the same one as in hers.

But what had the whole exercise meant? The nurse spoke to me in Thai with a bureaucratic voice, as if she had forgotten that I didn't understand. More confusion, then San translated, "Need doctor's order." She then added her own contrapuntal thoughts: "Not true...don't wait for the doctor...they want me to die...that's what the doctor ordered...don't you get it?"

I looked back and forth from San to the nurse and made my decision. "I'm taking her." I placed five hundred baht in the circle of lamplight on the table, and the nurse looked at the illumined money.

"No," she responded. But not firmly enough to convince me. She was negotiating. I put another five hundred baht on top of the first five hundred. "Get your stuff, we're going," I told San as I took hold of her. Once again, she was a marionette pulled here and there by others, but this time it was me doing the pulling. She jerked her head. Was it in agreement? Was it a psychotropic tic?

"I don't have any stuff," she said, looking at me, her speech clearer now, undoubtedly stoked by adrenaline and our pending escape. It had been unpredictable how San might behave in this unscripted situation, but I realized I was counting on her being able to function, being able to help get us out of there alive. I had not thought in advance about what to do if she turned out to be a vegetable, because she hadn't been a vegetable on the telephone, even if a bit loony. She wasn't the San I'd known before, yet this strange, agitated person was functioning as a recognizable *version* of Sandra. Things wouldn't have gone this way if she hadn't been playing along, if she hadn't been pulling her weight, however slight, if she hadn't exercised her special cleverness.

Chaos was breaking loose around us as the other inmates chattered loudly, sensing the unusual goings-on, but San kept her green eyes focused on mine, staying in sync. We were there together, and we both wanted to get out of there together.

A dark-skinned, shrouded woman emerged from the darkness and came toward us, singing beautifully. "She can't talk, she only sings," San said as she turned to the woman, petting her the way she used to pet her dog. "Yes, you go sit down now," San instructed to the singer, who tried to take hold of San's arm to bring her back to the group. Meanwhile, the nurse was doling out orders to me, to San, to the shrouded woman, to the whole ward. The place definitely felt like an asylum.

The nurse came so close that I smelled her curried coffee breath. She was showing me little plastic envelopes of medicines, touching me, making me look. San wasn't translating. She pointed at San and then put her hand up against her own head and waggled her outstretched fingers. "Your sister is crazy," she must have been telling me.

"She was saying I have to take these drugs or I'll be crazy," San finally translated.

"So we'll take the drugs with us, what's the problem?" I looked back and forth from one to the other while the question hung in the air. San was growing feebler now, strained by the effort of concentrating and translating while her fellow inmate was still singing to her and trying to pull her away, back into the fold. San spoke to the nurse in Thai. They argued back and forth for a moment.

"She says the drugs are very expensive."

I sighed. "Of course they are. I'll pay for them. How much are they?"

"She wants you to buy a month's worth."

"Okay, fine. We'll take enough for a month. How much will it cost?"

Despite unrelenting muscle spasms, San was still holding her pants up with one hand, her other arm pushing away the singing woman, who finally gave up and wandered back into the darkness. San let go of her fluttering pajama bottom, and it slipped to the floor. Her nakedness was exposed anew. Her bush wasn't red. She was completely hairless. What had I seen before? Why was she hairless? Was she shaved like a Muslim? Was she hairless from the medications? From starvation? Manic in my focus, it was only then I remembered I had brought clothes for

San—the Chinese jacket and pants from her hut on the island. I opened my bag and pulled them out.

"Put on these clothes and tell the lady we'll take the drugs and ask her how much they are." San looked at the clothing stupidly, overloaded with instructions, her cleverness all used up.

"Sandra!" I snapped mercilessly. "Tell her we'll buy the drugs!" She registered my command with her eyes, concentrated again, spoke to the nurse, who went to her counter and began counting out pills and putting them into plastic Ziploc bags. The nurse called me over to her desk to show me four different kinds of pills in four separate bags. For each bag she held up one finger, then three fingers. What was that? One pill three times a day? I could read the writing on one of the packets. It was Thorazine. The others were Haldol, Prozac and lithium, all the names printed in English, although the packaging somehow didn't look authentic. Maybe the drugs were fake, like all the designer-label clothes for sale on the streets of Bangkok. If the pills were the real thing, then they were, as far as I knew, very powerful psychotropic or antipsychotic drugs. If they were fake, they could be anything at all: salt, sugar, methamphetamines even. I guessed that the nurse was telling me to dose San with each drug three times a day. Enough to kill her. At least enough to kill her appetite so she would finish starving to death.

"How much?" I inquired of the nurse, who now

miraculously spoke enough English to understand me as she took a pen and wrote, "4000" on a piece of paper.

"Four thousand baht?" Incredible. That would be about one hundred sixty dollars—a lot for something I was going to flush down the first toilet I came to, but maybe not so expensive when the goal was to get away as quickly as possible. I gave the nurse the four thousand baht.

Our exit was a blur. We were soon walking alone through the jungle on the narrow road I had ridden in on with the flunky, only it was darker now. It was also brighter, as the darkness was illuminated by shafts of moonlight. We could basically see where we were going, so I took the opportunity to stare at this new Sansan, this woman who, aside from her flashing pale green eyes, looked nothing like the woman I had last seen maybe ten years before.

She could hardly walk. She wasn't walking at all really. She was *lurching* along in teeny steps, elbows glued to her sides with her hands and forearms extended out front. She was cutting a path for herself with her hands. It was the walk you see in an asylum, people heavily drugged…the Thorazine shuffle they call it. She was holding her hands and arms as if she had her thumbs in the straps of a backpack, only she had no backpack. She was limited to this spastic mode, so we went very slowly. When I tried to help her walk, we swerved and fell down again, this time hard on the pavement. After that, we both saw that she was better off not being held up, but instead, allowed to maintain her own balance.

We passed the first low building I had seen on the way in. The jungle birds and monkeys were silent now. The mosquitoes hovered in thick clouds around each of us. Before leaving the hotel, I had covered myself in mosquito repellent, and I tried now to spray some on San's arms, but she seized the spray can and sprayed it onto her face, directly into her eyes. I grabbed the can back. She didn't seem to notice what she had done. She blurted out a long speech: "Did you see the blind women...in the back row? They're all Muslim. Did you see? The lower classes. Wrong religion. Despised. Dogs. Me and the dogs. I'm...dirt...not part of the ruling family now, just a dog, a pariah, a Muslim."

"But they call you Class Lady."

"Because I'm white."

She reached out her foot to scratch some invisible dog and twitched her head and drooled, her tongue hanging out. "I'm dead...I'm already dead. Are we dead?" She grabbed the mosquito repellent and sprayed another hit onto her face. "Dead. Dead dog. Dead dog," she repeated, staring fixedly into the void before her eyes.

"Kitcha," she uttered.

I was frightened. I was scared of her. I snatched the mosquito spray out of her hands, took her in my arms. She gave back a little. The back of her neck smelled of orange blossoms. San had always smelled good. It had been one of her outstanding qualities. Back in Portland, she had smelled of Chanel No. 5 found at Goodwill, of rose blossoms, or of olive oil. She had found scented treasures for Sammy back in Portland to give me—fossilized pine resin, ambergris chunks, desiccated camel cud redolent of frankincense. She had always known about smells, good smells and bad smells. Resourceful Sansan had found a way to smell good even in her jungle prison. As I held her, I could feel her gathering back into herself.

Something screeched in the darkness. My teeth chattered involuntarily.

"Don't be afraid," San whispered into my ear, becoming attentive to me now. "It's just monkeys."

"I'm not afraid," I assured, and so I wasn't. The screeching rang out again when we resumed walking. "What *is* that?" I asked, a little frightened again. The shrieking was punctuated by the chattering of teeth, as if to mock my own clattering jaw.

"Monkeys...aren't they wonderful?" San replied zealously, a tattered guide. "I lie awake and listen to their wisdom." Her voice cracked. Her face shattered and splintered in the moonlight. The monkeys were laughing now, attuned to our tragicomedy.

"Do you want some water?"

"Yes," she said, and we stopped. She was panting. She took the bottle of water from me and drank sloppily, sloshing herself and then splashing water over her face, down her back, using it all. It was an extravagant Sandra performance, she who never thought to save anything for later when it could be used now. That's how she'd been in Portland—give her three cigarettes, and she smoked them one after the other. If she sold a treasure, she spent the money, then called to ask you to take her to dinner. And everyone was always delighted to do it, just for the pleasure of her company. San always lived in the present, no thought for the future, and I both loved and resented her for it. The water on her scrawny arms flashed in the strange light. She was so emaciated that I was reminded she had mentioned bad diarrhea. I had to get her to a doctor as soon as possible.

"Do you want a cookie?"

"Yes, a cookie."

I gave her the package, and she fumbled with it. I took it back, opened it, gave her one. She took a bite but choked on it, coughing and spitting. She hawked, spit again, pounded on her chest. She was starving but couldn't eat.

"Water," she demanded.

"But there isn't any more water," I said, my heart sinking. I felt panicky again, tried deep breathing. We stood there together, a pathetic unit of two. She finished coughing and her breathing calmed. We resumed our jerky trek out of the jungle to the highway.

San didn't complain, she understood that it wasn't going to get any easier. Which made it possible for us to keep going. All around us in the dark, the monkeys chattered and screeched. They swung through the jungle canopy, escorting us through their territory.

San and I plodded along. There was a new sound, more like a growl, closer to ground level. "Are there any animals out there besides monkeys?" I whispered.

"No…nothing…it doesn't matter…the jungle is a concept." She muttered the words in a descending scale, trailing off, her voice dying on the word "concept." What did she mean, *the jungle is a concept?* The monkeys fell quiet. We moved along in darkness, not talking for a long while. The monkeys swung overhead in the canopy. *Swish, swish, swish.* San rasped as she shuffled along, forearms extended to cut a swath through empty space.

She stopped suddenly. "Did you bring me cigarettes?"

"God, no, I'm sorry. I didn't think of it."

"I haven't had a…cigarette…since they threw me in prison." She was so poignant.

"How long has it been?"

"A long time… I guess…I guess I did have a few…in the other prison. But not here."

"So why start again?"

I hadn't brought any cigarettes. What an idiot I was. I was not cut out for saving people. Cigarettes would have been better than cookies, yet I had walked right past the cigarette shop in the hotel lobby and bought cookies instead.

"Why not?" she answered, her breath hard and ragged. "Why not smoke, I mean."

Out of the jungle on the highway, we waited only five minutes, not long enough to start worrying about the bus never coming. San addressed the oncoming bus with purpose and lifted her arms to signal the driver to stop. She lost her balance and fell over sprawling. I took over and did what she did only without falling, and the bus driver braked, drew to a full stop, not a running stop like the bus driver on the trip down. This driver actually stopped and waited, with unexpected concern for two *farang* in the middle of nowhere, and for San especially, who got herself upright and moved her spent body up the steps of the bus with a helpful hoist from me below her. We would never have made it onto a moving bus.

Flopping into a seat, San started in about her drugs. "It's time," she warned, jiggling nervously.

She was in need. That nurse and her cohorts back there had made San dependent on her pills. She coughed and spit phlegm on the floor of the bus.

"Give me a cigarette," she requested of the people around us. Our fellow passengers were all men, and not one of them offered her a cigarette. Half of them were wearing Muslim head coverings; the other half, bare-headed, must have been Buddhists. They were seated on separate sides of the bus. Both groups treated San like a crazy person, each man pulling away from her as she drew near. One man studied her, his body drawn backward, away from her, then looked at me accusingly, as if I were responsible for her, for her condition. The idea made me tired.

Failing in her search for tobacco, San jolted her way back to our seat cursing under her breath. She fell sideways, pulled herself up, came back to the subject of drugs.

"Just give me one cap," she whined. "I don't need them all...sometimes I threw away the ones they gave me...I didn't take them all...really I didn't...just give me one," she slavered.

I didn't know how to behave. I hadn't come to Thailand so Sandra could beg me for drugs. I had never seen her so submissive, didn't like her that way, and that in and of itself was alarming—the fact that I was not liking her. I didn't know what to do. I didn't want her taking enough drugs to make her worse, yet, on the other hand, just looking at her and using common sense, I didn't think it was a good idea for her to go cold turkey either, although the four psychotropic drugs we had were baffling. I didn't know whether mixing those drugs together was risky, possibly fatal, fatal tomorrow or next week, or just common practice. It seemed likely that bad things were bound to happen no matter what we did, no matter whether she continued or stopped. It was what it was. I didn't like having the responsibility for what it was. The heat of the night had me sweating. I wiped my face on my sleeve, made a decision and said, "How 'bout just one?"

I took out a plastic bag (the one labeled as lithium it turned out), opened it and extracted a single blue and white capsule.

"No." San looked at what I was offering. "I take two of those. One's not...strong enough."

She sounded very sure of what she was saying, but also very desperate, very sick, very like an addict.

I rebuffed, "I won't give you two. "Take a Thorazine instead." I almost laughed at the ridiculousness of telling someone to take a Thorazine instead, when I knew nothing about what I was doing. Nevertheless, I put away the lithium and took out a Thorazine capsule.

"Okay," she conceded, accepting the offer. How wrong it felt, not only to blindly give San a drug, but also to blindly assuage her that way, not to treat her as an equal, as a rational person. She took the Thorazine and swallowed it with her own drool, looked at me then and nodded. Meaning what? That the nasty pill went down. That I did good. That she was going to be all right, now that she had gotten her fix. That the Thorazine had been a good choice. Something else? God, it was maddening. I was very uncomfortable with the situation, which had become focused on the dispensing of drugs. She reached and took hold of my hand between her clenched fists, as if she had no fingers. She clutched my hand to her chest with her fists and rocked in place. She was pulling me into her animal-like rocking, her animal talk, rocking and cooing, rocking me with her. This physicality seemed familiar, felt good actually, like the old, uninhibited Sansan. I'd forgotten how small she was, so much smaller than me that I felt big and powerful next to her. I started thinking we would get her out of this mess.

"I'll stop taking these pills…I will, just you watch," she cooed, rocking, purring. "I know how much you hate it." We rocked together, and it felt nice. She made animal sounds, and we moved back and forth in our primal, bus seat waltz. After a while, her singsong took up a new tune, and then words, then a new idea. This was the new idea: "We'll get some Thai stick…at the hotel… I'll stop the pills…it's bad, really bad…but the stick is good here…the best…you'll like it too!" She tilted her face toward mine and beamed. It was the first time I had seen her smile in ten years. It was touching and warmed my heart. I smiled back at her. Why not? I mean, why not? It was so much work being tough, being responsible, so tiring.

"But I don't want to get any dope," I said, overwhelmed by doubt, my smile fading. "No unnecessary risks." Amazingly, she appeared to catch the nuance of my thinking. Even half-dead, she was still clairvoyant. I flirted with the possibility of trading places with her, letting her be in charge for a while.

"It's safe, don't worry." San pressed my hand between her fists as we rocked. "No one cares what we do. You'll see." She looked at me with a cat smile which made me wary. I felt like a mouse. I wanted her to shut up for a bit. I could see why they'd thrown a net over her.

The bus hurtled on to Songkhla by the sea. The coastal port was a bustling marketplace at night, busier than during the day, with heavy foot traffic— sailors everywhere, fishmongers, dock workers and the general public. Everybody out buying food, eating, doing their business. The bus inched along crowded streets. In front of one fish market was a huge octopus spreadeagled on the pavement, maybe twelve feet across. San noticed it first.

"Look," she said, alert, curious. Everywhere lights were dancing on the end of sticks, attached to bikes, rickshaws, tuk-tuks, or held in peoples' hands as they walked. San danced her hands and pointed gracefully—her gyrations had lapsed. Was it the

Thorazine? The moving lanterns cast animate shadows on the iron-gated storefronts, many of which were under pillared galleries enveloping the sidewalk, thus concealing the exact nature of human activities transpiring within.

The bus stopped near the same wharf I had embarked at a day earlier. Exhausted, San disentangled herself from our monkey grip, rose out of her seat, danced down the aisle and descended from the bus unaided and regal. With the flick of a wobbly wrist, she flagged a tuk-tuk. She looked like she knew what she was doing. The tuk-tuk driver was a young man who looked very old, or maybe it was an old man who looked young. He carefully helped San up onto the tuk-tuk bench, and I showed him a piece of paper with the hotel's name. Later, when we arrived at the hotel, the only real hotel in town, he just as carefully helped her down, even though, by then, she was frothing at the mouth.

Sandra had erupted upon seeing the hotel, spewing words and spit. She stuttered, shrilly repeating sounds louder and louder, all of it without meaning for me. She kept at it. She might have been saying something important, yet it was as if its importance hampered her ability to say it clearly. Her outburst was like the downtrodden Lucky's diatribe in *Waiting for Godot*, in which every fifteenth word or so he utters is part of a sentence he's formulating, and you can delete the extra words to arrive at his desperate meaning. Maybe San's vocalizing was coming from her reptilian brain, and her outburst was a warning, like a snake's rattle. It also generated waves of drool and exhausted her. Viscous slobber was hanging down from one corner of her mouth like a swinging stalactite. The elongated, slimy mass swirled madly about as she sputtered and thrust her head in a frenzy.

"Five star!" San spit out finally, splattering me with gobs of saliva. "Look! There! Five star!" The hotel was five star? What? I was on the ground running toward the hibiscus hedge to gag and rub my face with a blossom to get San's slobber off. San was back there in the tuk-tuk gurgling "five star" over and over. She was thrashing around, but when I finally looked, the driver was handing Sandra down to the hotel doorman, who spoke sharply to her, saying, "No five star" firmly yet politely, as if she weren't a freak at all but someone he knew.

Paris, France

It took time after Sansan's incoherent frenzy in front of the hotel in Songkhla for me to piece together its significance. Also to recognize and, more importantly, to acknowledge the danger San and I had been in. While I was focused on finding the woman who had spiked my leap into the unknown long before, the situation we were in had nothing to do with that. The actualities had grown threatening even though I was unaware of the details. Facts began to surface unexpectedly over the next few days.

To begin, the hotel where I had taken a room was a place where San had gone with Tip Nohting. Thus, it had nostalgic value for her—with her lingering and unresolved feelings for him—as well as shock value, since she now feared him. Arriving there had stirred up intense emotions in her, the way it might for any of us, going back to a place where we had spent time with someone who was important in our lives, someone who had then soured on us and who later posed a risk to our emotional stability and to our life.

It was also a fact that the hotel in Songkhla belonged to Tip Nohting, the invisible. He owned it.

Coming there, we were moving into his territory, and there was reason, I would learn, to be fearful about that. The hotel was a five-star hotel, yes, but Five Star was also one of Tip Nohting's names, the one used by people who knew what a hotshot player he was. Tip was a five-star kind of guy, so his friends called him Five Star. San knew him as Five Star. That's why she was wailing those words when we pulled up to the hotel. She knew what she was saying, even if I didn't. And when the hotel doorman told San, "No Five Star," he was telling her, in response to her fear, that no, Tip wasn't there at the hotel that night, that she wasn't going to run into him.

If I'd known at the time these facts about Tip and his hotel, I would have wanted to house us elsewhere. What a perilous move it was for us to show up at a hotel where Tip often hung out.

Still, he wouldn't have been caught by surprise. He would have been informed by his people that San had left the asylum and was now making a scene in front of his hotel. If he had wanted to be seen at that moment, he would have shown himself. There was never any likelihood of running into Tip by accident, even in his own territory. He was always in control of any encounters. But I knew none of this.

As for us *wanting* to encounter him, Tip would have assumed that Sansan had told me we were in a hotel that belonged to him, as he probably didn't know she was in such a bad state and unable to tell me much of anything.

So he would have assumed we were there purposefully. When he heard about it, he would probably have interpreted our coming there as an attempt to confront him. He would have heard from his network of informants that I had been asking about him on the island. And all this was happening after he had denied San his protection, left her in prison, let the demonizing process take its course. He would have assumed an encounter with us might be contentious. We were probably a real irritation, walking in there like that. Or an enigma.

On the other hand, maybe we were neither. Maybe we were like little marionettes, whose strings Tip was manipulating. For example, I was doing exactly what Ha—and who else? Tip?—wanted me to do: direct affairs in regard to Sansan. Get her out of there. Affairs were being directed. One step at a time, we were getting out of their hair. My aptitude for eliminating their problem was something the Thais I had encountered were responding favorably to with no real grasp on my part of their reasoning. But I was observing it. Everyone was letting us continue on our way, neither helping us nor harming us, as long as we were doing something in their interest.

As it happened, San was unable to get any words out that first night in a way that shed light on these subjects. In the following days, she suffered a kind of post-traumatic stress pathology (that was the way I understood it), with a resulting amnesiac blank-out of stressful subjects. She was shellshocked because of the violence she had known in Asia—first in Nepal, with Marty beating her until she ran from him, then in Thailand, as she lost favor with Tip and Song, was thrown out and then found her dog dead upon returning to her hut after major surgery. She had been in that devastated state when she assaulted Rudy Zuur and ended up in prison, abandoned by anyone who might have helped her. They all wanted her to disappear.

Songkhla, Thailand

After that first night in Songkhla, San started to blurt out disconnected fragments, the way a computer partially recovers a crashed file, so I heard some of the story of her first encounter with Tip Nohting in that hotel. The occasion had been an international business rendezvous between Tip and Marty, the sexy beast she'd gone to live with in Nepal. The story of the meeting went like this: Marty had been looking for a place to stow some ill-gotten money. He had heard through the Asian underground economy grapevine that a Thai named Tip Nohting wanted to exploit evolving global tourism and develop a resort on the northern peninsula of his island in paradise.

Marty had come to Songkhla to meet Tip and to consider an investment in that tourist resort. He'd brought his American Class Lady, Sansan, along with him.

It was long after that when Sansan fled Marty and went to Thailand, and it was an even longer time later that I went from Paris to Thailand to rescue her. It was even later that my unwavering former sweetheart, Sammy, in Portland would show me a photo of San that someone had taken of her in Nepal when she was in love with Marty. Sammy had loyally kept strong links with everyone from earlier times, no matter where they had ventured, and Sansan had mailed the photo to Sammy from her outpost in Katmandu.

The photo shows a Sandra who is no different from the woman who had impressed me years earlier. In the photo, she fulfills her myth—a striking exotic beauty, red hair pulled back from her tall forehead to reveal a pronounced widow's peak, a Class Lady. She is rich and thin, her slender body encased in silk green like the garden around her, green like her eyes. She fits into the ruling class, is very elegant. When I saw the photo years later, though, I saw a fragile look about her, as if she might bruise easily, like tropical flowers whose petals turn brown at a touch.

When Marty had taken Sansan along with him to the island that first time, Tip surely noticed her. He wouldn't have been able to take his eyes off her, and San had naturally fanned the flames with her famous sidelong glances. She and Marty had received royal treatment from Tip and his wife, Song, who noticed San, too...with nascent jealousy I would imagine. Not unlike my own when Sammy had talked so passionately about Sandra. With Tip and Song and Marty and San, there would have been a complicated dance. The foursome had sailed on Tip's yacht to see the peninsula where Tip wanted to develop a resort. Sansan had found the voyage outrageously spectacular, like Vegas, with the best liquor and food, kickboxing and gun shows staged by Tip's bodyguards, who fired off all kinds of weapons as the yacht lay at anchor in a lagoon under the full moon.

After the gun show, Tip said to Marty in a breathy Peter Lorre voice, "I get you any gun you want. I am the king of guns." Marty and Tip had then begun to negotiate, sniffing out one another for a deal.

Another photo that Sammy showed me after my trip to Thailand was a snapshot taken on that very yacht. The photo shows the foursome on deck. Sansan is wearing a turquoise cheongsam. The camera has caught her with a startled expression—a deer caught in the headlights—as she shifts her cigarette from one hand to the other, pale green eyes alarmed, all ten red fingernails on display in a transactional gesture with her hands. This was not a woman who kept her hands demurely folded in her lap. What was she thinking as she looked at the camera? Was this an unusual situation for her, or was she blasé about it after years of exotic situations? Was she already impressed with Tip? Was she in over her head? There's no telling. Marty in the snapshot is a full-lipped blond with high cheekbones, wearing a black shirt with the sleeves rolled up, head down but eyes up, nailing the photographer. What was he thinking?

Tip Nohting was handsome, beautiful even, with a quizzical expression, not the older man I imagined him being when I had first read what San wrote on the out-of-the-blue postcard or in ten-page, laboriously-handwritten-in-turquoise-ink letter. Someone who loved her and found her fascinating, a rich businessman and landowner, she wrote, and I had conjured up a wise, older consort.

In the photo, Tip was no older than Ha was when I met her on the island twenty years later.

He looked like Ha. They were obviously related. Tip was wearing a dark polo shirt open at the neck, smiling an ironic fake smile for the camera. There was a distance between what his mouth was doing and what his eyes were doing. He had striking eyes, deceitful eyes. Song was wearing a fake smile also, but a tough one. She was wearing a cheongsam, like San's, only blue, and sitting in the yacht's captain's chair, the real captain of the outing.

Three other men in the background were staff or bodyguards, dressed alike in black and brandishing automatic weapons over their heads. The bodyguards were smiling. Bottles of liquor sat on a sidebar. Champagne chilled in a bucket, although in the photo the group appeared not to have started drinking yet.

So that was the scene. Sansan and Marty must have been an interesting couple for Tip and Song to meet. Both were charming and seductive, both capable of swallowing sophistication straight. Questions of money were important to all four of them. They were well matched. If Tip paid attention though, and he probably did, he observed Marty's Cockney bully persona dominating Sansan-from-San

Fran's end-of-the-road defiance. Tip would have seen that Marty had the upper hand in their dynamic, that San was subjugated. Perhaps that's what intrigued Tip, that San was made passive by Marty. I personally had never seen the passive, subdued Sandra until I went to Thailand.

Marty was a tough guy, full of authority and dash, who had grown up wretched in East London council flats. But, being bright, he had gotten a scholarship to Sandhurst, the military college where the upper classes mix with royalty (including, at the beginning of the twentieth century, King Rama VI of Thailand himself). Marty was a king too, in his own circles. But for all his cleverness, the Sandhurst training would prove to be only a veneer.

Before San left him, the two of them had spent a decade together in the villa in Nepal. Marty had carried on his unspoken activities. He had also gambled regularly with people high up in the Nepalese police, as well as with the royal family…for pleasure (he often won big sums), but also for protection. Sansan stayed home and bonded with her servant, DeeDee. It was Sandra's way (just as it was Queen Victoria's) to prefer the company of servants. Sansan described DeeDee and herself helping the poor of Katmandu in letters to friends in Portland. She and DeeDee invested Marty's money in vaccinations, and Nepalese parents brought their children to the villa for shots. Sansan was a healer of sorts, with familiarity in herbal and Chinese medicines.

In a flea market in Hong Kong, she had found a medical book titled *When There Is No Doctor* to help her diagnose and suggest treatment to the Nepalese who came to her for advice. That was how her Nepalese sojourn was understood by her Portland friends, and she had written long letters or stories about one family or another who had come to her for treatment. The stories corresponded to her friends' memories of her in Portland, where she had assembled herbal remedies, putting herbs in capsules or in gauze teabags and distributing them to her friends or to the old people who lived in her run-down apartment building. She was the one who had told me to take vitamin B when I was exhausted. I did so, and I felt better.

The hot, humid evening when Sansan and I found ourselves outside the five-star hotel near Songkhla, when I was bent over vomiting in the shadows of the fragrant hibiscus hedge, San was swinging her viscous pendulum and deliriously shouting, "Five Star" over and over. Five star. It was a mystery what that could have meant. The hotel was five-star, but so what? It was just gobbledygook, part of the voices she was hallucinating.

"The voices say five star!" she insisted to the doorman, keeping up the ruckus. "The voices say five star! The voices say so!"

The doorman regarded her with disgust and dropped her arm. He was looking at her the way Ha's scary boyfriend had looked at me, with hard eyes. Those hard, Thai eyes get your attention. They are full of condemnation. The doorman stepped away from her. He was fed up and turned to see where I had disappeared to. What I got out of San's rantings was that the voices were still talking to her. While I cowered in the flowering hedgerow, she spoke of her son, Eddy. "The voices say that Eddy is dead. He's dead they say."

She looked over at me pressed into the hedge and accused, "The voices say you're lying about Eddy...he's dead, and you're a liar. You're a liar. You're a liar. Why are you hiding, you liar?"

She was demoniac. It was easy to understand why the Thai locals living around her hut on the island might have demonized her if this was how she had been behaving. Was there anyone aside from the doorman hearing the fracas, anyone who could help us? Or anyone who would get angry and cause worse trouble? San didn't stop, but got louder, and I heard her say, to an unseen interlocutor (her invisible sidekick?) that I—"That woman over there in the bushes"—was trying to kill her. She had forgotten who I was. That set me off. This had gone far enough. I walked over to where she was standing in the roadway, grabbed her by the arm and barked at her to shut up.

She looked at me in full, pale-eyed mania.

Amazingly, she shut up. I had never before talked to her like that. Silence prevailed in the heavy night air while we stared at each other. With my handkerchief, I wiped away the slime hanging from her mouth, then tossed the snot rag in the gutter. She was silent, staring at me.

"The voices," I said with authority, "are not real. They are not real. You hear me?"

San's hard look had gone soft. A docility settled over her, a slippery disconnect from what had gone on just before. Her eyes sought out mine.

"The voices aren't real?"

"No. The voices aren't real."

She sagged against me, her wind gone. Her frothing and vibrating came to a halt. I desperately wanted the Sandra I had known before to come back. Our little world was waiting for her to come back.

"I forgot to be careful," she said in an entirely lucid tone and pulled herself up to look into my face with the hint of a smile.

We walked, almost normally, toward the hotel entrance under the doorman's gaze. I was focused on the detail of the dark wood in the revolving door, the blue tile of the lobby floor. San encased my arm like a sleeve as we crossed the hotel lobby. She had let go of the voices, or stored them away in her unconscious. She had become passive, not just calm, as if she had no identity, a ghost of herself.

"Don't slip away," I begged her, and looked her in the eye. She tried to focus. I had to get her some cigarettes. Something simple for her to do. We steered toward the smoke shop, where I leaned her against the wall like an ironing board while I bought a pack of Marlboros and a lighter.

"Marlboros not so good," she remarked, noticing what I had bought. She took them anyway and I lit one for her. She smoked enthusiastically, lasciviously. Nothing else mattered. She smoked. I watched. We were an island in a sea of blue floor tiles. I had no idea what might happen next.

Sandra continued smoking, and it was helping her, slowing her down, slowing down her hands, helping her get control of herself. She was inflating herself like a balloon, taking on volume, glancing around the lobby, taking note of her surroundings. She wasn't coughing, even though she was smoking. In those extraordinary circumstances, smoking a cigarette revitalized her.

Looking at each other, we moved through emotional depths that we weren't able to express with words, all of it facilitated by a pack of Marlboros. It reminded me how easy we had been with each other in earlier times. The Thailand trip would never have happened if I hadn't idealized her, if she hadn't always liked me and thought me sympathetic and smart, or felt some connection with me. Whatever it was San was thinking about as she smoked allowed me to feel less worried as she took on substance, puff by puff. I helped her light another cigarette off the stub of the first one.

I noticed I was starving.

"I'm hungry," I verbalized toward the end of the second Marlboro. "Maybe you could eat some soup or something, some rice?"

"Yes." She went on smoking her cigarette down to the filter, tossed the butt on the tile floor and stepped on it with her flip-flop. She tried to pick up the butt and fell over.

I collected both her and the butt from off the ground, found a lobby ashtray to dispose of the latter and we sailed off rather smoothly toward the hotel's restaurant, which turned out to be a flashy Vegas-style lounge.

Inside the lounge, there were only round tables for ten or twelve, as if this were the standard number of people who might be eating together, rather than, say, two or four. Chinese restaurants in the States always have similar big, round tables. Here in Thailand, the three occupied tables had extended families around them, dining in the middle of the night. All around the sides of the vast room, there were deep, plush booths upholstered in turquoise and flamingo pink that looked so inviting, something to sink into after a long day. A prancing young Thai girl who swung her long ponytail and hips like a model on a Paris runway showed us to a booth. My watch said it was two o'clock.

"Meat, I want," San sputtered, grooming herself. She wiped her drool with a cloth napkin, spit into it, then threw it on the floor.

"I don't know if meat's such a great idea, San. How about some rice?" A starved stomach would surely have trouble with meat, wouldn't it? She stared at me. Why did I think meat would be difficult? "Fine," I said. "Have meat. Why don't you order for us?"

"Cognac, I want." Her sentences kept coming out backwards. I didn't know at the time, but learned later that Thai sentences are structured that way. We sat for a minute before I pressed her into drinking just water. She was fragile but she didn't seem to know it.

"Just drink water, okay? Your stomach might be sensitive," I sort of stuttered out. I hated acting as her caretaker. I wanted not to be concerned with how she behaved but couldn't stop. I wanted the old Sandra to be there so I didn't have to worry about her. She looked at me uncomprehendingly.

"Order what you like, okay? Your favorite Thai dishes."

The waitress swung back to us, pert and smiling. San proceeded to order iced coffee and beer and cognac and soup and five or six different dishes of mutton this and beef that and two kinds of fish, plus stuffed something or other. It was fine with me. I wanted her to have everything she'd been dreaming of for weeks. We sat without talking while she smoked another cigarette. The mutton dish arrived first. I tasted it, found it sickeningly awful. The mutton was urine-soaked, I was sure. I spit my mouthful into a napkin, gagging.

Laughing, San took hold of the dish of mutton with verve, but she spilled it on the table and in her lap, her hand too shaky holding the dish. She set it down, *plop*, in front of her. She tasted it and didn't find it bad, or at least pretended not to, shrugging, "Not…what I ordered…take it back."

When the waitress returned with a plate of fish, San picked up the mutton dish and extended it toward her, saying, in Thai, that it wasn't what we ordered. The waitress backed up, *not* pert and smiling now, *not* taking the plate, as San lurched toward her, extending it with all her waning strength. The smelly food spilled off the plate and onto the florid carpet. Sandra didn't see that she was humiliating the waitress, nor did the waitress see that she was humiliating San. The girl spoke harshly to San and pushed away the plate, which banged onto the table. The rest of the smelly mutton splashed down the length of the surface. A mess.

"Never mind," I said, laughing, because it actually was funny despite everything, despite all the humiliation. Both San and the waitress looked over at me laughing, but neither of them was amused. Then

Sandra repeated the same routine with the fish, a dish I liked and was quite willing to eat, but which an increasingly obnoxious San insisted she didn't order. The waitress held her ground, brushing San off, and the plate of fish clattered down the already soiled table to join the mutton—*kerwhack, splash*.

I was still laughing, but I was laughing alone. The waitress stalked off, no longer swinging her body. Sandra absorbed herself in another cigarette. I ate a few bites of the piece of fish that was still intact on the plate that had landed near me. It was filet of white fish with garlic and ginger, and it was tasty. Now that the waitress was gone, San started snickering a bit.

"What a bitch I am," she admitted, looking me in the eye, then glanced with interest at the rice in a blue bowl. Good! It seemed so obvious that a starving person should lay down some rice in her belly to cushion anything more exotic also going in.

"I always eat rice," San declared, self-righteously now, as if she had invented eating rice and eating rice had done her some good. Even as she sat there drooling, half-dead and out of her mind. *Eat rice, and you will turn out like this*, was what she was saying. I didn't believe she always ate rice, even though she was currently doing so.

"I do," she insisted. "I do always eat rice." She was defensive. My class lady was an unreliable narrator in her present state. It was disconcerting. She said she didn't get what she ordered, for example. Did she speak Thai or didn't she? Did she know the food or didn't she? Had she really put down roots in Thailand or had she spent the past months as someone's slave? What was the point of what we were doing here?

When the bill came, I paid for the whole mess, including two dishes we'd never touched at all. It wasn't much, compared to Paris prices—forty dollars or so, which included a huge tip, but I didn't have much money left. I was a low-level wage earner traveling on a free ticket. My presence in Thailand was an act of fate. I was not normally a five-star kind of gal. I was uncomfortable about the money, about running out.

"We can't do this again," I said sternly.

"Do what?"

"Eat like this, order too much. I don't have very much money."

She looked at me blankly.

"Never mind," I sighed.

"You have money," she bullied. I wondered where her energy for an argument was coming from.

"How in the hell do you know if I have money or not?"

"You always had money."

"I always worked! Come on, let's go." I couldn't stand the argument, wanted out of there. "Come on, move!" I ordered.

"The waitress can pack it to go and I'll eat it in our room if that will make you happy," San said sarcastically with a spastic dramatic gesture that took in the whole sloppy table. She couldn't let me have the upper hand. And I guess I couldn't let her have the upper hand either. I couldn't keep my feelings inside any longer. It wasn't just a question of San always ordering the most expensive beer back in Portland when someone else was paying—that was funny when it happened and people would chip in, no big deal. No, I remembered another time, much more acute, when my mother, whose house was across town from mine in Portland, had just moved to an assisted living place. I decided to have a dinner party at her house—my childhood home—before it was emptied and sold.

We were seven for dinner, all friends of Sandra's from earlier days. I made rice with curried chicken, and everyone but Sandra complimented me on the food.

This is what Sandra had to say: "The recipe called for saffron, but she was too cheap to buy any, that's why the rice isn't yellow." She announced this as she pointed at me. And for what reason? Because we were sitting in a nice house? With drapes and a painting on the wall behind me? What was it with her?

Issues of money, or class, always made San aggressive, and issues of money made me defensive.

In the Vegas lounge, San looked toward the crowd of Thai diners and, with an over-the-top gesture directed at me, warbled, "Why does she do this to me?"

"Why do *you* do this to *me?*" I retorted.

There was a long silence.

"I don't know why I do what I do to you," she finally said. "I would like to know. But right now, I am going to rise above it." The way she moved her body as she pronounced this, puffing out her emaciated chest, not acting feeble at all, she was very funny, very clever, very self-aware, playing on her words like in *commedia dell'arte*. She still had it in her to be a good performer, no question.

I was won over by her self-parody and forgot my bad feelings. I was laughing that night in Thailand when the waitress came back again. I didn't want to fight. Apparently, San didn't want to fight either and was laughing too. *We* might have been in stitches, but the waitress was not. She was still hard-eyed. San ignored her hardness, spoke to her nicely about something and the girl left. San and I sat quietly smiling for about five minutes, waiting, each with our own thoughts.

The waitress came back and began dumping that execrable mutton mess into a plastic box, which was what San had evidently asked her to do. She scraped up what was still on the tabletop. Clutching the plastic container in front of her like a battering ram, San mustered up some dignity as we shuffled out into the lobby past the desk clerks who stared at her, then at me. I was impressed she was able to carry off such an exit despite being a wreck. She had more energy than I did. I was so tired. In the room, I tore off my dress, washed it in the bathroom sink and hung it up to dry.

San went into the bathroom right after, turned on the water for a bath, then came back to beg me for drugs. I was already flat on my back in bed. I got up and gave her a red and white Prozac capsule. I also gave her five hundred baht in cash, so she could control some money, and we could avoid clashes on that subject. "Oooo," she responded, coquettishly pushing the bills into her red satin bra which was all she had on now. I no longer winced at her sallow, skinny nakedness and was instead thinking she had merely gotten down to her fighting weight.

I needed to contact the U.S. Embassy. Also, I wanted to call Renard to say I was safe. I dialed his number in Bangkok, figuring he could tell me what to do about discontinuing or continuing the drugs we'd gotten from the asylum. I didn't want to go on making decisions haphazardly. I could take San to a doctor in Songkhla the next day, but it would be good to talk to Renard first. It was three a.m. Renard's phone rang and rang. No one answered. I hung up, deflated, and stared at my disappointed self in the mirror on the hotel dresser. My curly hair was reddish brown in the lamplight. Sansan's calico hair—brown, white, red—was very curly, too, because of the humidity. San would surely want to dye her hair red again.

On the television set, there was no news in English, only a manic variety show in Japanese. What happened to CNN? What happened to the BBC's "News of the World"? I would have liked further information about the bombing in Oklahoma. Or about the police shooting at drug dealers in the south of Thailand. There might be a reason to be concerned about our safety where we were.

Before San got out of the bath, I took the drug-filled plastic Ziploc bags out of my purse and put all but two capsules of the lithium in with the Haldol. I put the bag with only the two lithium back in my purse, set it on the dresser in plain sight and tucked the other plastic bags with the remaining drugs under the mattress on *my* side of the double bed. Then I went to see what was happening to San in the bathtub.

She was stretched out full-length in the tub, smoking, and she smiled at me with genuine affection. She was inhabiting her body now, herself, it seemed like, and she looked so young with that smile, so like a baby smiling. She appeared innocent. I smiled back at her. She asked if she could use my toothbrush. "I haven't brushed my teeth for maybe two months, can you imagine?"

"Sure, I'll get another one tomorrow. You can use anything you want," I told her, indicating my cosmetic satchel. "There are pills to take if you have diarrhea. I'm going to bed now."

"I'll be right in," she said, not moving. She was a skinny burlesque of the vamp she used to be...prematurely worn, but still sexy. I bent down and kissed her on the forehead. We had kissed on the mouth back in Portland, like everyone else. Everyone had kissed everyone all the time. "You sweetie," she purred lovingly. "This is a five-star hotel...you see the soap? French perfume, hmmmmmm."

I had fallen asleep, drained, by the time San got in bed, but I woke up the instant she lit a cigarette. I had gained an appreciation for the pleasure and security and rhythm she had drawn from the act of smoking. I had observed that smoking allowed her to reflect and sort out conflicting information she'd been getting...or imagining.

But I could not tolerate anybody, not even Sansan, smoking in the bed I was trying to sleep in.

"You *cannot* smoke in bed!" I growled, pained by my own creepy lack of generosity. I was already getting out of bed to retreat from the smoke. "It makes me want to strangle you," I heard myself saying, "I can't help it. If you want to smoke, go in the bathroom."

Without hesitation, she got out of bed. Maybe she preferred banishment, she moved so quickly. She ended up spending the night in the bathroom with the door slightly ajar, the fan on, while she slept on the tile floor, which was not so different from what she had been doing in the asylum. Before I fell asleep again, I listened to San colonizing the bathroom, smoking again, then running the water for another bath. Before she got back in the tub, she ate some of the food, and that foul mutton dish smelled even worse than before. Then she threw up and flushed the toilet several times.

I had drifted off when she came out of the bathroom and woke me up asking, "You awake?" followed by, "Could I...look in your purse for the drugs?"

I didn't answer. I didn't need to; she would find what I'd left for her. I didn't want to engage anymore. Too tired. She would find what she needed. She opened my purse on the dresser. In the dim light, I saw her pull out the plastic bag with the two lithium capsules in it and heard her snort ironically to herself, taking note of my stinginess, or my generosity—which was it? Then she went back into the bathroom for the night.

Songkhla, Thailand

Thump, thump, whomp, went the muffled sounds from inside the closet. There was a secret escape route through it. Sansan had found it and was calling me to follow her. We were escaping from Thailand down a plunging vertical wall by grabbing onto suitcase handles sticking out from the it. I woke up. There really was thumping and pounding from outside in the hallway. San was banging on the door to our room and calling my name.

"What are you doing out here?" I asked when I opened the door. It had never occurred to me she might leave the room. She had seemed too frail, too handicapped, too satisfied with the bathtub to go out. Yet there she was outside in the hallway.

"I went out at six…the sun came up, so I went out," she explained rapidly and clearly, not slobbering, a recovered woman. "I always get up at dawn." It was true she had always gotten up at dawn in Portland. This morning she had fixed herself up, put on lipstick and eyeliner, creamed her face, shampooed her hair. Her hands were already less claw-like, more relaxed.

"I'm speeding," she said, laughing, excited, eyes flashing, talking breathlessly like Marilyn Monroe—like the old Sansan. I kissed her on the cheek, she was so delightful. "Oooh," she breathed and smiled her sidelong smile of yore. I thought I was still dreaming.

"I had three double espressos. They were delicious. Oh yeah, coffee is a wonderful drug. Up, not down. Clear-thinking, not crazy. And I met a man in the bar." She shook her finger at me, warning, "Never marry a man you meet in a bar. Ha, ha. I did that once! Well, this man bought me a glass of wine. He was nice." She made a Betty Boop moue, bounced her eyes sideways.

"He's Thai, a businessman probably," she went on. "They're always drawn to me. I don't know why. He wants to come upstairs, up here." Eyes wide open in mock astonishment, she looped her hand up and around and down, finger pointed at the floor, right where we were standing, up here.

"You understand? He wants to come up here...and fool around. Ohhhh! But I scared him off." She giggled, put her hand over her mouth, a stand-up comic.

"You *are* pretty scary," I confirmed, remembering how grotesque she had been the night before and imagining what reserves this new performance was drawing upon.

"Yeah, I'm scary, I guess," she said with apparent lucidity, shuffling past me to pull open the heavy curtains, which, for her, was a daunting physical task. I didn't help her, just watched... transfixed. She didn't ask for help. I was a spectator, and she was the show. Like the good old days, only now it was spine-chilling.

The curtains finally opened. She looked out the window and down, her hands and lips pressed against the glass like a child, like a monkey peering out through the bars of its cage.

"He said he would wait for me." She laughed melodramatically and turned to face me in profile. "Ha, ha, ha. By the pool. Is he down there? I can't see that far. Ha, ha, ha. Is he there?"

At the window, I looked ten floors down at the pool, saw that there was, indeed, a man down there amidst a sea of white plastic deck furniture. A man in a gray suit, idling, smoking, staring into the pool.

He turned and looked up at the sky, perhaps in anticipation of a coming cloudburst. Then he looked directly up toward the tenth floor. Maybe he saw me. He squinted—blank, open-mouthed. He brought his cigarette up to his lips, closed them around it and dragged languorously, exhaled, still appearing not to see me but squinting right up in my direction as I studied him. Just then, the morning's towering dark clouds let loose with a pounding tropical downpour, and the man disappeared inside.

Was he headed up to the tenth floor? Had he been sexually aroused by Sandra's spastic jerkiness, by her facial tic, by the moisture gathering around her buccal orifice? Perhaps she had told him there were two of us.

"The man's not there," I lied to San, who, evidently, couldn't see that far herself. Besides, he wasn't there anymore by the time I was saying it, he had gone inside. "I don't see anyone down there. Look at that rain come down."

"I think he had a gun," San remarked, disconcerting me even more. A gun. This was unexpected. A gun. Everything was flying out of control.

"I think I'm going to barf," she said then, also unexpectedly, and went into the bathroom. "Shut the door," I called after her. "I don't want to listen to you barf." She shut the door, but I heard everything anyway.

I circled the room trying to think what to do if the Thai man came to the door with a gun. San had always been good at throwing me off balance, usually with some sexual motif, and there she was, doing it again, although now it took more to make me uncomfortable than in the past, but now there was more, and it was still about sex but also about guns. I didn't like the idea of a guy with a gun coming upstairs hoping to have sex with two women.

Who was he? Hired killers are cheap in Thailand. San had said on the phone to me in Bangkok that someone was trying to kill her. Is that what this guy with a gun was about? It seemed more real now than it had then. Had this guy been sent to get rid of San once and for all? To get rid of both of us?

I tried to calm down. I reconstructed the scene from the night before to see what I had missed. San had come out of the bathroom and found the lithium in my bag where I had deliberately left it for her to find. I had drifted off after that. The bag was still on the dresser in the same place it was the night before. I went through it to see if anything was missing—any money, for instance. Not that I would remember how many baht I'd had...

Nothing was missing. I lifted up the mattress. The plastic bags of drugs were still there. She hadn't found them. So far, she was accommodating the arrangement we'd tacitly worked out, wherein I was her dealer, a role not to my fancy.

I decided not to leave the plastic bags of drugs under the mattress any longer, in case the maid discovered them, or in case I wanted to leave San alone in the room. I put everything in my purse, leaving two lithium capsules on the dresser.

As far as I knew, San had taken no drugs for seven hours, unless she had gotten something from the guy with the gun beyond a psychological boost, a glass of wine and three double espressos. Discounting the possibility of additional drugs from unknown sources, I figured she'd had two lithiums, one Thorazine and one Prozac—all from me and all within the twelve hours since I'd found her. I thought this was less than what she'd been taking at the asylum, but I didn't know, and I also didn't know if the drugs were compatible. I knew nothing. I didn't know if it was a real doctor who had ordered those drugs. Because what kind of real doctor would mix all those drugs together?

I took back one of the lithiums I had just put on the dresser and decided to leave only one. But then I took that one back, leaving none at all. No more drugs for Sansan until we had more information.

My watch indicated it was too early to call Renard in Bangkok, too early to call the U.S. Embassy. So I called room service, ordering cereal and toast and eggs and orange juice and tea for two. When San came out of the bathroom, lipstick freshly applied, breath sweet-smelling, I went in there to shower and took my bag. Carrying the stash around with me was my only choice.

In the shower, I heard people talking outside the bathroom door and panicked. Was it the man who'd been standing by the pool, the man with the gun? I stuck my head out from behind the curtain to hear San speaking throatily in English, then in Thai. It was room service. Cups clinked on a tray. She and the room service man were standing right outside the bathroom door talking; it was a warm exchange. I got out of the shower and found there was only a washcloth to dry myself with. All the towels were strewn in a messy heap on the floor.

Outside the door, Sansan was now whispering to the room service guy. I was certain she was asking him for some Thai stick…and this was in the middle of a government crackdown on drugs. The man said something to her, and she chuckled throatily. She was in her seductive mode. He was probably on the younger side, touching San's arm, looking deeply into her eyes. Sansan murmured a flirtatious-sounding remark in Thai, and the man answered in a soft and low tone. Just as I was straining to hear the rest, he (or they) left the room. My ear was pressed onto my side of the closed bathroom door.

"Sandra?"

She opened the bathroom door suddenly, knocking me aside, stuck her head in and saw me drying myself with a washcloth. "Oh, excuse me," she cooed in the same voice she'd been using on the room service guy. "I am so bad, I used all the towels, there was no towel for you!" Sizing up my naked body, she made a two-handed curving gesture, sort of like a sculptor might. Then she saw my bag hanging on the back of the bathroom door and exclaimed, "Oh, *here's* your purse!" She could easily have grabbed it with all my money and all her drugs and shuffled away fast, down the hall to a rendezvous, to a new adventure, a new life, but all that was just in my imagination. That's not what San was doing. She was standing there, holding my bag close to her chest. I glared at her stonily, baring my teeth like a primate.

"Can't I just...?" she pleaded in a baby voice, tilting her head, her eyes rolling dreamily down toward the desired object.

"*No!*" I lunged for the bag. "Don't touch my purse and shut the goddam door and we'll talk about it when I come out!"

Sandra withdrew submissively. Her docile switcheroo in response to my aggressive behavior was like what she'd done the night before, when I'd made a scene about her smoking in bed. She had backed off, cowering. If that was our only possible dynamic, I hated it. It reminded me of those mangy dogs on the dock on the island. It was so fatiguing, so boring. Is that what she had learned from her bloody Brit? How to cower?

In a spiraling rage, I stalked over to the toilet with the plastic bag containing the Haldol and the lithium and emptied them into the bowl, flushing them without a nanosecond's hesitation. The purple Haldol and the blue and white lithium circled colorfully in the water, going down in a swirl of final glory.

Soon after, I was dressed and eating breakfast in heavy silence. We needed more order in this strange scenario, or we would both go mad. I had to think.

The eggs were cooked up into omelets garnished with ginger and green onions, and mine tasted good. San didn't touch hers. She was standing up, too agitated to sit down. She made toreador passes at the food tray on the dresser, and, in between those passes, shuffled around the room with whatever she picked up off the tray, cutting a path for herself with her forearms as she had done the night before. She buttered and jellied a piece of toast which she held between her teeth as she flattened herself against the wall. She ate the toast, then flung herself forward to get another hunk, piling on the butter and jelly. She took this new creation and went over to the chair, circling around it like a dog trying to settle.

Finding that chair unsatisfactory, she took the toast to bed, where she ate propped up against the pillows. The food and the chewing made her drool, so she wiped her face with the sheet and pulled herself upright using the twisted linen as a rope. Standing, she shuffled over to get a cup of tea and added six cubes of sugar. She glanced over and noticed me watching her, so she stopped her manic sugaring, as if I had accused her of something. Like a peasant, she held her teacup two-handed and drank standing up, gazing out the window into the distance, contemplating the horizon.

As always, her physical behavior was interesting, not static even when she was motionless. What I was reading in it was that she felt trapped there in the hotel with me. If she could, she would leave.

"Nice sugar, very nice," she mused to herself before reaching for more, popping two cubes in her mouth to suck on.

I cleared my throat. "San... Who was the doctor that gave you those drugs? What kind of a place was that nuthouse? Is it where people go to vanish?"

"Yeah, right, that's what it was, yes, a place where people vanish. You do see things clearly. That's what I always liked about you."

"No, I don't see things clearly. Really, no. I don't know what's going on." She looked at me, so I continued. "For instance, that man you picked up in the bar. Was he someone you had seen before?"

"Oh, he was..." She shrugged, drifted over to the mirror to look at herself instead. She shifted her shoulders and head around, as people do when they want to get a sense of how they really look. I took it as a positive sign. She was weighing her assets.

She reached up to touch her three-toned calico hair. "My hair..." she grunted and chuckled, then smoothed her Chinese clothes, which nicely concealed her thinness. They made her look almost classy.

"You look good," I complimented.

She looked back at my reflection in the mirror and gave me a real Sansan smile, full of life.

"So tell me about that guy," I said to her reflection. "You mentioned he had a gun. Is one of us gonna catch a bullet?"

San was still smiling, but now scoffed at some invisible third party. She grumbled, "I bet she thinks I'm falling for all this...don't you think?" She went on joking to this nonexistent other person in the talking-to-her-sidekick way she had done back in Portland when she was onstage, laughing and saying funny lines to an unseen accomplice.

She stopped doing it then and looked at herself in the mirror. "They all have guns," she said, picking up the earlier thread, still looking at her hair, which, combined with her slanted green eyes, made her seem altogether feline. It was easy to imagine her washing herself like a cat, licking her own long legs. She poignantly touched the worn skin on her face, which was drained now—not the animated Betty Boop mask of earlier, no longer the joking, laughing Sansan. She was crashing. In the mirror, her features were again wrinkled, sunken, and her teeth and jaws were as prominent as those of a skull.

"What do you mean 'they all have guns'?" I wasn't about to let go of that. "*Who* has guns? Come on, San! Everybody in the street has guns? Everybody in Thailand? What are you saying? You said last night you had forgotten to be careful. What are you mixed up in?"

"He was sent by Tip...maybe...I think..."

"The guy you picked up in the bar was sent by Tip? To kill you? Tip knew we would end up here in this hotel? Come on. What are you saying? You think Tip had us followed? You think someone followed us from the nuthouse?" This was starting to feel like a game of charades as I hammered on, "You think someone was on that bus? I suppose the gangster sitting in his car up at the wat on your island was monitoring me too?"

"Gangster up at the wat on the island?" Sandra pronounced the words slowly and with care.

"Yeah, I went to the wat," I confirmed, my voice strident. "And there was a guy in dark glasses sitting in an expensive car parked sideways across the road just before you get to the wat, like a roadblock."

"You shouldn't have gone up to the wat," she said in the voice of doom.

"Why the hell n—?" I started to screech, but stopped myself and went to the window to calm down.

I felt at risk, following her into the world of voices that told her people were pursuing her. Was she a guide or wasn't she? Could I have been listening more precisely to what was behind what she was saying, as if every syllable meant something different from what it normally meant? But how could I listen any more precisely? I hadn't missed a single thing, not a twitch, not a tic, and it seemed like San was trying to deal with some real danger to herself, a danger not just in her head, but a genuine danger to both of us, something she couldn't quite verbalize, something ominous.

Our adventure together had taken on a frightening dimension. It was crucial to hear the things San was saying on several levels—as truth or partial truth, or as exaggeration, or paranoid fantasy, or clairvoyant vision, or all of them at once. I had to sort through it if I wanted to get us out of that place alive.

Thailand was a violent place, where drug dealers were shot wholesale, where body sweepers gathered up dead people killed on the streets of Bangkok, where dozens of Muslims were rounded up by the police and stuffed into military trucks to suffocate. It was Dominique Renard who had told me when we first met in Patpong that Thailand is a dangerous place. At the same time, Thailand is a land of peaceful Buddhist tradition. How does all that go together?

San, meanwhile, was caught up in the sight of herself in the mirror.

"Sandra?"

"Yes?"

"Do you think you're being followed?"

"I…"

"What have you done? Did Tip send someone to follow you? Who are these gangsters?"

She turned away from the mirror and looked

at me confusedly, not following the thread. She had gone off somewhere again.

"Tell me what Tip wants," I said, trying to get her back. We looked at each other, waiting. Outside the door, the sound of voices flowed as people walked by. San froze. I saw a thought forming in her mind, but she didn't speak.

"Sandra!" I shook her by the shoulders, to jolt the thought out of her.

"It's the voices," she panicked, seizing, it seemed, on the voices outside in the hallway. If red lights had flashed, she would say it was the red lights. Who knew where her ideas were coming from, what was stimulating them? The moment lingered on. We finally broke our locked gaze, and San looked for and found a pack of cigarettes on the dresser, a fresh pack she must have bought that morning. She shakily lit one and inhaled deeply, seeking relief. I left her to smoke while I piled the breakfast dishes on the tray.

"The voices aren't real San," I said conversationally, sitting back down.

She looked at me with a half-smile, fixed on me with a serious expression, thought for a moment, then spoke elliptically but earnestly.

"How do I know...you're telling the truth? They...are...real to me. They say that Eddy is dead...and the baby, your baby with Eddy...the voices...tell me...people turned against me...angry people are here...maybe to kill me."

"The voices are not real San. They are *not* real. You're hallucinating. Bad things have happened to you. Bad things are still happening to you."

I was thinking San's voices were brought on by excessive doses of drugs, which had stimulated a psychotic state, or by other real mental or physical threats to her. Also, I was thinking—new information leading to a reinterpretation of the old—that San had a way of seeing things that I, that none of her friends in Portland, had ever recognized in her before. I was no expert, only a friend who had washed up onto Sansan's shore and found her afflicted.

"Eddy is *not* dead," I emphasized. "There was no baby. I never had a baby with your son Eddy. I never had any babies at all. And I don't know who they are, the people who might be following you. We'll have to figure that part out together, okay? If the voices are back, it's related to the drugs, don't you see? The drugs stop the voices. Or maybe the drugs cause the voices. Do you understand? It's a vicious circle. Your mind is being messed with. The drugs are messing with your mind. Do you understand what I'm saying?"

She looked at me blankly.

"San, the drugs are killing you," I summarized.

"Of course, they're trying to kill me," she replied, switching the words around to fit her own line of thought.

"I'm saying the drugs themselves are killing you.

I don't know about the people. Look at you. We have to get you to a doctor."

She turned back to look at herself in the mirror again as she smoked.

"No doctors, you understand? I will run. And I want to get my own money out of the bank." She was addressing her reflection in the mirror. The mirror worked for her, as if I were her double, her sidekick. At the same time, I thought she knew I was there, a separate person from her, knew it was me.

"You have my bankbook, don't you?" She was truly on task now. "From the police? Give it to me."

Sandra was onto the survival thread. Or the money thread. With her own money, she wouldn't have to get drugs or anything else from me anymore, she could step out on her own, which was desirable from both our perspectives. It occurred to me San might be figuring out how to ditch me. Her ditching me might be what I now wanted myself. An end to the episode. Once San got her own money, I figured she would be better. But it was hard to know, it was hard to get a foothold in such treacherous territory.

"Here," I said, foraging in my diminished cache of psychotropics for a Prozac. I found it and held it out to San. "Take this and why don't you take another bath, too? It calms you down. And you can think things over. Wouldn't you like that? The bankbook's right here in my bag. Here it is. Take it. Go have a bath. I need to make a phone call."

She snatched the bankbook and the proffered pill which she downed with a gulp of tea, tossed her head back extravagantly to swallow and choked, pounded on her chest. When she did that, I thought of Harpo Marx. She got control of her coughing, poured herself another cup of tea, dropped in five cubes of sugar, looked at me accusingly and said, in a kind of delayed reaction, "Who are you calling?"

"A doctor I know, a French doctor."

"I'm not going to a doctor. It's too dangerous. They're following me. They're listening to your phone calls. Now they'll follow him."

"This doctor is in Bangkok. He's a friend of mine. I just want to talk to him. I want to ask him how I can help you. Trust me, please. Go. I'll get the maid to bring fresh towels."

The fresh towel thing worked. San always responded to promised comforts. Or maybe my tone had changed to something more reassuring, more confident, more cool, less hysterical, and San responded to that. With a pleased look, she nodded and headed for the bath, taking her tea, cigarettes and bankbook.

Maybe she was tired of fighting with me as much as I was tired of fighting her. I poured myself a cup of tea, called the concierge for fresh towels, looked at my watch. It was almost noon. A good time to call Renard? I dialed his number hopefully.

"*Allo*," Dominique answered after the first ring.

He wasn't surprised to hear from me again, sounded more than pleased that I was safe, and listened as I related how I had sprung Sandra from the asylum and described her current behavior, as well as the drugs they had sold me at the psychiatric facility.

"What kind of place do you think that is Dominique? Do you think a real doctor prescribed those drugs?"

"I couldn't say. Anything could be true or not true. Anything at all."

I snorted at this.

"Where are you now?"

I gave him the name of the hotel and the telephone number, then walked over to the window and looked out. Down below, steam was rising off the pavement around the pool, the rainwater evaporating in the hot sun. The man who had been idling there earlier was gone.

"You can't get Sandra into a hospital there in Songkhla?" Renard asked from far away, across the Gulf of Thailand.

"I don't know if there's a hospital here, and I don't think Sandra would go to a hospital in any case. She's fighting me every step. She might be in some danger, I'm not sure," I answered, slurping my tea as I talked. "Also, she's here illegally. Her visa expired long ago. She could be thrown in jail just for that, you know. You know this country."

"Yes. Have you contacted your embassy?"

248

I explained that I had been planning to take her to the U.S. Embassy in Bangkok, to get her repatriated to the States, but that San was not of the same mind and might be trying to escape.

"Hmm." Renard put down the phone to light a cigar, puffed, then came back. It was reassuring, listening to him puff like that. "Can you stay there in the hotel a few days? You have money?"

Renard explained to me how to bring about a soft landing for San through incrementally reduced doses of her drugs so that we would be able to travel to Bangkok and get her repatriated. He said to do exactly what I had been doing with the drug doses, spacing them out, only now to increase the intervals between pills. He thought it was good I had flushed the Haldol and lithium down the toilet so that we had less product to deal with. I felt buoyed listening to his professional advice.

When I told Renard that San weighed only about seventy-five pounds, we stumbled over how much that is in kilos. After he grasped how thin she was, he told me to ply her with liquids, that sugar was okay ("You remember? I gave you sugar?" he said), that alcohol and coffee weren't a good idea, that rice was the best thing, that eggs were excellent. I told him this was more or less what she'd been eating, though she hadn't abstained from coffee and alcohol.

"So you are a doctor yourself and don't need me." I could hear him puffing on his cigar. "You must call your embassy and ask them to help you. Do you want me to come down there and join you?"

"No," I said, then "yes," then "no" again, then "yes" again, not certain he would come if asked.

I hardly knew him. I did want to see him again though. "I think we're okay, just the two of us, for the time being," I finally verbalized. "But thanks. I'll call you again. I'll call you when I come back to Bangkok."

Renard was too good to be true, I was thinking after we hung up, already regretting not just telling him "yes." I looked around the hotel room as if I'd never seen it before, unable to imagine how San and I had gotten ourselves into such a mess... although, knowing San, I could imagine that much of her life had unfolded in similarly messy territory. I rubbed my jaw where the muscle ached. I'd been clenching my teeth. I lay down on the end of the bed to sigh and stare at the ceiling and think about how it would be to have Renard as my traveling companion.

Instead, I had Sansan, who was so destroyed. I did want to do the right thing for her, to be a good person, to get her into the hands of someone competent. There was no thought in my mind of abandoning her. I was inspired by Renard's kindness.

The maid knocked, bearing fresh towels. San was in the tub, her head reclining on the headrest. For an instant, I thought she was dead but then she snored slightly and twitched, lifting her hand out of the water onto the long scar on her belly. She had crashed. She looked comfortable, physically peaceful. The headrest had a lip on it designed to keep sleeping bathers from drowning, and it was doing just that. Half-submerged, San looked like an otter floating on its back, or some kind of sea creature captured and brought home as a pet.

I went out for some fresh air to collect my thoughts. San would sleep for at least an hour. I wouldn't go far in any case. Outside the building, the intense heat was welcome after hours of air-conditioning. I poked around the grounds, examining all the flowers without really seeing them. I startled a hotel employee who was doing something behind the bushes. He giggled.

The change of perspective felt nice. I'd been scared upstairs, and now I was less scared. The ominous horizon as seen from ten floors up was less sinister at ground level. The earth felt good underfoot, and smelled good too, for it was the smells that finally drew me in—wet soil and jasmine, frangipani, hibiscus and cut grass. I looked around and saw the gorgeous place I was in. A splendid array of orchids had been planted by someone who knew them well, knew they would complement one another in full flower the way they did now. And there was an empty Lipovan bottle in the dirt.

It seemed like a bad idea to stay ten floors up

in the air with San. She was so unbound. Being ten floors removed from the real world certainly couldn't help her stabilize. And what was worse was the two of us isolated together ten floors up. No wonder we both wanted to bolt. Sansan had bolted countless times in her life, and that was just during the part of her story I knew. And me? I would have thought I was the more likely one to bolt from the current situation with San, to tie up loose ends rapidly in a relationship of diminished equality. But the situation with San was a commitment. And I had never bolted from commitments, from jobs or assignments, from deals or contracts, so I was not likely to start now. I bolted when communication was nonexistent, but that was not the case with San. We were having our good moments along with the bad. In Paris, when people from earlier periods in life had visited me and turned out to be unable to adapt to the cultural circumstances, I had sometimes bolted. San's stop-off in Paris nearly two decades before had been very good. We had endeared ourselves to each other forever during that visit. We had marched arm-in-arm in a demonstration on the anniversary of Franco's fall, walked the canals in the gritty northeastern part of the city, dressed up in the vintage clothes she had with her to sell to finance her travels. I had felt bereft when she left for Afghanistan.

San was out of the bath wrapped in a towel and watching television when I came back upstairs.

She had found CNN and was watching an update on the drug-related killings in South Thailand. The image showed the director of the Thai branch of the human rights NGO called Civil Rights International.

"*Ying ting*, that guy said, you hear that?" San was saying. "*Ying ting*." She was stimulated, as if she had drunk three cups of espresso or done some drugs. But I had left nothing for her.

"What is it?"

"*Ying ting, ying ting*, it means they kill you and throw you away. How many times have I heard that before?" she sang out.

"*Ying ting?*"

"Yeah, that's what Song threatened me with..."

"Song?"

"Tip's wife," San reminded, quieting so she could hear the TV. I wanted to hear the Thai story too, so I let the questions go, but I didn't want to lose track of the *ying ting*.

The Thailand drug lord story was on television only because an NGO like Civil Rights International had called attention to it in the name of, well, civil rights. Otherwise, the TV people would never have covered it. No one would have ever heard about hundreds of gangland drug dealers in Thailand dying, shot at point-blank range without an NGO piping up. And how strange, because the obvious issue was whether the larger public could ever care about gangland drug dealers being shot. NGOs can be odd sometimes. As an employee of an NGO myself, I was thinking that drug dealers dying was a problematic story to get behind. Try to raise money for that one.

The CNN anchor went on to the next story, an update on the Oklahoma bombing. San looked up at me, her face filled with disbelief.

"How did they get there so fast?" She tensed up, twisting her body. She was spewing a frantic flow of words and saliva now, the way she'd been doing when we arrived at the hotel. The television was showing footage of the damaged Oklahoma City federal building, where a day care center was on the first floor. San was screaming. I could hardly hear when the TV anchor in Hong Kong reported that a truck with explosives had pulled up and parked right outside the federal building. Two hundred and fifty people had been killed, lots of them kids.

"*How did they get over there*?!" San shouted. She hadn't been at all shocked by the story about hundreds of shooting deaths right there where we were in Thailand, but she was hyperventilating about an event in Oklahoma.

"How the hell did they get into the United States? How did they find that place? Two hundred-fifty kids?" She was snarling in a low voice, her teeth clenched on the stub of a cigarette as she struggled to light a new one off the old. The anchor once again blamed the bombing on Islamic terrorists.

"How did they get to Oklahoma?" she barked at me.

"Who?"

"The voices, they're in Oklahoma!"

"The voices?" She thought the bombers and the voices were the same people? I couldn't follow her anymore. It was too irrational. The situation required a professional. I had shifted my focus away from her madness while I was downstairs in the garden. And now it was as if I had forgotten how to understand her. Or maybe I didn't want to try to understand her any longer.

"I'm not going there," San declared definitively, as if she had figured everything out.

"Where? To the United States? You're not going there?" I shivered. It was the air-conditioning after the heat outside.

"I'm not going there," she rasped at me, coughing, pounding on her chest like Harpo Marx.

"Where are you not going? To Oklahoma?"

"*No!*" she shouted, frustrated. "Not Oklahoma!" She was angry at me, annoyed that I couldn't or wouldn't follow her anymore. Exasperated, she pushed and pulled against my arm, trying to force me to be there with her again.

"Where are you not going? To Bangkok?"

She spit out her words one by one. "I am not going to the United States... They're already there...you saw? The voices. We're safe here. They're not mad at you and me. They're mad at the United States." She stabbed at the screen with her cigarette. "I'm not going back to the States."

"San, you *have to* go back," I insisted in an altogether wrong voice, long-suffering instead of compassionate. "Look at you. You're sick. You need care."

"No, they...take your passport, and you're stuck."

"Who?"

"The U.S. Embassy."

"They take your passport?"

"That's what they do when they...repatriate you...until you pay them back. Give me...my passport."

She seemed lucid again. All I had to do was not listen or not help out for a minute, and she became lucid. That was the way it worked. When I faded, she picked up the slack. When she had to, she performed. Which was good, because I needed her assistance. I was not exactly on top of what was happening. There was a silence while I contemplated this news of hers about not wanting to return to the States.

"So where do you want to go?" I said finally. It hadn't occurred to me that Sansan wasn't yearning to be safe in the bosom of her own country. How dumb of me. I had misjudged who she was. I was a bit overwhelmed. I dug out her passport and gave it to her. She grabbed the document and clutched it, claw-like, in one hand.

"I'll stay here...go underground," she declared. "Go south."

I couldn't help but be impressed by her willfulness. Now she was looking for something else in my bag. She had already thought about all this, it looked like. She already knew what was in my bag and pulled out the plastic Franprix sack I had stuffed my underwear and bathing suit into. She dumped out the contents and took the sack. In it, she placed her passport, her bankbook and a fifty-baht note she pulled out of her red bra.

San took the plastic sack with her when we went downstairs to the Vegas lounge for lunch. We sat at a table and I ordered rice, hot chicken curry and a fish cooked in coconut milk wrapped in a banana leaf. I no longer wanted to depend on San's choice of food.

We both ate heartily, but I got more food in my mouth than she did. Sadly, her drooling was stimulated by eating. We talked about her plan to go underground, but we were talking at cross-purposes, like a parent and child, switching roles back and forth, neither of us willing to comprehend the other's arguments.

"What if the man is still following you?" I posited. She went blank. I was beginning to understand that going blank was San's way of going forward. When she did speak, it was to take up an unresolved point from the day before.

"They killed my dog. I have to get my dog's body. I want to have her skull."

"I saw Manley, San, at the gym on the island, and I think your dog died of old age and a broken heart, and because you were gone too long. I don't think they killed her."

"I wasn't gone that long."

"How long were you gone?"

"A month maybe. I had an operation. They took out my tumor."

"Was it an abortion?"

"*No*, it was a tumor...a parasite."

"Really?"

"Yes, really. It was a benign tumor."

"Well..." I said, not knowing what else to say. I switched back to the other subject. "Kitcha was an old dog, you know."

"Then why won't they give me her body?"

I had nothing more to offer on that subject either, so we kind of petered out. The opportunity to get answers from Sandra was slipping away.

"Why did Tip throw you out?"

She rose self-righteously in her seat. I thought for an instant she was going to get up and leave, or maybe take a swing at me. Good for her. But she continued the exchange. "Because...I screamed at the Germans...because I saw the Muslim man...burned with third-degree burns...Song was leaving him to die...I spoke up...tried to take care of him. She said he'd burnt himself up, and I knew nothing."

I didn't quite get what she was talking about. "Who was leaving the burned man to die?"

"Tip's wife, Song."

"Is that how you offended her? You wrote me something about offending Tip's wife, that you spoke out of turn."

"Doesn't matter. Stranger in a strange land."

"Ha!"

"I wasn't vigilant," she admitted.

"Was the burned guy a terrorist?"

"Doesn't matter."

"Was he a police informant?"

"Doesn't matter."

"But you're saying you wanted to take care of this burnt person when Song was going to let him die? So you interfered or something? Was this a humanitarian act on your part or were you trying to get in a fight with Song?"

"What do you mean?"

"I mean...I understand you were trying to do the right thing, but this was your protector's wife we're talking about, and...sometimes you're such a pain in the ass."

She was shocked and stared at me. I was shocked at myself, but I didn't back off, with little regard for San's feelings by then. I wanted to goad her. I wanted her to defend herself. She had to be able to defend herself.

"What was that gangster guy doing up at the wat on the island, blocking the road with his car?"

San looked intently at me. "I really don't know...I don't know."

"You sent me a picture postcard in Paris of that very wat. Why do you act like it's the wrong place for me to go? You were kind of pointing it out to me, sending a postcard, no? Maybe it was the right place to go? Maybe you were trying to tell me something, sending a postcard of that particular wat, telling me that something was happening up there, or something was *going to happen* to you up there?"

She looked hard at me, her eyes glinting fleetingly. But it passed, and she was blank again, silent.

I tried something else. "Well why did you try to kill Rudy Zuur? He seems so harmless. Why him?"

She pondered me like I was a police interrogator, just as Rudy Zuur had done. "I didn't...try to kill him. I wanted...my manuscripts. He stole them."

"Your manuscripts?"

"Everything I wrote in Thailand."

"But…but you wrote in a letter to me that you sent them to the States."

"What? I wrote what? I did nothing of the kind. I don't know what you're talking about."

"In an unsent letter to me that I found in your hut…you wrote that you shipped your manuscripts to the States."

"I did?"

"You did. You want to see your letter?"

She was dumbfounded. Not embarrassed, so much as sort of stopped in her tracks.

"No, I believe you. Maybe I did send them…"

We were interrupted by the waitress clearing our dishes, putting them on a trolley, asking if we wanted anything more. When she was gone, I started up again. "San, if you go to the States, you'll probably find your manuscripts, wherever you sent them."

"I'm not going to the States," she reaffirmed. "Don't try to pull a fast one. Don't try to trick me like that. I'm not going to the States. I'm staying in Thailand." She mopped the saliva hanging from the side of her mouth with a flourish, then said, "I've gone Asian."

We had been close to something, but it slipped away. San slid out of her chair, pushed herself upright and navigated out of the restaurant cutting a swath with her hands, thumbs locked onto the straps of the immense invisible weight she was carrying on her back. It was like the scene we had filmed in

Portland years ago, when San had said, "I'm going to Asia" and walked out. In the scene we filmed, she was wearing a silk celadon cheongsam with spike-heeled sandals. Now she was wearing a green silk Chinese jacket and blue silk trousers, both tattered but serviceable. She was also wearing the mismatched blue rubber flip-flops I'd found in her hut on the island—not classy at all. She needed the spike-heeled strappy sandals I'd left behind in her hut to complete the picture. If only I'd brought the classy sandals instead of the stupid flip-flops.

Songkhla, Thailand

Bringing the classy spike-heeled sandals would not have made things easier for us. That was just a fantasy. San would have broken her ankle doing the Thorazine shuffle in spike heels, and things would have been more complicated than they were already. We were just barely hanging on as it was. And she didn't need the actual sandals when she could act as if she were wearing them and when her only witness could *imagine* she was wearing them. And once both of us imagined the sandals, it was destined they would be in the story, their image pixelating in and out of focus like truth itself.

Lunch hour in the lounge was over. I stayed on, caught up in regret, wonder and fatigue. San's ability to remind me of my lack of picaresque imagination had struck again. Those high-heeled sandals were just the sort of inspired indulgence that had drawn me to her in the first place, and in not choosing them I had inadvertently denied her a little harmless pleasure.

Cocktail drinkers and a few extended families were my company in the lounge as I lingered there trying to work out what to do, drinking another creamy iced coffee—never did I drink so much good coffee—and studying the solitary lounge lizards scattered around the place smoking as they examined their thoughts. There were also two Asian men standing and smoking across from me toward the exit.

The shorter one was wearing a gray suit, the taller one a black polo shirt and gray slacks. The man in the suit was looking at me. He looked like the other man's assistant, and they were both about fifty. The taller man in the polo shirt was sizing up the lounge. The man in the suit pointed in my direction when he saw me looking at the two of them and said something to the taller man, who glanced casually over at me, caught my eye across the lounge and locked me in his gaze for a long moment. Something was wrong. What had San done now? Who was that man?

The man lifted his arm as if he were going to wave me over, but then didn't and let his arm drift slowly down as he instead paced purposefully toward me, circling around a table, holding his gaze. He strode confidently, like a prince, a half-smile on his lips. The people sitting at the tables he passed fell silent, and they all turned to look at him go by. My heart pounded an alarm. The prince kept coming.

I stood up from the table. The man stopped, and we stood facing each other, about ten yards apart. I lurched clumsily forward a couple of steps as if drawn to a magnet.

A look of amusement crossed the man's features, but he lifted his arm again, open palm facing me. *Stop right there*, the palm said. I did stop. Then he gestured me toward the exit, almost insouciantly.

Go, he was saying with his eyes. *Go help your friend. Go out there and direct affairs.*

In the time it took me to pick up my purse, the two men had disappeared. I thought the handsome man in the polo shirt might have been Tip. I felt connected to my mission again, having seen the man, having been under his spell ever so briefly. When I came out of the lounge, San was there, adrift in the middle of the lobby, just standing there, waiting.

That might have been as far as she got after her own exit from the lounge sometime before, or she could by that time have ventured outside the air-conditioned hotel, found the heat exhausting, come back in and beached herself. She was waiting to be dealt with by whoever, like Blanche DuBois waiting for the kindness of strangers. Had she seen the two men? Or had the men seen her without her seeing them?

San at least noticed *me* coming and nodded her head in compliance, as if I'd said something, given an order. What did she think I'd said? That I saw those two guys? But no, she didn't really communicate anything like that. She looked drained, empty, a very sad sight. The moment resonated forward and backward in time like a cruel payoff, as if her recklessness were finally extorting a high price, as if rebellion would always and forever lead to grief.

Probably San was not thinking she was such a

sad sight or that she had washed up there in the lobby. She was probably thinking I was awfully slow getting out of the restaurant. I was sure she hadn't seen the two men. She wasn't alarmed, just tired. Whatever the difference in our thoughts, information, perspective, it didn't matter.

"I won't ditch you," I promised, and she sagged, relieved, into a nearby lobby armchair.

"Let's figure it out then," she said matter-of-factly, ready to do business.

I knelt on the cool blue tile floor in front of her. "Okay. I would like to take you to Bangkok and go to the embassy and get you repatriated. Can we do that?" I didn't expect her to want to do that, but I felt like asking one more time.

"No, we can't do that."

"You want me to leave you here alone when I go back to Paris?"

"I do."

"You want to stay here, without a visa?"

"Not here, I'll go south, to Malaysia. I'll get my passport stamped at the border, then I'll come back into Thailand. I'll find a new scene." She gestured jerkily to the south, her hand contracting and releasing, contracting and releasing, like a butterfly opening and closing its wings.

"But if you aren't able to make things work, if you can't find a new scene...?" We had to strike a better deal. "Who would be responsible for my soul if

I left you here and you were dying? I won't be able to come back and rescue you again."

"Good try, but I won't blame you if it happens," she said quietly.

The refreshing coolness of the tile floor came up through my legs. I could happily have sprawled out there and let everything slide. I never wanted to decide what San should do. She was a strong-minded woman making a decision, so I had to respect it.

"I don't think you should do that San. You're so fragile."

"It's my choice."

"I can't leave you alone when you're so frail."

"Yes, you can. Think of me as a big fish you caught, but now you have to throw me back."

"Yes! But you will go under, you might drown."

"I take responsibility for this decision I'm making."

Was that enough? Would I regret this moment forever? "It's like taking responsibility for your suicide," I said.

"I take responsibility for my death, whenever or however it happens."

"Fine," I surrendered.

She touched my shoulder gently. "I knew you would get what I'm saying."

"I didn't come here to capture you." I wanted her to do things in her own way, as she had always done. She had been right to leave the United States when she did. She had gone Asian. We nodded in agreement.

That afternoon, we went downtown to the local branch of San's bank to withdraw her money. We went there in a plush air-conditioned *automobile* taxi, as her time for struggling with the elements was later, when she would be alone, not now, when I was still there...and the taxi didn't cost much in any case. I was beginning to see how San could survive in Thailand with even a tiny amount of money. There were people around who were used to being paid to fetch a bottle of water or dinner for very little money. Life was not expensive there, away from Bangkok. San had a pension, from her father's death or something, about three hundred and fifty dollars a month. I could see how she had survived for so long in Asia and how she would continue to survive.

The modest small-town bank was ingenious in its simplicity. A soaring ceiling rose to the heavens over a tiny floor space, so the volume made the place look important. The stone floor was refreshingly cool underfoot even though the bank was not air-conditioned. Dark wood had been fashioned into a rich, long counter with windows behind which women sat like orchids in boxes, beautifully dressed in bright silk cheongsams. The men wore dark Western-style suits. The place was silent. People whispered when they spoke.

As we waited silently in line, San was nervous, glancing around, head jerking as she mopped her face. We were both sweating. She presented her passbook to the teller and asked to withdraw all her money. The woman looked at San with wide-eyed repugnance, then went away to check the current balance. San had rivulets of moisture on her upper lip, sweat running down her forehead and her hands were shaking. When the teller came back and said, in English, that the current balance was ten thousand baht (about four hundred dollars), the delicate-featured beauty registered San's glad relief. The woman looked us both up and down and let it be known as she counted out the bills that ten thousand baht was a significant sum.

She fixed her eyes on San and touched a talisman at her neck, the way you might touch a cross to ward off the devil. She was not sweating but was deliciously moist-looking, like a fawn, with huge brown eyes. San replied in English to the young woman, saying that it was indeed a lot of money, and then she said something in Thai, perhaps the same thing. With her unsteady hands, she counted out the bills again herself before accepting them as the correct amount. She finished counting, looked up at the girl and nodded her head ever so slightly to indicate the money was right.

"That's great, you got your money," I exclaimed as we walked outside. San looked at me in bewilderment, as if she no longer knew where she was. She had been so exacting in the bank and was now so lost. The transaction had taken everything she had. In the sticky heat and dust of the street, her energies drained away. She breathed raggedly and coughed, shook her head, *no, no, no*. She couldn't go any farther. Did she really imagine she would be able to survive on her own, having been exhausted by a limited effort like going to the bank? There would be so many efforts to make on her own. There would be limits to relying on kindness from strangers, even with money in her pocket, just as there were limits with her friends, even with the one who had come halfway around the planet to save her.

Roger, in Paris, had looked across the courtyard at my closed shutters while my phone rang two hundred times. That was kindness, but Roger wasn't a stranger. He was a close neighbor, a friend. I could not be a neighbor to Sansan from a distant country. *She has to find some neighbors*, I was thinking as we moved up the grubby Songkhla sidewalk, slow as tortoises. Neighbors were the solution.

What about Dominique Renard, almost a total stranger to me, not a neighbor, having saved me when I fainted? How did that compare? It had been nice, but hardly a matter of life or death, and besides, Renard was in the business of saving people. It was his vocation. It was philanthropy. Still, Renard was wonderfully kind, an inspiration, someone I would want as a neighbor, a friend...or something more.

These were my thoughts as we happened mercifully on a coffee house. A modest, rundown-but-elegant establishment, it was not unlike the bank—high, soaring ceiling, white walls, cool stone floor, dark wood, not air-conditioned, humid. A ceiling fan barely turned. Customers moved in and out at the speed of the fan. The place was full but muted, languid, like an eddy in a river where people got sucked in for a while and then eventually oozed back out into the mainstream. Those seated around us were not sweating, and they stared at San and me as we both sweated profusely. A drop of sweat rolled down my nose and dripped off. San was twitching and drooling and clenching her hands, symptoms I had grown accustomed to and now found normal, but which, I was now reminded, were a real drawback.

The ceiling fan whined. We ordered, had no conversation; people continued to stare. Through straws, we gulped sweet, creamy iced coffees and glasses of water. After her coffee, San wiped her face on her sleeve and whirled around on her chair to study the place.

She was cunning, checking it out, and knew what she was looking for. She did have an idea what her needs were and how to get them met. This was the resourceful Sandra. With her eyes, she mounted the handsome, creaky wooden staircase leading up to a mezzanine that ran across the back of the room. She squinted up there at two young boys leaning against the railing looking down at the customers in the coffee house. They looked servile. They weren't globalized teens like Ha's brother, Tung.

San smiled at the sight of them. "Ah, ha...good," she chuckled, recognizing minions who could perform services for her. She could move in there and "direct affairs" as best she could until she was ready to move on. Catching sight of something else, she rotated around on her chair to squint at a large painted sign hanging down from the underside of the balcony. The sign had one long word in Thai script.

"They have rooms to let here," San read out loud in a tone that confirmed what she had already figured out. "I'll rent a room here, a few days, until I'm ready to travel south." The question of what to do was settled that fast. I was wondering if San had sensed Tip's presence in the area and was wanting to make contact. Probably not, though. She wasn't *that* cunning.

We sat for a moment and drank in the atmosphere. I paid the bill, and we made our way over to the wide staircase and up to the balcony, where we entered a long, dark, windowless hallway illuminated by two dim lightbulbs, one of which was shooting off sparks like a sparkler.

Open doors lined each side of the passageway,

and the heavy-set cleaning woman, maybe the proprietor, was standing with her mop at the end of the somber hall, watching us draw nearer. The tiny, dark rooms on each side of the hallway were like cabins on a boat. Each contained a bench and a polished dark wooden platform bearing a thin mattress. In one cabin, a feeble lightbulb was on, revealing closed wooden shutters over what might have been a window (or maybe just an airshaft) and a ceiling fan that turned slowly.

As we passed another cabin, an old man got up off the bed and approached the doorway to look at us. He appeared to have come to the end of the road there. He stared at San. I did too and, to me, she seemed almost serene. We continued down the hallway. I could hear people arguing in some Asian language behind closed doors. Everything was clean and polished, but the heat was stifling.

San turned toward me and asked, "When are you leaving?" She was breathing with difficulty in the extreme, stuffy heat. "It's going to be cheap here," she predicted.

"Friday. Day after tomorrow."

The stout proprietor of the boarding house accepted a week's rent in advance from San, starting on Friday. "She sick?" the woman asked me in a high-pitched voice, pointing at San.

"No, she'll be fine."

Back downstairs on the street, San was almost

light-hearted. She laughed, said I was a real sweetheart and blew me a kiss. We took a cab to our hotel and slept for a couple of hours until after dark, both of us in the big double bed. San kicked out at something in her sleep once and raked me with her long toenail. It stung, so I got up and put antiseptic on the scratch. She had drawn blood.

That evening when we got moving again, we went to the night market. It was a vast, open-air kitchen where hundreds of people were doing their shopping or eating outside at pushcarts and low tables or standing and talking. It was a practical idea to have the market at night in such a hot climate, but it was also a festive notion. White paper lanterns with lightbulbs inside were strung on stalls or mounted on upright sticks, swaying in the breeze as they lit the way. The temperature had dropped to eighty degrees Fahrenheit.

We stopped to buy some fruit, not a smelly durian, but mangosteens—round rubber-like balls that held gooey oyster pods with a sliminess that made me gag.

San ate five or six of the fruits and threw up soon after in the gutter. It didn't matter. We were having fun together for the first time. She was genuinely cheerful. We ate a little bit of this and a little bit of that and tried all her favorite things, the best being a sweet pancake made on a griddle and filled with chicken curry and spicy saffron rice,

274

topped with chutney. We sat down to eat our pancakes and drank several tiny glasses of beer, two swallows of beer in each glass. We got up, laughing, and moved on to the next stall, and the next, slipping in and out of the crowd. Sandra pointed out the differences in facial types among those living in this southern city, the predominant Malay with their almost Polynesian features, the Thais closer to Chinese. She explained about the Sino and the Thai people counterbalancing each other in Thailand. She talked about growing tensions between Muslims and non-Muslims there in the South, where we were. She was still the same Sandra, zeroing in on geopolitical realities.

It was dark so people didn't stare much as San shuffled by, grinding her jaws together, taking hold of things to steady herself as she scooted along in the stream of humanity. She was so surefooted that we walked arm-in-arm.

"Remember when we marched in that demonstration in Paris celebrating Franco's death?" she said breathlessly, grabbing my arm more tightly. We fell into step, chests and chins high, the old militant drill. It felt real for a split second until I opened my eyes. People watched us and smiled as we marched along in the crowd.

San laughed gaily. "You were wearing your blue French policeman's cape that day, the one you stole from some gendarme, you remember?!"

I laughed, ha, ha, yes.

But I stopped laughing because, as nice a detail as that would have been, wearing a stolen cop cape in a march in Paris, I had not been wearing my blue policeman's cape stolen a few years before from a Paris cop when I was a student. As for how I obtained it, a policeman had stashed his heavy, wool felt cape in a tree while he directed traffic near the Champs-Elysées on a warm day, never imagining somebody might steal it.

The cop was right to assume no French person would steal his cape. It was an American who did it. I'd acted on impulse, thinking, rightly or wrongly, that I could talk my way out of trouble if I got caught. It was youthful arrogance or ignorance. It was youth thinking it's invulnerable. In any case, I was scared afterward, my heart pounding hard until I got that cape hidden safely in my room near the Champs de Mars. Even then, I remained on high alert for a couple of days, but the police didn't pound ominously at my door. I relaxed then, began to imagine myself wearing the cape in Portland and, at the end of the school year, the cape went home in my trunk to the States.

Those navy-blue capes were easily identifiable—you could never have worn a stolen one in France back then. In Portland though, I wore it for years and felt like a bandit each time I wore it. I had never, ever, worn it in France.

"No, I wasn't wearing it San, I never wore that cape in Paris, only in Oregon."

We were still marching arm-in-arm through the Songkhla night market, as if we were in a political demonstration. She was drawing on her bottomless reserves. The cape business didn't really matter.

"Yes, you were wearing your cape," she insisted. "I remember. You looked fabulous, you just don't remember."

"But I wasn't wearing the policeman's cape. It's impossible. I never wore that cape in Paris. I might have been arrested. I wore it in Oregon, because it was cool. To impress you, don't you see? You see how much I impressed you?"

"You were wearing that cape in Paris when we marched against Franco," she said. "You were fabulous."

For years after our march through the Songkhla night market, I couldn't see my policeman's cape without thinking about Sansan; she had created such an effect with her fantasy. Shaping reality to suit her vision was perhaps her strong point. What she saw in her mind's eye was how she spun a myth. A cape weighted with lead in the hem swinging menacingly in a crowd was a strong image that could somehow bring Franco's intimidation to life for people listening to San's stories, people who didn't live in Spain or Paris, people who would never have known anything about Franco if San hadn't told her story and included my policeman's cape. She was a storyteller, not a scholar—a creator of historically relevant, imaginative fiction.

That night in the Songkhla market marked the first time I heard her stolen cape elaboration. It caught me off guard, confused me. I began to doubt myself, my grasp on reality. The night market's white lights spun and bounced around like in a discotheque, shattering the darkness with their photon shards. I felt dizzy, wanted to go back to the hotel, wanted to get some sleep. Most of all, I wanted to get some nice white rice in the Vegas lounge to calm the growing queasiness in my stomach.

It was nearly three a.m. when we got back to the hotel, and we went straight to the lounge for my rice. That was my plan. San had a different idea and immediately pointed out the Thai man who had picked her up in the hotel bar the morning before. He was sitting just a few booths away from the one we were sliding into. He was the man who had bought her multiple espressos and glasses of wine, who had wanted to come up to our room, who was probably following us for Tip Nohting, and who had us in his sights now. He was the guy with the gun.

How could she see in the darkened Vegas lounge if it was the same guy or not? San hadn't been able to see well since I rescued her, but now she was sure it was that guy. Her eyesight seemed to come and go. I wondered about her vision. Could she see, or couldn't she? She seemed unreliable in that regard as well. I wanted to get her some glasses the next day, before I left her.

"Look," she said. "He's having a drink."

I craned around to look at a guy having a drink, but couldn't say if it was *the* guy I'd seen from ten floors up the day before. San was certain it was him. She was getting excited and went into her "coquette mode." Just like that, a femme fatale radiating sexual energy at the sight of a man who attracted her.

"I'm going to ask him to join us," San informed me as she slipped gracefully out of our booth. She could now control her body and make use of it, just because of that guy. She actually looked pretty good as she walked over to where he was sitting and bent down to say something into his ear.

I looked away then for a few seconds. I was embarrassed, felt like a voyeur. When the two of them sat down opposite me, he was interested only in her, not in me at all. When he finally looked over at me, I said to San, "Ask him what kind of business he's in." She did ask him, but in a seductive, Lauren Bacall sort of way.

I pondered how I could make my exit but also stick around like a fly on the wall so I would know how the immediate future was shaping up. I stayed for a while. The words "refrigerator" and "Scandinavian," which the guy said in English, figured in his brief reply. I seized on the two words I understood and imagined a shady deal with money laundered through an exchange of kitchen appliances via Sweden. I had read in a magazine in my seat pocket on the plane to Bangkok that exporting arms to Thailand for distribution in Southeast Asia figured into Scandinavia's relationship with Thailand. The brief article had also referred to weapons trafficking in the Southern Thailand, where the local mafia was selling weapons to gangs and Sri Lankan and Northeast Indian insurgents in the area.

I had read all that on an airplane before coming to the place where this activity was supposedly happening. My mind was now fixed on the mysterious lounge lizard in front of me, although I didn't hear him say anything about arms trafficking. He was, in fact, just mumbling, drunk perhaps, or drugged, and San was struggling to understand him. I was doing my best to put it all together, but my eyes were starting to cross. San was listening with interest to whatever the man was telling her, or else she was very successfully feigning interest. I decided it was time for me to go, so I got up, went upstairs and left the room door unlocked for San. I passed out shortly after.

I was asleep when she came into the room much later and woke me up.

"Are you awake?"

I yawned and rolled over to face her in the darkness. "I am now."

"I think this guy will take me on," she said, looking almost beautiful now in the shadows.

"That guy? Right now? Take you on? What do you mean?"

"He touched his genitals," she expounded. "We were standing up to go, and he put his hand on his genitals. They do that. It means they want to sleep with you."

I was strangely aroused, hearing her say that he put his hand on his genitals. Did he really want to sleep with her in her current state? But there would have been many factors at play, many I knew nothing about. Leave it to Sandra, I thought. "Are you interested?"

"I don't know. I don't think so. You think I should go with him?"

"It's entirely up to you."

"Is it a good idea?"

"You have to decide for yourself," I said, shifting in the sheets, yawning.

"I don't think I'm interested in going with him."

There was a long silence and then San spoke again. "I was in love with Tip, you know, right from the beginning. There was an erotic spark between us. We touched each other a lot, even in public. It was very intimate. When he wanted a cigarette, he would reach into the pocket on my breast to get one and leave his hand there, and sometimes he put his hand on his genitals, right in front of Song."

I said nothing, but I was thinking about Tip's hand resting on San's breast pocket, on her breast, his head tilting down to look at Sansan, her head tilting up to look at him. I rolled over facing the wall, away from San, who was still standing near the door. I pulled the covers up tight around my head. After a moment, the door quietly opened and then closed.

"San?" But she was gone, there and then not there, like the aromatic grilled sardine of Roger's childhood, swinging back and forth across the table past everyone's nose, the enticement that made the bread a banquet.

Songkhla, Thailand

In the morning, San was stretched out on the big double bed facing me from the far edge. I had slept through her coming back and getting into bed. I must have wanted to stay asleep. And she must not have smoked. When I opened my eyes, she was quietly waiting, staring.

"I woke up happy," she whispered conspiratorially. "The first time in ages."

"Peace, laughter and innocence?"

"Ha, ha." She laughed, then frowned.

"Who said that?"

"You did. You wrote those exact words in a letter to me in Paris. You were still with Tip. You said he brought you peace, laughter and innocence. Was it true?"

There was no answer, so I yawned and stretched and got up, leaving San to her thoughts. In the shower, I thought about the guy down in the lounge putting his hand on his genitals. I wondered what had happened between him and San when she went back downstairs. I confess I wanted to know the details.

I felt ambivalent about whether she should go off with the guy, but I didn't want to dog her every move. She seemed so much better, both physically and psychologically.

"That's great San," I told her a few minutes later

when I came out of the bathroom, my hair twisted up in a towel. "That you woke up happy, I mean."

She was still on the bed, lying on her side, looking peaceful. It was a relief to see her that way. She generated so much pleasure for so many when she was happy. If she was happy, I, too, benefitted. The world would benefit. She would weigh in on the upside of things rather than the downside. Having an option on the horizon was making her happy…not necessarily this particular man and not drugs (or at least, not any drugs she was getting from me). I'd stopped giving her the drugs from the asylum. I had flushed them all down the toilet. She'd had no hard landing and had stopped asking me for more after we made our deal squatting down on the floor in the hotel lobby. But since she'd met the guy who was now making her happy, she had stopped hearing the voices, which was even more important. It was beginning to look like she was going to pull off her magic survival act once again.

Doctor Renard had given me solid advice on the telephone about reeling somebody in. He was a good doctor, pretending to be only reluctantly available to the melancholy and needy, yet very available to me, so far. I began to wonder how much more he might be available once I got back to Bangkok.

Downstairs in the lounge for breakfast, there was no sign of those two men from the day before.

San didn't bother to pretend she could read the menu. She picked it up, fanned herself with it, put it down to light a cigarette, picked up the fan again.

The place was air-conditioned, but she seemed to be having trouble getting enough air. She was rasping like an old refrigerator compressor, wheezing, spitting into her napkin. She had probably spent half the night smoking and drinking, not waiting until she was healthier. But that was her choice and her way.

"Do you need glasses? Can you see? Are you going to be able to see?"

"I can't see anymore," she admitted, coughing. "I can't see to read, and I can't see far away either. I want to buy some magnifying glasses, reading glasses. I had some. They were at my place on the island. Did you find them?"

"No."

San sat smoking her cigarette, thinking. She suddenly burst out, "Those peasants on the island stole everything nice a person could get for herself. They had no idea what an effort life was. Isolated...no money for two months. Checks held up because she has no address. Kids taunting, saying, 'Why don't you sell your pussy, or is it too old?' No help or harm, that was Tip's decree. Except free food once a day in the noodle shop. She becomes a pariah."

Sandra was speaking about the community I was in only days ago, but she was talking about it in the third person, as if from a great distance in time and space. As an abstraction. She was already making something we were in the middle of into a story, as if I hadn't just been at her hut, picking through her rags, as if it hadn't been a matter of life and death for her in the asylum only days before. The episode was already a story, a myth in her mind. She went on declaiming about the cruelty of peasants.

"I am a pariah," she said, finally speaking in the first person, inhabiting her own story. Something had made her switch, a sudden realization that gave her a personal connection to her own story.

I ate my Thai sticky rice. Fried pieces of pork were embedded in the grains, the whole delicious thing tasting like the aromatic banana leaf it had been cooked in. San talked and I listened, offering no disagreement. After a while, she went back to coughing and spitting. She was a relentless smoker once again, pumping two packs a day into her tired lungs. No wonder she couldn't get any air.

After she quit coughing and drank some coffee, I asked what we needed to do that day. "This is my last full day here," I reminded.

"Your last day here." She nodded. She took a puff on her cigarette and inhaled deeply.

"Okay," she said.

"Right, so what do we have to do?"

"You leave tomorrow?" She seemed surprised I was really leaving. It probably hadn't registered before.

"Yes."

"For Bangkok?"

"Yes. Want to come?" Getting her to Bangkok and to the embassy was too much to hope for, but I tried.

"No," she said flatly, lighting another cigarette off her stub. She inhaled sharply and blew the smoke out as she glanced rapidly around at the people in the Vegas lounge with us. "I want to dye my hair black, get some clothes like the Thai ladies here wear."

"Black?" I hadn't imagined her dying her hair black. I had pictured her going back to red, tarting herself up, going after that guy or another one. "Not red anymore?"

"I must become invisible."

"You want to pass for Thai?"

"Yes."

"But nobody here has green eyes, San."

"I'll wear sunglasses."

"Blinkers on your flashing orbs?"

She snorted. We were both thinking about her being an illegal in Thailand with her visa expired, something Thai officials readily arrest you for. She had to at least *try* to be invisible.

"Do you feel you're being followed?" I asked.

"Maybe. I'll slip out of here and go south."

She was fearless. I willingly forgot my concerns as we went downtown in a taxi to a road lined with shops selling cheap clothes like the locals wore, the racks spilling out of open-air gallery stalls onto the sidewalk.

San knew where to search for her new identity. She wanted to look like the local women who were wearing black or dark blue, Mandarin-style cotton tops with straight, dark, floor-length skirts, printed pieces of cloth wrapped around their waists and tied.

The cloth on the racks all around us was heavily starched, rough to the touch. San tried on two things, held others up against herself for a look in the mirror, didn't like what she saw, gave up on the idea.

"It doesn't work," she sighed to her reflection in the long, narrow mirror hanging on the wall of one of the stalls. San wasn't a physically vain person. In Portland, she hadn't been inclined to fuss over her appearance beyond keeping her mane shiny. The mirror revealed a white woman, skinny as a toothpick, playing at dressing up—a *farang*, not a local.

"I have to get those sunglasses," she declared, as if they might really make a difference. Half of our day was already gone, and we'd made no progress.

On the way back to the hotel in a taxi, San saw a beauty shop sign down a side *soi* off the main road, not far from the hotel. She had the taxi driver do a U-turn and go back.

The shop was rural, a rustic beauty parlor with a

dirt path and tall grasses leading up to it. Inside, two middle-aged ladies wearing the kind of clothing San had been considering sat talking to one another. One might have been a customer who had just gotten her hair washed and combed. The other was the beautician. San got control of herself and explained to the beautician how she wanted her hair to be cut short and squared off. She pointed at a faded technicolor photograph on the wall showing a Thai lady, her sleek black hair just as San described: short, squared off. The other two faded photos showed blonde Hollywood types with tightly curled, fifties-style hairdos. It seemed doubtful the beautician could reproduce such a curly blonde look on a Thai customer. Probably the photos were just decor.

The beautician and her customer chattered with San, who seemed comfortable with what was happening, in her element now, with real people.

The beautician settled San in the chair, placed a towel around her shoulders. San pronounced a single syllable, and the lady picked up a box of black hair dye that was right next to her and showed it to San, who nodded. There was continuous chatter among the three women, a glimpse for me of how San must have lived in Thailand when things had been going well, when she'd been at ease under Tip's protective wing.

The beauty parlor smelled of jasmine, orange flowers, and another familiar perfume, the frangipani.

There were long frangipani leis dangling from the edges of a large mirror positioned in front of the customer's chair. Farther up on the wall, more frangipani festooned a large photograph of the King of Thailand, displayed there just like it was everywhere else in the country—although people seemed to avoid pronouncing his name, out of respect perhaps... or for fear of being misunderstood, fear of reprisal over any perceived disrespect.

"I'll come back in an hour and a half." With that, I left San and walked and walked, looking in shop windows, thinking it would be easy to find sunglasses and magnifying reading glasses to buy. I found neither. Either I was on the wrong streets, or the town didn't have those items for sale. I couldn't get a positive response from anyone I asked. They just shook their head no. I decided to give San my own sunglasses the next day when my plane left.

I took a tuk-tuk back to the beauty shop, but she wasn't there. The client or neighbor or relative—whatever she was—was still there with the beautician, and the two were now playing a board game on a table. They indicated that San had left and walked off in the direction of our hotel. That set me on edge, the idea of her walking any distance at all in that humid afternoon heat. I made my way back to the hotel, half-expecting to see her slumped over somewhere along the shoulder.

Instead, I found San sitting in the hotel lounge

having a glass of vodka. She was easy to spot from across the room, her white skin framed by a coal black hairdo—short and squared off, just as she had requested. She wasn't invisible at all, but rather, seemed to be flaunting her new appearance. She was relaxed and smiling at the man she was drinking with, that guy again, the one with the gun. I sat down with them for a minute. The guy smiled warmly at me this time. He nodded his head in my direction a few times. He and San talked comfortably with each other. She was making a real effort to please him, and they were content. He had already become a character in the life she was improvising for herself.

Upstairs in the room, CNN had the story of the bombing in Oklahoma, now told through interviews with distraught survivors of the explosion, or with parents of children killed in the attack. There was no mention of terrorists anymore, suspected "Islamic terrorists." I guessed, rightly it would turn out, that the authorities—the FBI or someone—had gone off half-cocked, saying it was the work of Islamic extremists. Now they were pulling back. That Islamic terrorist characterization must have panicked people in the States. Where I was, in the Muslim-filled deep south of Thailand, people's imaginations were stimulated by piracy, or by rising militancy, or by government crackdowns on drug dealers. The U.S. scarcely existed for them. Asia was what existed for them. Asia was the center of their universe. On the television, a Muslim cleric from Iran said he resented Americans for blaming Islamic extremists for blowing up their federal building when there was no such evidence. He said American authorities were foolishly planting ideas like seeds, which would sprout and grow in the minds of real Islamic extremists. Or so the voiceover translation in English said.

San came up to the room later, waking me from a deep sleep. It felt very late. It was dark, and there was no noise at all, not even outside in the hallway. She smoked a cigarette in the bathroom, then got into bed with an unlit one.

"Hi."

"Oh, good…" she cooed at me meaningfully. There was a long, pleasant silence during which I pondered what she had meant by "good."

So I asked her, "What's 'good'?"

"Oh, I wanted to…you're…?"

"What is it?

"You're…"

"Are you all right?"

"Yes." We were silent again. She seemed to have forgotten what she was going to say. "So what is it?" I pressed.

"Oh…" she trailed off, and then finally dredged it up. "Tell me about Kitcha."

San had trouble talking about Kitcha. Kitcha was the consequential subject that got stuck in her craw, but now she had regurgitated it, she had said it: Kitcha. She hadn't been able to listen or hear when I'd told her about Manley telling me that Kitcha had given up, but now, protected by darkness, now that she was about to lose access to me, she wanted to know more. What she thought she knew was fanciful, to say the least: that they—Manley and Jimmy? The people who were following her?—had killed her dog.

San had been shaken to her core when she had come back from the hospital and discovered that her dog was dead. I was sure she'd gone mad on the spot as a direct result. Because she *was* Kitcha. She herself was that beast, Kitcha, the living thing that filled the space around her own physical self, like an extension of herself, an outer skin. And then, coming out of the hospital where she'd been operated on, still recovering, coming back to her island, and going, first thing, to Manley's to pick up Kitcha. The dog had been even more important after San had been thrown out by Tip's wife, or by Tip himself. Whatever Manley and Jimmy had done to the dog, they had done to San as well. Even if all they'd done was ignore the dog to death.

At the gym on the island, Manley had told me that Kitcha died curled up under a chair refusing to eat or drink for days. He had begged her not to die, he had told me convincingly, and his story was believable to me despite his unconcealed lack of feeling for San. I had even sensed, when Manley told me about Kitcha dying, that he felt much more for the dog than he did for San. Plenty of people like dogs or cats more than they like humans. Manley might have been one of them. But Kitcha was an old dog, perhaps an ancient dog, and San had been at the government hospital for over a month. She had written in the unmailed letter to me that Kitcha had "bought the farm" while she was in the hospital. So. The slang phrase for dying didn't imply that San was light-hearted or indifferent about Kitcha's death. It was Sansan-from-San Fran talking. Her letters were always true to her voice.

San had wanted to see Kitcha's body. Manley had been thrown by that, so he'd raged his guilt onto her. She'd gone nuts. A normal response I would say—I would have wanted to see the body had it been my own animal, just to be sure the animal was really dead, not just lost, or stolen. I would have needed to see the body just to get started with the mourning process.

So, now that Sansan had finally asked to hear about Kitcha, this was what came to mind: San's jungle hut where she'd lived with Kitcha and the little girl who had bounced in and out of view, who had inched closer to get a better look at me and, flying through the understory, a short-legged dog, its ears straight out, like wings.

"Kitcha had puppies, didn't she?" I finally asked after a long silence. "Didn't Kitcha give birth to puppies in the cave you were living in before the hut?"

"Only one puppy survived. Aura's her name. She ran wild in the jungle there. She wasn't really mine. Everybody took care of her. The people all loved her. They loved Kitcha's baby."

"I think I saw Aura when I was at your hut," I said with a rush.

"You did?" San shifted eagerly in the sheets.

"Describe her."

"Golden, very short legs...she was leaping through the underbrush on these incredibly short legs, ears straight out like wings."

"That was her! You saw Aura!" San wriggled with pleasure, bouncing her feet on the mattress, squealing.

"So a piece of Kitcha is still there...she's still part of that place where you were. They're taking care of your baby," I suggested.

"Yes...Aura ran wild."

"She was flying along, leaping through the undergrowth, in perfect health."

San didn't reply. She might have stopped listening. We were silent again. A laughing couple passed in the corridor; a door slammed. We were quiet, breathing in and out. Ten seconds longer and I would have been asleep, but San broke the silence. She wasn't through.

"You're a cat person, aren't you?" she whispered,

the first time in Thailand she had asked me anything about myself. My slide into sleep halted. I rolled onto my back to focus on the cats I had known, my own animals, who, in my mind's eye, helpfully lined themselves up on the ceiling in the darkness, each one a Siamese jewel, a chain of cats with emerald and sapphire eyes, all of them dead now but each one illuminated. That was how I described them to San.

"Don't you still have one?" she wanted to know.

"No, my last one died, in Paris, last year. She was nineteen."

"It's terrible, isn't it? But why don't you have a new one?"

"It *was* terrible. I buried her in Père-Lachaise, across the street from where I live. A violinist friend of mine stood fifty yards away playing music to draw all the people away from where I was digging the little grave. You can't bury animals there, but no one saw me. And we burned some incense from the Oregon high desert where she liked it best."

"That's beautiful. What was her name?"

"Her name was Snatch."

"Oh, I remember her."

"You do? Little blue point with a round face? I don't like Siamese cats with long snouts, just the round-headed ones. Have you noticed all the Siamese cats here, all striped?"

San sighed. "You miss her?"

"The vet who came to my apartment to help her

die told me I would be better off loving people from then on, instead of cats."

"He said that?"

"He did."

Both of us made sounds of incredulity. Animal stories, books and leaps into the void were three things San and I had in common. But I didn't stop at animals. I went on to people, to the lecture I had been wanting to give her for a long time, about responsible behavior, only it wasn't a lecture anymore, more like a plea. I told her she had to stop depending on people from afar to take care of her. She had to attach herself to people around her, wherever she went, I implored, so that she could depend on them. Not just animals. But people nearby. Better to depend on people than on pets, and it should be people right around where you are. Neighbors. Don't count on people halfway around the world anymore, I told her. And don't depend on your family either. They're far away too, and they're busy with their own survival. We all move around a lot, so we have to depend on strangers, I said to her, knowing I was really talking about myself but, still, there wasn't going to be another chance to tell her what I wanted to tell her. Create a little group of them around you, I went on, talking in the dark, not certain if San was still awake or what. Work at it so they're not strangers anymore. Colonize a group of strangers. People who will help you out. Neighbors. An artificial tribe.

They're the ones who will save you when you need it.

"Yes," she said, very much awake.

We were silent for a while, but now I wanted more. I was stoked.

I shifted to face her in the darkness. "Why did you come to Thailand when you left Nepal? Why here?" I wondered If she would remember things to tell me, now that we had started. "Did you think you had a tribe in Thailand?"

She was silent. It had been too much of a leap, and I'd lost her. Her bolt out of Nepal had probably been one of Sandra's better moments, but I had disconcerted her, and she rambled on about why she had come to Thailand. Then, all of a sudden, she remembered something important and, in the darkness, chopped the air the way she used to do as a younger woman.

"Tip set me up like a bowling pin," she exclaimed, and that line triggered the sequence that followed, which came out like a narrative, with a beginning, a middle and an end.

This was the story: Tip's con, San explained, was getting foreigners to invest money in development projects—like getting Marty to invest in that resort project out on the peninsula where'd they all gone on the yacht. But the con was that, before construction could get underway, everything would come to a halt. There would be some reason why the

298

work couldn't continue, such as having no freshwater at the site, or no permit from the government to excavate, or something. Tip would tell the investors he had to pay baksheesh to the local authorities to get permission to continue, but all the money paid out came right back to him, because he owned everything around. He *was* the local authority.

"And then, what do you know," San said, gesturing in the shadows, "the investors' money vanished...." She went on in a dramatic voice, a magical voice, "When I got here, Tip told me I could live on the peninsula where they were going to construct a resort."

There was no freshwater out there though, so Tip said he would bring it to her, along with food supplies. She set up house in a makeshift hut. She was happy, bodysurfing a lot, and Tip had given her a small boat so she could make the trip back and forth herself. Tip told her he was looking for a hydraulic engineer who could solve the freshwater problem.

"Of course," San broke into her story to say, "I didn't know it was all a scam then. I only learned that later, after I got to know Tip better. At the time, I thought he really was looking for someone, and I said I knew people who could fix the problem for him. I needed a place to stay, right? And I did know a guy who could fix the water predicament. Tip was impressed and told me to invite the guy to come to Thailand and take a look, and I did. And that

299

was when my romance with Tip became compromised."

It was terrific listening to San tell a tale again and I didn't want her to stop. She explained that some guy she knew had come from the States, a friend of hers she thought would be able to solve the problem. But the guy coming from the States had been the beginning of the end for her, as he—San's suggestion, remember—had no idea at all how to solve the freshwater problem. Tip was no longer impressed with San, saw that she couldn't come through for him. It was the last straw. Or maybe it had been a trap. Song, who had never liked San, was eager to be rid of her.

"So they threw me out. Tip was a pirate. He loved a rumble." She laughed, pounding herself on the chest.

"Did Tip really think you knew the kind of people who can build water systems?" I asked rudely.

"Well, I told him I did. I guess he believed me. Or he loved me. Or he thought there was something in it for him. Or he was mistaken."

"Tip owns that whole island, doesn't he?"

"He does."

"And Ha is Tip's sister?"

"His cousin."

"His cousin. Hmmm. So is she terrified of Tip?"

San was silent for a long moment, then said,

"Ha doesn't openly go against what Tip wants, but she is very smart and has her own life. Ha always knows how to take care of herself."

"And so do you, San," I told her. "You know how to take care of yourself. Don't you?"

"So do you," she parroted back, glowing in the dark, not answering my question.

"But how did Tip throw you out?" I asked after another period of silence. "I mean, how exactly were you thrown out? Who said what? Who did what? You were physically manhandled?"

"No, no, of course not."

"What do you mean 'of course not'? Given the violent individual we're talking about here…"

San then talked about how she'd gone on a yacht with Tip and Song for a cruise with some Germans, new investors. The bodyguards did their gun show routine, and San was sitting next to Tip, and he was saying to one of the Germans (in that Peter Lorre way of his), "I am the king, of…and then he turned to me and said, 'What am I the king of, Sansan?'"

"I was supposed to say guns," she whispered, "but instead I said…extortion. I don't know what came over me. Nobody spoke to me after that. When we got back to Tip's house, I saw the burnt Muslim guy on the ground outside. And I asked Song about him. She was already mad. She got furious. She threw a bottle at me. I caught it. She was screaming at me, saying 'Bitch. Bitch. You always fuck around with everything! Get off my property, you whore!' I thought she was going to kill me."

"Kill you and throw you away?"

"Right."

"*Ying ting*?"

"How do you know that?" San asked, jolted. "*Ying ting* means kill you and throw you away. How do you know that?"

"You told me. On television, the story about the drug dealers being killed by the police in Thailand. They called it *ying ting*, and you told me *ying ting* means kill you and throw you away, don't you remember? I wrote it down."

San stared at me in the dark, her mouth opening to reveal her twitching tongue, her luminescent green eyes narrowing, like a rattlesnake ready to spring. The only thing missing was the spine-chilling rattle. I couldn't imagine what she was thinking in relation to what had gone just before.

"That's the Thais," she chortled, "the gentlest people on earth, but also the fiercest. Just watch out. *Ying ting*. Right. You're done for." She let out a hearty guffaw that made the bed bounce.

Waiting for her to stop laughing, I asked, "So did Song really call you a whore?"

"She did. She called me a whore. Classic, huh?"

Just when I was about to fall asleep, San shook

me out of my peaceful state again. "You know why I can't go back to the States? I am too weird. I don't fit. I never did. Simply stated, I don't like the way people over there think."

The next morning, we didn't talk at all in the taxi that took us to the boarding house where San had paid a week's rent. Neither one of us had slept much. It felt like we'd said all there was to say. Before San got out of the taxi, I gave her all my Thai money except for what I needed before my departure from Thailand. I also gave her my tube of face cream and my sunglasses. She was grateful and smiled and kissed my cheek. She put the sunglasses on. They were lopsided on her.

"You're not afraid of running into Tip?" I asked.

"Not at all," she said, then whispered as she got out of the taxi, "I love you, whatever that means."

I got out to hug her. "Me too. Send me a postcard!"

She promised that she would, as soon as she was settled, and she disappeared inside the boarding house we had stumbled across. That was it. She didn't look back.

As always, she wasn't into denouement. I *was* into denouement though, so I was obsessing about what would happen to her. I was thinking about what that kid had said to her when she'd been thrown out: "Why don't you sell your pussy, or is it too old?"

How long would she be able to keep up her survival mode as a seductress, growing older in a changing world?

I looked back as I got in the taxi. How could I not look back? I was *still* looking back as we drove away, but San had already gone inside, so I was looking back at my last memory of her. I was creating a memory of myself looking back at where I'd last seen her.

Paris, France

Ho Tay and I were having bowls of pho in Belleville surrounded by Chinese and Vietnamese people speaking their languages and also eating pho. Outside, people drifted by in the Paris rain. I was eager to tell Ho Tay about my trip since it was she who had given me the plane ticket. But my story was skimpy, lacking in coherence, because many of the finer points didn't come my way until later, when I went to Portland and made inquiries, especially with Sammy, the community organizer.

When I got to the part about meeting Renard in a Patpong bar and then running into him again in a tailor's shop, Ho Tay found the story preposterous.

"And what was that about working with boat people?!?" she tossed at me. I had no details. Renard never talked about his line of work beyond saying that saving desperate people was tantamount to stealing their melancholy. Ho Tay thought he was too perfect to be true.

"You must be projecting your thoughts onto this doctor," Ho Tay ironized. "Isn't that it?" She had her head down, eating, but after a pause looked up slyly at me. I didn't like her summing up my experience that way, reducing it to *that*. So much was left out. She was too second-degree (and French) for my first-degree state of mind. I was swimming with emotion.

"What are you saying? That I'm the last to know everything?" I said very loud, alienated. Now she was stealing *my* melancholy. My chopsticks hung menacingly in midair. My eyes caught hers in an accusing way.

Ho Tay put up her hand for a truce, reached for her bag and removed a set of tiny color photos she had taken on a recent visit to Hanoi. "Tell me what you think of these," she commanded, pushing the photos across the table. I stared at each one a long time and slowed way down. It was like reading a book instead of an email. Each photo was a portrait of a single object in its real or natural setting. The pictures oozed outside of their frames to embrace the observer, me in that case. Oyster-like mangosteen fruits lay in a round, mother-of-pearl dish sitting on a turquoise enamel surface. The mangosteens reached up and grabbed me by the throat. I saw San gorging herself on mangosteens and throwing up.

"Thailand was visceral," I told Ho Tay, who was ready to listen.

Thailand *had* been visceral, and Renard was part of why. I did call him from the airport when I went back to Bangkok. When I told him where I was, he said, "Take a taxi and come to my place. I would like to see you. This is the address." He spelled out the long street name and told me how to pronounce it.

In the taxi, I remembered I had met Renard at a sex show in Patpong. I had forgotten that part. It

306

was my first night in Asia when I'd stumbled into the Patpong bar in the middle of the night and, in the darkness of the bar, sat down next to Dominique Renard. He ended up telling me how the prostitutes of various cultures differed, while a Thai girl on the stage popped ping-pong balls out of her vagina. I had forgotten all that in my focus on his life-saving characteristics, and the intriguing sound of his smoker's voice on the phone.

Now, back in Bangkok, the taxi drove by Patpong 1 and Patpong 2, and soon after turned down a *soi* and stopped. The *soi* was across from the Oriental Hotel where I had gone for a drink only ten days before, right down the street from my own hotel, which itself was within walking distance of Patpong. Renard and I were neighbors, which explained everything, as far as I was concerned.

Renard was perfect when he answered the door, nervous, like I was, but visibly pleased to see me. His eyes lit up, he moved close and smiled. His salt-and-pepper hair was unruly and damp, as if it were drying after a shower. He'd cleaned up for me. Still, he was wearing the same rumpled white linen pants, or maybe an identical pair, and he had on the red shirt I had seen him in days before, but now the shirt looked freshly pressed.

He offered me some tawny port, probably his personal favorite as he already had a glass of it and served himself again as well. We drank right where we were standing, by the refrigerator next to a bar that separated the kitchen from the salon, where there were chairs with white cushions, a marble floor, a television and a white couch. I would have liked to lie down on the couch and be taken care of, watched over as I slept, sung to. There was something about Renard that was familiar, as if he were an old friend.

"What a perplexing country this is," I observed.

He snorted. "Perplexing! And full of adventures, yes."

"Is this just a *travel adventure*?"

"It is a little bit…but also another kind of adventure."

He smiled and shifted his head to look at me more intently.

"But I have gone through many things since I last saw you," I said.

"You have turned white since you came in here," he joked. "Are you going to faint again?"

"I've turned white?" I put my hands up to my face. It felt hot. It should have been red, not white. "Show me."

He took me by the hand and led me to the mirror covering a wall in the salon. I looked at myself, and Renard, who was standing behind me, put his hands on my shoulders. The two of us looked at each other in the mirror. I looked pale, it was true. It must have been stage fright. He had an expectant look and a looseness around his mouth like someone wanting to be kissed.

"*Voulez-vous m'embrasser?*" I asked his reflection. He laughed, delighted, and put down his cigar in the ashtray. I turned around and put my arms around his neck and kissed him. I loved his smell, which was of the cigar but also of sweat and soap, and orange blossoms. He kissed me back, very passionately. He led me over to the white couch, sat down and pulled me next to him, drawing my head onto his shoulder, encircling me with his arm. It was exactly what I wanted, to be protected. How did he know? I turned my head and looked at him. He leaned in and kissed me again. Then he stopped.

"I can't do this," he said, and there was fear in his voice.

"Can't do what? Can't kiss me?"

His face touching mine, he put his free hand between my legs and pressed his fingers on my pudendum and held them there. I came, very fast and very hard, shuddering as if zapped by a continuing electric shock. I burst into tears. He moved his face away from mine and looked at me with tenderness. We stayed that way for what seemed an eternity until I slipped into sleep.

Later, Renard woke me up while I was snoring. He put a cushion under my head, covered me with a light blanket and went off to another room to sleep. The next morning, he called a taxi to take me to the airport. *I love him, I love him*, I was thinking all the way there.

The shirt I had ordered from the tailor was waiting for me at the airport, just as arranged with Apache John. At the boarding gate stood a delivery boy with the shirt, a kid about twelve years old holding a garment bag bearing a sign with my name on it. It had been only ten days since I'd fainted and then regained consciousness in Apache John's shop. I had forgotten about the shirt and felt like a child with my new custom-made, blue-striped cotton shirt with a band collar.

I had no Thai money left for a tip, but I gave the kid a ten-dollar bill, which pleased him. It was then I remembered my green snakeskin high heels, which I'd checked at my hotel's baggage room. I'd forgotten to go by and pick them up. I would never get to wear those exotic shoes in Paris, or anywhere else for that matter.

Back in Paris, I found a message from Renard on my answering machine. His interesting voice said he was going on another mission in Bosnia, but he was coming to Paris soon to see his father for a few days before going away, and wanted to see me as well. Listening to him, I visualized him still wearing the same rumpled clothes as he took a puff on his cigar, exhaled, said, "*Tu me manques.* I miss you. *Je t'embrasse fort.*" Where did that come from? He was suddenly so romantic! I was outrageously excited by the phone message and had fantasies of the very best sort.

I felt like a changed person now that I was back in Paris. I felt older, wiser, more able to see the larger picture. My apartment was as it was before, but I didn't look the same to myself in the mirror. I tripped over and bumped my head on things I'd lived with for years, like the shelf over the telephone. And my last Siamese cat's ghost was no longer staying put in Père-Lachaise.

At the office, things seemed at first to have changed for the better. Right after I got back, the boss openly threw his favor my way when, in front of everyone, he thanked me for the work I was doing and gave me a huge orchid plant with four stems of salmon-colored flowers.

I realized after a couple of days that everyone at work had halted what they had been doing before I left and had turned their attention to getting sympathetic candidates on the ballot in every legislative precinct in France. My issues were no longer of importance. I no longer had a role there.

I felt out of place even before hearing from the press attaché that the kid who didn't like me was demanding that my salary be liberated to hire somebody to work on the election campaign. Then the kid himself strode into my office and informed me I had to quit. "The boss agrees," he added for maximum effect.

"No," I said, not buying into it. I was not prepared to lose my job, even though I'd seen it happen abruptly to others.

"Yes," he rebutted, unflinching. I was blindsided, even though I knew that you can't be fired in France...not just like that. There are laws against it. They have lengthy procedures.

I went looking for the boss, but he wasn't in the office.

"He's not here," Blondie, his assistant, told me, peering conspiratorially over the top of her horn rims. "He's working at home."

"To avoid me? He can't tell me in person he's pitching me overboard?"

Blondie puckered her mouth and hunched her shoulders in mock pain. Still, she didn't say anything. I was on my own. That's what the orchid had been about. It had meant thank you and goodbye. I hadn't understood the gesture. What a misunderstanding. The kid had won. They do it differently in France from how they do it in Thailand, but I was being tossed out just like Sandra was. Well, not just like Sandra was, but I was on edge and vibrating in a nasty register, so I saw nothing good about my situation.

"It's about negotiating your exit in a way that provides the most benefits for yourself," said Isabelle, the lawyer I went to see over near the Champs-Elysées. She listened to my jittery version of what was

312

happening at the office. I had no backup plan for my life, for my financial survival, in France or anywhere.

Isabelle was telling me the compensation I would receive would depend on how well we played the end game. "You have some resources here," she noted, tapping my dossier. "You must hold firm. There's no reason to be frightened. And it's perfectly normal for you to pursue your case in court if the process wasn't correct. It's not considered vindictive or arrogant. It's your right. It's a right French workers demanded for themselves and won. Many of these laws go as far back as Napoleon."

Isabelle's long nose twitched whenever she had an interesting thought. She was sophisticated, bright and efficient. She had lots of interesting thoughts.

"Write down for me what has happened to you...think of it as a story," Isabelle advised while examining my work contract. She was very calm. "Don't quit your job, and don't make any mistakes at work, as they will be able to fire you if you make a single *erreur professionnelle*, as defined by the French legal code. If you don't make *une erreur*, they can't legally fire you. They must offer you a settlement if they lay you off and can only do that with legal cause. Stick it out. Sorry it's so unpleasant for you, but that's the point—they are trying to bully you into quitting. Don't do it. Let them make the next move. We're waiting for an offer. Keep me informed of everything that happens."

Isabelle's fee for her services was a month's salary, whatever my salary had been. That struck me as enlightened. Without her, I had nothing. With her, I would negotiate a beneficial exit or at least one I might be satisfied with. When her contract for legal services came in the mail a couple of days later, I signed it along with a check for a month's salary, thereby drawing my bank account down to two figures.

I told Roger about some of it. I had told him earlier about the anonymous phone calls threatening me, so of course he asked me how things were going at the office when he invited me to dinner two weeks after I was back from Bangkok. Sitting at his table together, he raced me through my Thailand story so fast it sounded like pulp fiction.

"Roger, you're so hard-nosed," I objected. "It's not funny. It's very sad. Sandra almost died."

"Well. I knew it was a dog story." Then he cooed at the Siamese cat he was holding in his hands stretched up over his head. The cat dangled up there passively. Two other Siameses were in his lap, one on top of the other. The rest were heaped on Roger's mother as she lay in her bed staring at the ceiling. I'd gone to her bedroom to say hello when I came in, but she didn't answer, didn't look away from the ceiling. She was in Algeria.

314

"And this doctor in Thailand," Roger continued, lowering the elevated Siamese onto the pile in his lap. "I don't think he was really a doctor. Did he show you something to prove he was a doctor? His identity card or something? Why do you believe your doctor was any more real than the doctor who gave Sandra those drugs?"

I didn't want to pursue it. Every time I told my story it became grist for someone's mill. I wanted to eat my *couscous merguez* and go back to my side of the courtyard.

"*Tu l'as baisé?*" Roger badgered, as if clamped onto prey. "Did you fuck him?" His freckled, pale face and scalp reddened with anticipation. What a clown. He should have had a big red clown nose to put on at such moments, or some kind of inquisitor's mask. He'd been locked up too long taking care of his mother, I was thinking. Everything was a joke to him.

"No," I replied. I didn't want to hear what he might have to say about my relations with Renard.

Roger pretended to lose interest in the story then and began chattering about the cats. There were gaps between us that weren't bridgeable. How could there not be, considering our cultural differences, our backgrounds? How do people from different cultures ever successfully communicate at all? I was beginning to think they don't.

Roger touched my arm. "I'm sorry," he said, and everything was suddenly all right again.

I still had my neighbors. I still had my little colony. My little tribe. Not like San having no one in Thailand that understood who she was or what she was saying. San and I are quite different from each other, I told Roger, as if we'd been talking about that, and he nodded, puzzled but accepting. My French friends accepted me the most when I became enigmatic.

I left the apartment, never having told him much of anything about how things were going at work. Once outside Roger's door, my sense of panic returned.

My stomach was unsettled as I crossed the courtyard to go to my own apartment. I changed course and went to the well in the far corner of the cobblestone courtyard. It was dark, but I found the edge of the heavy wooden cover and pushed it aside about a centimeter to hear the tinkling of water rushing downhill far below. Along with the sound, a gassy emanation wafted out of the opening, the smell of mold mixed with gas from the underbelly of Paris.

I made it upstairs to the toilet before the diarrhea hit. After the first attack I looked around for the antidiarrheal caps I'd taken to Thailand and brought back to Paris with me, minus the ones I'd left with San. I took one with a couple of glasses of water. In the morning I would feel bloated, but stabilized.

At work, I completed now-pointless tasks. It was a holding pattern, I told myself, forcing my way through the process, wanting to bolt, unsure if I could stick it out in a place where the good guys looked at me sympathetically and the bad guys no longer spoke to me at all as they moved through the narrow corridors.

I locked myself in my office and wrote an intelligent letter to the people at the Ministry of Foreign Affairs in Thailand, to keep the door open.

When I went to fax my letter to the ministry in Bangkok, I found this fax already sitting in the machine:

Dearest,

Am going down. Sick of mind and body. Went south, heard of an island supposed to be cheap, it was upscale instead and no one was interested in me. I came from there to Bangkok, they are checking visas so am trying U.S. Embassy. So far I just sit and wait, haven't seen anyone yet. I run out of money in ten days, if my expired visa is found, I go to jail.

If you don't wish to help, let me know by fax. I realize this is out of order, this rescue thing, am very sorry, I misjudged my situation a lot and its near impossible to get to someone in the embassy.

I will keep trying, please be well, I miss your charm.

Love, Sansan

I juggled an array of emotions. I was relieved San was alive, glad she missed my charm. Glad she realized she was out of order, asking to be rescued again, glad she was asking anyway. She really did have a sense of perspective, even humor, in the worst of situations. It was endearing. Of course I had to help her out. I couldn't turn away from her.

Long-distance information gave me the number for the U.S. Embassy in Bangkok. As the phone rang halfway around the world, it occurred to me I might be committing a "professional error," according to some French legal code. What I was doing was responding to a friend in urgent need, but from work, on an office phone line. Would the French code define that as a "professional error"? I personally would have said that it wasn't one, but I was biased. This was an emergency as I saw it...though maybe that wouldn't be the Cartesian or Napoleonic assessment.

There is a French law requiring people to help someone in danger—a civilized social measure, *non*? Or is helping people in danger not civilized when it has to be legislated?

Whatever, if my actions to help San from the office could in any way have been interpreted as a professional error, I decided to keep it strictly to myself. I kept the door closed and took advantage of the fact that I still had an international phone line.

It was the middle of the night in Bangkok, so no one answered the phone at the embassy, what was I thinking of? The embassy in Paris informed me when I called that they couldn't intervene from here. They explained that San had to be interviewed for repatriation by the U.S. Embassy in Bangkok, since Thailand would be paying for the plane ticket.

San had no choice but to go to the embassy in Bangkok. I faxed her telling her to go there, to wait until she was seen, to camp out until her problems were solved. And to ask for medical help. And to give them my phone number in case they needed any information, adding that I would do whatever I could to help her.

I faxed Repatriation Services at the embassy in Bangkok asking them to see Sandra Sandra for an interview immediately as she was in ill health, both mentally and physically. I recommended her as a person of outstanding qualities. Next, I sent a fax to our beloved Sammy in Portland.

"What are you going to do from there?" I asked Sammy, handing off the baton. It was somebody else's turn to direct affairs. I didn't know if Sammy would step up, but I needed help from Portland.

I had another attack of diarrhea, which smelled awful and befouled the ladies' room. The experience was debilitating. Was it just nerves or did I have a slight fever as well? Back in my office with the door closed, I drank a liter of water, then decided to go to the Institut Pasteur, where I'd gotten my vaccinations. It wasn't a professional error to leave work when sick. Especially if I told Blondie where I was going, which I did. Maybe it was malaria. I had taken the antimalarial tablets every day just as the doctor at the Institut Pasteur had instructed: for a week before going to Bangkok, during the whole time I was there…and I was still taking them during the follow-up period. The literature they'd given me at the Institut invited me to come in immediately if I experienced any problems after my trip to a tropical zone.

The waiting room at Institut Pasteur was full of people who looked sapped, ashen, all of them worse off than me. It was like a secret meeting of germ hub operatives come together for the exchange of bacteria after we had successfully spread disease in the streets and buses and subways of Paris on the way to the clinic's waiting room. Our germs were mating and mutating.

"I'm going down," I told the doctor once we were in his cubicle. Sansan's phrase about "going down" resonated with me, so I said it again: "I'm going down." She was feeding lines to her sidekick from afar.

The doctor asked where I'd been during the preceding month, asked if I had ever fainted during that time. I told him the story about fainting and waking up in a tailor shop next to a Dr. Renard, a French doctor in Médecins Sans Frontières. The Institut physician stared at me incredulously, doubting what I was saying. Was it the fainting, the tailor shop, or the Médecins Sans Frontières idea that bothered him?

"But I don't even know if he was really a doctor, he could have been an impostor," I added, moving the exchange to absurdity's door.

The man rolled his eyes, did not open that door. He asked no further questions, gave me two pills and left me alone to rest. I eventually felt stable enough to go to the bathroom and produce the necessary fecal sample, followed by a blood sample at a nurse's station down the hall. I was already feeling better because of the pills. In a week, the test results would show what repulsive thing was growing inside me. It was probably delayed rage.

I went home, stopping on my street to pick up some rice from the Chinese takeout place, which I ate with two eggs and a liter of water. Spartan existence.

The next morning at the office, Blondie gave me a fax. "I saw it in the machine and rescued it for you." Her blue eyes were glued on me over the top of her glasses. "You never know who might have seen it and thrown it in the trash." She smiled wickedly, then remembered I'd left sick the day before and rearranged her face into concern.

Like the press attaché, who eavesdropped and then tipped me off, Blondie was helping me...but only up to a certain point. They wouldn't go so far as to intervene with the boss, but Blondie was being very good to me. She had been the boss' secretary for eight years and was very loyal yet nevertheless torn. She had also known me for five years by then. She had observed that when I first came to work there, I had nothing to wear—only one set of clothes for important meetings. She was the one who had told me what clothes to buy for professional occasions when I had enough money, what the protocol was, how to behave. She and I had come a long way together. She made it obvious she hated the mess I was in, but she was also dubious about her own future. Now that I was getting dumped, she could easily imagine herself being dumped, too.

"Is the boss here?" I asked Blondie. "Or is he staying away until I'm gone?"

"Something like that." She reached for a glass sitting next to her computer. It was whiskey. The J & B bottle was right there on her desk. Blondie had her own way of dealing with the shifting sands. I raised my eyebrows exaggeratedly. "Why not?" she shrugged and flicked a lock of her hair. "No one's here but us sheep." She was right. Just us sheep.

Cartons of campaign material were piling up. Campaign worker sheep were spreading their things out on every desk and table. Sheep were talking on new phone lines, having meetings, shouting and arguing, flocking through the hallways, butting heads. Blondie was getting drunk, and the boss was running things from home.

As I walked back through the gray corridors to my office, I read the new fax from San:

Dearest,

Went to embassy, they will pay flight back but want someone to pay immigration fine ($800). They have your card, so you will hear from them. Don't let them harass you about the fine. I have bad cough, trying to avoid hernia. Please don't worry.

Always, Sansan

No point in going wobbly at the last moment, I thought. I took a sheet of paper and wrote again to Sammy in Portland to tell him he had to raise eight hundred dollars somehow because I couldn't. I made it sound as urgent as it was.

He must get San's son, Eddy, to do it. Yes! He could pay San's fine, I wrote, adding for maximum effect that if no one paid the fine, San would go to jail again and not survive. None of her friends would ever see her again. I closed by saying that I was taking no further action on my end.

Early that morning, the embassy in Bangkok had rung me up as I slept the sleep of the dead. The low-level diplomat (with a Boston accent) on the phone said he'd read my fax recommending Sandra Sandra to the repatriation staff.

"How did she ever get that name, Sandra Sandra?" he inquired in a chatty way.

"Her parents named her that."

The man went on to say that he had interviewed San since then. While I yawned and stretched and tried to follow him, he finally got to his point, which was: who was going to pay Sandra Sandra's visa fine? The embassy's policy, he succinctly explained, was to loan money for emergency plane tickets but not to pay fines incurred in foreign countries.

I referred him to Sammy in Portland for further help. Before hanging up, I spelled out for him what an extraordinary person Sandra Sandra was, despite her wretched state, and how people in three countries were counting on him to deliver his fellow American safely home to Oregon.

San was still counting on me to direct affairs, that was clear. She was having her way with me. My fellow American in Bangkok closed the long-distance conversation by promising to help.

At the office, there remained things to do before I lost the opportunity. First, a fax to San encouraging her to stay engaged in the embassy process, assuring her they wouldn't abandon her now that she was in their pipeline. I offered to wire her fifty dollars. I told her my fax number might change but that I would let her know in a later fax. No point explaining my deteriorating situation to someone whose situation was worse.

I had to wait a couple of hours before the fax machine in the mailroom was free. Interrupting the work of the political campaign would probably have been a professional error, and the kid was hovering, waiting for me to make a misstep. I called a friend to come by the office the next day with her wheeled bag so, along with my own, we would have two wheeled bags to fill up with papers and files from my five years' worth of work.

The next morning, my office was occupied, the contents of my desk in cartons in the corridor. My friend who came with her suitcase helped me go through everything hastily. We got everything important into our two rolling suitcases and made a zany exit. It was only later, going through the stuff at home, that I discovered my Rolodex and address book were gone. My leather address book, with its red and purple pockets in the back where you could accumulate special notes and cards.

I'd had a couple hundred business cards at least, from trips and meetings in many countries. This was of course before the era of various electronic gadgets. All those contacts taken. Confiscated. Stolen. I would never get them back. In that era, the French equated your value as a colleague with the size of your address book. Whoever took it had done the predictable thing. I was disgusted with the whole mob. With myself! I went back to the office the next day to try to retrieve what was mine, *High Noon*-style.

The guy who ran the copy room whispered to me the name of the person who had my address book. He actually knew who had it, and he actually whispered. I went right to the thief's office—he was an inexperienced, new recruit, but an older man, and he already had his own office. I planted myself right next to him as he sat behind his desk.

"Give me my address book!" The words were meant to be stinging and full of authority, but they came out all wrong. I was no good at fighting French-style, the wordplay, the fronting off, the aphorisms, the insults, the snide demeanor. You have to grow up in France to get it right. My role models for defiant women were brash frontier types, not aristocrats.

The thief was himself patrician, elegantly white-haired, clad in an expensive tweed suit. He could have passed for a gentleman. Nevertheless, he shouted at me, "Get out of here, you bitch!"

He lunged out of his chair, pushed me against the wall, took hold of my arm and hurled me toward the door. I hit the doorframe with my shoulder and felt a sharp pain down to my toes. My bad shoulder it was, as rotten luck would have it, an old injury.

I asked a witness to come with me, and we went down the street to the police office. We stepped into a tiny foyer and sat on a wooden bench to wait. It was my second time in a police station in less than a month. I had circled halfway around an island to get to the last one—no proximity police in Thailand—and ended up getting pretty much what I'd gone there for at not too high a price. How would I fare in France?

A young, floppy-haired detective came in, introduced himself and lifted the counter so we could pass under it into the cubicle behind.

He seemed comfortable with his hole in the wall. He was wearing a black leather motorcycle jacket over a white t-shirt and had an Auvergnat accent, and when I commented on the accent, he said mine was rather charming too. He pointed at a calendar from Auvergne on the wall and fetched it to show us clever Auvergnat cartoons for several different months. Provincials like him were common in the Paris police for some reason. It had probably been some innocent Auvergnat like this young fellow whose cop cape I had stolen years before. Paris cops hailing from elsewhere in France wasn't necessarily a bad thing, because they had fewer assumptions or established loyalties than someone reared locally might have had.

"So you know who my boss is?" I asked our guy.

"Yes. Everyone in the neighborhood knows who he is. Office down the street."

"Is this the first time you've had a complaint?" I queried.

"No. I think we had something just the other day," he divulged but stopped there. "So what happened to you?" His pencil was poised over a stack of square paper with three holes punched down the side. When I asked what the other complaint against my boss had been, he screwed up his face like a kid, shook his head and repeated, "What happened to you?"

So I told him my story. When I faltered, he elicited, helped me along, made me talk like I was at ease in a bar. That is how the French police accumulate what's called "general information" or intelligence, also known as informants' revenge. He wrote down what I said, reading aloud each part and then rereading the whole thing for my approval. He explained that this process is called a *main courante*, a handwritten account. The resulting four handwritten pages would be inserted into the station's big black intelligence ledger, he said, pointing at the one sitting on a shelf behind the counter. I got no copy of the *main courante*.

"Copies can be purchased through a Court of Justice," the cop offered as he dated, signed and stamped the pages. "Are you going to have a doctor look at that shoulder?" he asked conversationally as he stood up, the interview over.

I was aghast. "Aren't you going to do anything about the guy who threw me across the room?" I couldn't believe that's all there was.

He clamped his mouth tightly. "We'll wait a couple of days, see what happens."

My story was nothing at all to him compared with what else came in the door. I was supposed to absorb the insults at the office and carry on. We left, and I took a taxi home, not having gotten what I went to the cops for. Getting my story in the police ledger seemed like nothing. I didn't understand at the time how much those pages in the ledger might mean later on, in my lawyer Isabelle's hands. At the time, I felt baffled about life in France, as opposed to the seemingly clear-cut life in Thailand, where things are simply bought with baksheesh.

That night, my boss called me at home around midnight, waking me up. After a good shoulder massage by the *kinésithérapeute* on my street, I had gone to bed early. My boss had been drinking. Our conversation was short.

"I heard what happened to you today, and I'm really sorry…" he was saying as I interrupted him.

"Tell it to my lawyer," I snapped as I started to hang up.

I could still hear him respond poignantly, "You have a lawyer?"

"I do. I'm sorry. Goodbye." It's very American to say, "Tell it to my lawyer." Direct and violent.

"Goodbye." His voice cracked feebly. It was genuine. He was shocked. What was I doing? After hanging up, I thought that going to the police with a complaint against my employer was possibly a professional error, at least in the employer's eyes. Maybe the whole episode was, if not a professional error, a cultural error on my part, even if I was within my rights.

I was dismissed the next day, in a letter delivered by registered mail, part of the legal abracadabra required by labor law in France. The letter had been sent before the boss had called me to say he was sorry. The letter said I was now persona non grata at the office, and that I would get two months' salary as a settlement. A few days later, Isabelle examined the letter and found legal fault with it. She said I should get a year's salary, which was standard procedure. The faulty letter turned out to be far more important to my legal case than getting tossed into a doorjamb, although Isabelle believed the latter added emotional weight to the former. She initiated legal proceedings against my ex-employers. She assured me I'd made no mistakes at all, cultural or professional. "This could take a while," Isabelle told me, "so don't be in a rush."

At the Institut Pasteur a week later, I was informed that my loose bowels had resulted from a simple case of food poisoning—E. coli bacteria, and nothing else had showed up in my blood test, except malaria antibodies. The doctor said I'd probably picked up the food poisoning no earlier than the very day I'd fallen ill. "There is no gestation period for E. coli, your malaise was French, not Thai!" he joked. He did point out, though, that the antimalarial bodies in my blood meant I'd been exposed to the scourge of the tropics, but that, thanks to the Institut's prep work, I hadn't succumbed.

In my neighborhood I found a little fax and printing shop and adopted it as my annex. The two men running it were ex-cops it turned out, or perhaps they were still cops operating secretly "in proximity." They were happy to receive faxes for me and phone me up whenever one came in. One of the two, Titi, an Auvergnat, tried out his English on me. "Hello Mrs. woman," he greeted awkwardly, a grin on his round face as he shook my hand. Titi watched while I wrote out a fax to Sandra giving her my new fax number. That one-page fax cost me the equivalent of six dollars to send, an amount that seemed large now that I was unemployed.

The next morning, Titi jovially called me up to say I had a fax back from Thailand. He presented it with panache when I went to get it. On the wall behind the fax machine was a poster of Coluche, the famous French comic who'd been killed in a motorcycle accident.

Titi was wearing a black leather motorcycle jacket and smiling exactly like Coluche. I got it and laughed, remembering that Coluche had hung out with cops. I was beginning to like hanging out with them myself.

While I read the fax, Titi watched with interest, the smile still lingering on his plump jowls. The fax was of course from Sansan:

Dearest,

Something is very strange. I leave for the States in a few hours. Sammy paid the fine, the embassy paid the ticket. What is odd is the consul is taking me to the airport. I believe I'm wanted for a serious crime in the U.S. It must have to do with Rudy Zuur on the island. Something is very wrong.

I know I am correct, it isn't at all normal for the consul to accompany me to the airport. I think I'm being transferred to U.S. authorities. It's too late now for you to help.

Love forever, Sansan

I wanted to tell San she was not being transferred to the authorities but to her loving community of friends in Oregon. It was too late, though, and she would find that out soon enough.

Titi was still watching me, his face full of anticipation. I realized that if he had tried to read the fax from San before I got there, with his marginal English, he would have noted the words "serious crime" and "transferred to U.S. authorities," which would be similar in French and which probably had aroused his interest, not to mention his respect.

The next morning, the Bostonian from the embassy in Bangkok phoned me to say Sandra Sandra had not shown up for her ride to the airport with the consul. There had been no further word from her and there was nothing they could do unless she surfaced again. "We'll hold her ticket," he said. "It's good for a year." I didn't think they would see her again. She had bolted. She had done it. She'd gotten somebody to pay her visa fine, so now she could start over. Ha! America could no longer hold on to its people. Brilliant. I was eager to believe San would survive. I forgot all my doubts about her. The class lady had done it. She had dived back in. The fish was back in the water.

Not long after that, I got a phone call from Renard. He was in Paris.

"I'm at my father's," he said in a tired voice, jet-lagged perhaps. "I am here to visit him. He lives alone, but a woman comes in to clean and make dinner. Would you like to have dinner with us tonight? Papa is very charming."

I was surprised, but also not surprised at all, because he still seemed familiar, accessible. "Yes, I would love to."

The apartment was near the Jardin du Luxembourg, and it was dark, elegant, a little messy, with books strewn everywhere. The odor of beeswax rose from the polished, creaky parquet floor. Dinner was simple, but rather magical. Dominique's father asked me what I was reading, and we talked about Christopher Isherwood's *Diaries*, which he had read in translation, about Montaigne's *Essays*—specifically the author's emphasis on the suspension of judgment in human interactions, and about Colette, who he said he liked to read when he wanted to lose himself in the past. Dominique and his father spoke rapidly to each other about a psychoanalytical interpretation they appeared to have been discussing before, perhaps for years. Papa asked me what I thought about it, and I answered. Time slipped by. I could barely look at Dominique, I wanted so much to touch him, to have him touch me.

Around ten o'clock, his father stood up, said good night to me, took my hand and lifted it to his mouth to kiss as he looked me in the eye. The two then left the room and went into another part of the apartment. When Dominique came back, he said "My father likes you."

"He is so kind."

Then he led me down a corridor to a tiny bedroom, like a maid's room, where a narrow, unmade bed waited in the corner.

"We will be quiet. My father..."

We were like adolescents in his father's house. We lay down together, were silent, not moving, not breathing, suspended on the edge. At my slightest spasm, he moaned noisily. He was funny, and we laughed. It was so good to laugh together.

In the morning, he wanted me to be there when his father got up, and I obliged, but then I went home. During the next two days, Dominique and I talked at length on the phone three times, but I did not see him again. Then he called to say he was leaving in an hour for Bosnia.

Sometime later, Isabelle won me a year's salary, a fair amount, not excessive, but satisfying. The *main courante* that the Auvergnat had so laboriously written out at the *police de proximité* had reinforced Isabelle's procedural arguments, as she had said it would. The money I won from the judgment was a surprise and made me feel rich, giving me permission to do whatever I wanted for a year or so. I decided to write about going to Thailand to find Sansan, but I worried at first about what might happen to me if any of the bad guys in the story happened to read what I might write about them. Would they contact someone in Paris to break my legs? Those thoughts can cripple creativity, and I eventually succeeded in setting them aside.

I wondered as I was writing about Sansan when or if I would hear from her again. I tried to imagine where she might have found a toehold. One day I would get a postcard from, say, Bélem, the town in Brazil on the lower lip of the wide mouth of the Amazon. The card would say, "Quick, come see with me the sheet lightning reaching down from the sky where the Amazon hits the Atlantic Ocean. There is someone here who may not wish me well."

One morning, the concierge slid a letter under the door for me. "You have a letter," she sang out from the landing.

"Thank you," I sang back through the closed door.

The letter was from Sammy, in Oregon, who announced that Sansan had arrived back in Portland.

The embassy in Bangkok had kept her plane ticket in case she showed up, and Sandra hadn't resisted or escaped this time. Sammy wrote that Sansan told him she couldn't handle the risk anymore. She was too tired, things were now too hard, the hippies were younger and had money. In short, it was too difficult to get by as beforehand. As I read Sammy's letter, I was thinking that of course San had also lost her beauty and some of her ability to manipulate people, including me no doubt. It's what happens to those who live as adventurers for years, never finding a niche equipped with long-lasting comforts.

Sammy's letter said that people were taking care of San, housing her, feeding her, letting her sit quietly in the sun. Sammy said she was silent and reflective, not talkative. She appeared to be in pretty bad shape. She had seen a doctor in Portland who told her that it would take time for her brain to recover from the excessive mixture of drugs she'd been force-fed in Thailand. "I was too good a friend to her before," Sammy wrote. "Let's see if I can still be a good friend to her now when she's no longer the person we all knew and loved."

Enclosed in Sammy's letter was a photo he'd gotten from Sansan. The photo had been in San's package of her writings which she had mailed from Thailand to him in Portland for safekeeping. Sammy wrote that Sansan had asked him to send me a copy of the photo, that it would mean something to me. It did. It was the first time I had seen the snapshot of San, Marty, Tip and Song onboard a yacht at anchor in a lagoon somewhere in Thailand, where they'd sailed to check out the property Tip was trying to lure Marty to invest in.

It was the photo where San was wearing a tight turquoise cheongsam and strappy high-heeled sandals, and was caught off guard, her pale green eyes piercing the camera lens as she dramatically shifted her cigarette from one hand to the other, all ten red-tipped fingers splayed kinetically in the air. Next to her, Marty menaced the photographer, while Song lingered aloof in the yacht's captain chair next to the bodyguards holding their Kalashnikovs aloft. It was Tip—so handsome—with one eyebrow lifted ironically, who drew my attention.

So. It *had* been Tip I saw that day in the hotel's Vegas lounge in Songkhla. It had really been Tip, the handsome prince, who froze me in place as he moved across the lounge toward me. He'd been bemused when I lurched clumsily forward. He had abruptly put up his hand to stop me in my tracks. I'd known intuitively that it was Tip, but I hadn't really known. Now I wondered if San had seen Tip that day? And if she did see him, that would add another layer to the mystery. Maybe one day I would find out, or maybe that would be one of those things San kept to herself.

I phoned San in Portland, and she sounded drained. She was probably way too exhausted to tell me if she saw Tip that day in the hotel in Songkhla. I asked her anyway. She cleared her throat but didn't say anything. There was a long silence. I broke it with, "Maybe I'll see you in Portland someday, but please, no more tricky situations from now on. Okay?"

"I get it," she said. Unconvincingly.

About the Author

Penny Allen, born in Portland, Oregon, discovered theater and created several shows in English and French before turning to cinema, where, still in Portland, she wrote, directed and produced two features, *Property* and *Paydirt*. She then lived in Central Oregon for nine years before moving to Paris, where she first worked on environmental issues and published two books, one on the environment, *Metaphors for Change*, the other a memoir, *A Geography of Saints*. She then returned to cinema with *The Soldier's Tale*, *Late for My Mother's Funeral* (in French and Arabic) and *The Didier Connection*. She has lived in France for thirty years and is working on a new movie.